# REVELATION

## The Future Human Past

Dr. Michael P. Masters

*I have begun to feel that there is a tendency in 20th Century science to forget that there will be a 21st Century science, and indeed a 30th Century science, from which vantage points our knowledge of the universe may appear quite different than it does to us. We suffer, perhaps, from temporal provincialism, a form of arrogance that has always irritated posterity.*

– J. Allen Hynek

# Acknowledgments

I would like to acknowledge the help and support of those who took time to read and critique this manuscript, and for their insightful and influential comments and suggestions that aided in its evolution. I am also grateful for those who contributed valuable guidance while navigating the nuances of this divergent form of literary expression. Most notably, these include Keira Masters, Dr. Hussein Ali Agrama, Cheyenne Crooker, Maggie Dallen, Dan Stirling, and Nick May. Thank you all!

# DEDICATION

This work is dedicated to Joan of Arc, Cathelyne Van den Bulcke, Galileo Galilei, Anna Kruger, Paul-Henri Thiry, Anna Göldi, Cayetano Ripoll, Susan B. Anthony, Alfred Russel Wallace, Thomas Henry Huxley, Friedrich Nietzsche, W.E.B. Du Bois, Bertrand Russell, Zora Neale Hurston, and John Lennon.

# TABLE OF CONTENTS

# CHAPTER 1
## DIRECTION – CAMPUS – TERRA
## 2035 CE

I wondered, what makes us human? Our bipedalism? Our brains? Our adept linguistic ability emerging out of these massive cortices? Of all the other species drifting aimlessly through space on the inbred island of Earth, how has this horny hairless ape risen to supremacy?

Fucking and fighting might be the simple answer, but nothing is simple. Not anymore.

Civilization without civility. An intergenerational house of cards. Empires rise and fall, but nothing is realized. Nothing changes. Ravening politicoreligious despots salt and scorch the Earth as the hungry wither, the thirsty turn to dust, and the chosen ones burn in the hell of their own creation. They vie for power in their own time and that of the future, sowing seeds of mind and body, ensuring the survival of their successes in the chromosomal culture of those who inherit their avarice.

But what now? This must surely be the decisive cycle. The final countdown. The Great Filter.

Earlier iterations of the political lek were primordial staging grounds for this unfurling chaos. But the arena is larger now, and the dances are blanketed in fire.
Empathy is unattainable.
This is unsustainable.

——— ◉ ———

**Markus Moksha:**

*jesus christ, it's hard to write sitting next to this halibut-perfume-scented candle. This chick sure went full on with the pretty pink princess vibe in here too. I doubt I've ever seen another dorm room like it. Although I do appreciate her commitment to cliché gender stereotypes.*

*And who is she again? Might as well crawl back in bed and have a little look-see. Oh yea, that whole thing. Hmm, not bad though. I see I wore my raincoat like a good boy too. Mom would be so proud. Dad would be too since she's hot. Although she clearly ain't one of those crazy christian types, so probably not.*

*I still can't believe that fat bastard kicked my last girlfriend and I out of a Thanksgiving dinner because she refused to say grace, or "the creepy prefeast cult chant" I think she called it. Too bad it didn't work out with that one; she had some balls on her. Among other notable physical attributes.*

*That fun family event likely had something to do with why me and the old man haven't talked in some years. Although, it also could have been that he started banging the babysitter when my brother and I were kids, leaving Mom and the two of us to fend for ourselves. She had a hell of a time finding work after the sperm donor took off with the homewrecker too, since she "wasn't allowed to work" while they were married, on account of his honorable christian belief that a woman's place is in the kitchen and at home raising kids.*

*I'm just glad I finally recovered from the decades of dogma-induced, brainwashed shame that used to follow the coital act. Sex should be fun, not something you feel worse about afterward relative to how you felt while doing it. Seems there are consequences for everything fun though. A sort of cosmic, energetic yin and yang, perhaps.*

*It is curious that the same reproductive act that helped eukaryotic life survive and prosper for over 1.7 billion years could ever be restrained by religious zealots. I can't help but wonder if it was the nerdy pious types who couldn't get laid that put all that monogamous marriage-induced misogyny bullshit into the bible.*

*I doubt I'll ever understand why people willingly rob themselves of pleasure in this life on the off chance that something better awaits them in another that may never come. All the while shouting from their 2-millimeter-tall soapboxes that the rest of us are damned to spend eternity in the fiery pits of hell with Hitler sticking pineapples up our urethras because we didn't take the 'backdoor to heaven,' or whatever that loophole was. Might as well enjoy this life while we are here and now.*

*I do wish I hadn't enjoyed it quite so much last night though. Damn, my jaw hurts! I can't believe this chick still brought me back to her dorm room after her boyfriend kicked my ass at the bar either. I guess that's one of few perks of being a college educator is there's a seemingly endless supply of hot willing participants.*

*May as well see if this one's up for a quick second round before we head to class. Gotta average down that beatdown somehow. An early morning shagfest might be the only thing that beats this hangover into submission too. god, it sucks I've gotta lecture hungover again, though most of my students look like they're high as shit anyway, so I doubt they notice. The jokes seem to come easier after a go-hard night like last night too. Well, better get after it. Time is short. And the wintry walk across campus is long.*

**Markus:** Hey, you up?

**Sheba(?)**: Ahhh no, very much asleep at the moment.

**Markus:** Oh, that's unfortunate....
What about now?

**Sheba(?)**: Still sound asleep, but hmmm, starting to feel slightly more awake somehow.

*Slowly migrating down below the sheets like a mighty African elephant leading her herd across the open landscape of the Kalahari.*

**Markus:** What about now?

**Sheba(?)**: Mmm, yea, if you keep doing that maybe.

**Markus:** The colossal pachyderm stops to snack upon juicy fruits from the mighty marula tree.

**Sheba(?)**: What?

**Markus:** Nothing, just some internal dialog that slipped out. We do have to make this quick though, I teach in an hour.

**Sheba(?)**: Right, about that, by the way. Umm, I'm not going to be able to make it to class today.

**Markus:** Well, if that's the case, I'm going to need to see a doctor's note.

**Sheba(?)**: You're a doctor. Will you write me one?

**Markus:** I'm not that kind of doctor, or any kind, yet. But yea, I'll write you one. Just this once.

# CHAPTER 2
## DISSENSION – CAMPUS – TERRA
## 2035 CE

*Damn, it's cold out this morning! And why did they build these dorms so far from my office? Somebody dropped the ball on that one. Guess I should have taken a fuzzy parka out with me last night. Although it's always hard to predict when one might be doing the walk of shame in the snow the next morning.*

*At least it's finally March now. I think I even saw some tulips popping up through the snow somewhere along this godforsaken, postcoital promenade across campus from Shiva's dorm. Sheba? Shahna? Shyla? Jedediah? Yea, Shiva sounds right. It'd be a lot easier if all their names rhymed with a part of the female anatomy.*

*I should check the attendance sheet when I get to class to find out for sure though. She could be a good one to keep in the back pocket in case things don't work out with Amanda... or her roommate. That was a fun item to check off the bucket list.*

*Oh shit, you've got to be kidding me! Out of the 30,000 students at this god-damn university, I run into this guy, right now?!*

*Maybe I can duck into Morton Hall before he sees–*

5

**Angry Boyfriend**: Hey fucko!

*Guess not.*

**Markus**: Oh, hey man. Great to see you again! My deepest apologies, but I didn't catch your name last night.

**Angry Boyfriend**: I fucking saw you coming out of her dorm this morning!

**Markus**: Who's dorm?

**Angry Boyfriend**: Sheila's dorm, you asshole! I know you went home with her last night!

*Oh yea, that was it. "Sheila." I think I liked Shiva better though.*

**Markus:** It wasn't me, bro. Besides, I was only visiting a friend who must be in the same dorm I wasn't just in. Didn't realize your girl lives there too. Crazy coincidence.

**Angry Boyfriend**: Fuck you man! I should kick your ass again, right now!

**Markus:** Well, it's 10:30 a.m., and we're in the middle of campus at the moment, but do what you have to. I kind of enjoy the pain.

**Angry Boyfriend**: Naw, it was too easy last night. It wouldn't be as much fun this time. I got a better idea. I Know you're her professor, so I'm gonna find out what class you teach and tell your department head that you're fucking around with your students.

**Markus:** I'll save you the trouble. I teach Proctology 6969, and my department chair's name is Dr. Ben Dover. His office is in Sphincter Hall, Room 420, and he'll actually be delighted when you tell him about this because part of our graduate coursework involves doing a residency in our final year so we can heuristically apply the knowledge and skills we learned in the classroom to the real world. In fact, I *assume* he'll be *assuaged* to hear about Shiva's *assistance*, as she was an *asseverate asset* and an *assiduous* but *assertive associate* in an *assortment* of *assignments asshole*!

*Thwap*!

**Angry Boyfriend**: Fucking prick.

....

**Kind Stranger:** Dude, are you OK?

**Markus:** What time is it?

**Kind Stranger:** It's like, 10:30.

**Markus:** No, I mean the *exact* time.

**Kind Stranger:** Oh, it's...10:38.

**Markus:** Nice. Thank you for waking me, kind stranger. What is your name?

**Kind Stranger:** Jared, and yea, no problem. I was just walking to class and saw you laying here, passed out, with blood all over your face.

**Markus:** Yea, weird. I must have slipped on the ice and face-planted. Thanks again though. I'll buy ya a beer sometime if I ever see you out at the bars.

———— ◉ ————

**Markus:** Bonjour Ryan. Are you about done with that copy machine? I've got to get these review sheets printed out before my 11:00 a.m. class.

**Ryan Roberts:** Morning Markus, and yea, I'm almost done. Cutting it a little close though aren't ya? It's 10:45.

**Markus:** Yea, late night. And I got chatting with an old friend on the way up here. You guys should have come out with us when we left the pub last night. Good times were had.

**Ryan:** Your black eye and bloody face would suggest otherwise.

**Markus:** Well, that part was admittedly less fun. Both times.

**Ryan:** Looks that way. I wanted to stay out, but I had to head home early. I've got the 8:00 a.m. class this semester.

**Markus:** Oh, right. That's brutal.

**Ryan:** You're telling me. By the way, wasn't that one of your students you left with last night?

**Markus:** Yea, she was the 'more fun' part of that cosmic energetic yin-yang.

**Ryan:** While I do appreciate your Confucian moralizing musings, I don't think you're supposed to date your students.

**Markus:** Oh, no worries there. I've been dating Amanda for the last year, and she isn't my student, anymore.

**Ryan:** Right. Sounds like a healthy relationship. Well, you had better hope Dr. Cohen doesn't find out. With all the recent funding cuts, the other Anthropology PhD candidates are clamoring for your position, and getting caught between the sheets with one of your students seems like a good way to lose it to one of them.

**Markus:** It's all good, mi amigo. I might be more worried about it if I was in the Proctology Department, but they'll never find me here.

**Ryan:** What? Why... and who?

**Markus:** Long story.

**Ryan:** OK. Anyhow, I'm just saying, watch your back. Noah would especially love to see that happen. He's always sucking up to the department chair, and I know he wants your 11:00 a.m. class.

**Markus:** That fuckwit!? Why would they let a linguist teach an Introduction to Anthropology course? They don't know shit about fuck. He could never cover the genetics and evolutionary anatomy sections.

**Ryan:** Politics, man. Squeaky wheel gets the grease, and the ass eaters get the teaching positions.

**Markus:** Whatever, I'm over all this bullshit anyway. After I defend my dissertation Autumn semester, I am gone. I can't wait to get the hell out of here either. I doubt there's any other occupation in this entire shithole country where 30-year-old scientists get treated like dumb kids.

**Ryan:** You are a dumb kid though.

**Markus:** Fair point. Ight, imma head out, I've got to get to class. Maybe I'll see you out at O'Hooley's again tonight?

**Ryan:** Doubtful, I'm not a go-hard like you.

**Markus:** Just takes practice. You'll get there someday.

**Ryan:** Hope not.

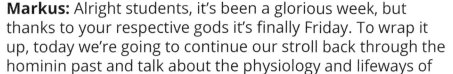

**Markus:** Alright students, it's been a glorious week, but thanks to your respective gods it's finally Friday. To wrap it up, today we're going to continue our stroll back through the hominin past and talk about the physiology and lifeways of *Homo erectus*, the inventor of Viagra.

*Crickets*

*Man, I swear I used to be funnier when I'm hungover.*

**Failing Student:** Um, excuse me, Professor?

**Markus:** Yes, Isaiah, what is it?

**Failing Student:** Um, is this going to be on the exam, and also, when is the exam?

*Holy shit, I really hate this job sometimes. I totally get why the tenured full professors make the grad students teach these little wankers in all the 101 classes.*

**Markus:** Yes, Isaiah, considering this is one of the most important stages of human evolution, both culturally and morphologically, this will obviously be on the exam. Also, being named after an old-testament prophet, one would think you could have telepathically precognized the future date of the exam.

*Hysterical laughter*

*Well, all right, hungover me has still got it after all.*

**Markus:** Although, even without prophetic paranormal powers, Isaiah, I have mentioned the upcoming exam date in each of our previous three classes, which I can only surmise you did not attend. The syllabus also provides dates for each of the exams, which for this one, again, is Monday. The exam is this coming Monday.

**Failing Student:** Oh, okay, thank you, Professor Moksha.

**Markus:** Not a professor yet, but close enough. Does anyone else have any other questions before we get to Viagra Boy? I promise to be less condescending in my response to your inquiry, assuming you are in possession of the course syllabus and you have been to at least one class in the last month....

**Slightly Better Student:** Professor?

*Swing and a miss.*

**Markus:** Yes, Bethany?

**Slightly Better Student:** I have a question... What's going on with your face this morning?

**Markus:** Good question, Bethany. I slipped on some ice and fell on my face...twice. Any other questions? Well alright, let's get after it then, the weekend beckons.

# CHAPTER 3
## INFLICTION – O'HOOLEY'S – TERRA
## 2035 CE

**Markus:** Bonjour again Ryan, I thought you said you weren't coming out tonight.

**Ryan:** Yeeea, sooo, you can only say bonjour to the same person once each day, and that was your second one. Freedom Fries bitch!

**Markus:** Duly noted.

**Ryan:** Anyhow, I didn't stay out late yesterday so I figured I'd try to hit it harder tonight. Also, your inspirational speech at the copy machine this morning moved me beyond words, so here I am.

**Markus:** You mean my inspirational speech where I said, 'maybe I'll see you out at O'Hooley's again tonight,' and 'it just takes practice, you'll get there someday?'

**Ryan:** Yes, that one. It was an impeccable motivational oration that filled me with a sense of passion and excitement I haven't felt in years. You should be a presidential speech writer.

**Markus:** I'll search for an opening tomorrow.

**Ryan:** Oh hey, quick heads up. I saw Noah here earlier, so don't go home with any of your students again tonight or he'll be all over your ass with Dr. Cohen.

**Markus:** That soggy ass twatwaffle? What the hell is he doing here? I always assumed he was allergic to beer, or he puts mustard on it or some asinine shit like that.

**Ryan:** He does, in fact. Horseradish too. Along with all perennial plants of the family Brassicaceae, also known as Cruceferae, which includes many genera, species, and cultivars that are raised for food production, such as cauliflower, cabbage, brussels sprouts, and broccoli, and which, most notably, are entirely human inventions that don't occur in nature.

**Markus:** Shit dude, I thought you were an anthropologist, how do you know so much about domesticated varieties of wild cabbage bred from undomesticated Brassica oleracea?

**Ryan:** I could tell you, but then I'd have to *kale* you.

**Markus:** Oh, your, god. Did you just tell me all that shit so I would ask how you knew that so you could make that terrible joke?

**Ryan:** Yes. And it was all worth it. Anyhow, Noah's bitch ass is running around here somewhere, so watch your back.

**Markus:** Oh man, I do not, under any circumstances, want to have to talk to him tonig–

**Ryan:** He's right behind you.

**Markus:** Fuck, dude! I thought you said you had my back.

**Ryan:** No, I said, *you* should watch your back. And you clearly did not.

**Markus:** Oh, hey there Noah, fancy meeting you in a place where nerds don't usually hang out.

**Noah:** Hi Markus, I heard you went home with one of your students last night.

**Markus:** No. No, I most certainly did not.

**Noah:** Well, that's not what I was told. And just so you know, the Board of Regents updated Section 6.2, Article 9, of the Faculty Handbook, which now states that no instructor can have an intimate relationship with their, or any other student on campus.

**Markus:** I'm not sure what you're talking about, Noah. And I doubt you even know what 'intimate relationship' means since you probably still live with your mom and have never had sex with a living creature, humanoid or otherwise. Why don't you bugger off and go round up two of every animal for another one of your little incest cruises. It's been a while since the last one.

**Noah:** That's highly blasphemous, Markus. Also, I have had more sexual intercourse with human women than you have pubic hairs on your tiny balls.

**Markus:** So, none then. Thought so. Anyhow, this has been a super fun chat, Noah, but I'm gonna go fetch a to-go cup for this beer so I don't have to be in the same building as you anymore. Oh yea, that reminds me. Hey Ryan, the rugby team is having a kegger in that big green house down on Mill Street a couple blocks up from the soccer fields. You wanna be my plus-one?

**Ryan:** Dude!

**Markus:** What!?

**Ryan:** Nothing, I'll tell you later. But yes, absolutely. I'll always drink free keg beer over the shit I have to pay for on a TA stipend.

**Markus:** Right on, let's roll out. See ya, Noah. I hope you find a human woman to have consensual sexual intercourse with tonight, ya mustard-loving prick!

# CHAPTER 4
## RECEPTION – TERRA
## 2035 CE

**Markus:** Damn, dude. I didn't realize the walk was so long to get down here from the brewery. Sorry about that, big buddy.

**Ryan:** No worries, it's a lovely evening for a stroll across campus. Besides, it's not your fault. They add a few extra bricks to the street each night once all the college kids are tucked into bed. It likely wasn't this long of a trek the last time you did it.

**Markus:** Hmm, yea, probably not.

**Ryan:** Besides, the Bavarian Illuminati secretly modified all standard units of measure in the late 18th century, so even if you had quantified it beforehand, that would have rendered it moot.

**Markus:** Right, I remember reading something about that in one of my undergraduate classes. Or on the dark web maybe. We are getting close though. In the meantime, here, take a hit of this. It'll make the rest of the walk seem shorter...and full of pulsating fractals.

**Ryan:** I'm good for now man. I'm starting to catch feels from that Molly we ate up at O'Hooley's, and I've got to keep my wits about me in case Sharron is at this party. I can't throw game for shit after smoking weed.

**Markus:** Oh, you're in luck then, cuz this definitely ain't weed!

**Ryan:** I'm still gonna pass for now, especially after hearing the way you just said that.

**Markus:** Wow, so it's getting serious between you two, huh? That's great man. She seems like a cool chica.

**Ryan:** Yea, she's fun. And she keeps me out of trouble, for the most part. The other day we even chatted about our plans for after graduation.

**Markus:** That's fantastic, my dude. I hope it works out for you two. I've got to admit, I'm a little jealy. I've never had a relationship like that with anyone.

**Ryan:** I mean, have you tried? It doesn't seem like you put forth much effort.

**Markus:** No, not really. I sometimes wonder if my dad running off with the babysitter when my brother and I were kids has something to do with my inability to form meaningful bonds with women, or anybody else for that matter. Maybe it instilled a sense that all relationships are ephemeral, and we should always be chasing something new and different.

**Ryan:** Is your brother the same way?

**Markus:** He was, to some extent. But he was younger when it happened, so I don't think it affected him as much. I could just have abandonment issues too. I don't really trust anyone, or myself, which makes it hard to love, I guess. Damn dude, look at us getting all real and shit. Must be the Molly talking—

**Ryan:** Oh fuck, look out Markus!

*Grr, woof, woof, woof!*

**Ryan:** Shit man, did that fucking thing just bite you?

16

**Markus:** No. It came damn close though....

*Grrr, ruff, ruff!*

**Markus:** He's a cute little angry fucker though, ain't he. It's hard to tell with his matted fur and all the mud in his coat, but I think he's a Great Pyrenees. Probably about five or six months old.

*Ruff, ruff!*

**Markus:** I bet he got abandoned by some shithead college kids who thought they could manage having a puppy in a house full of drunk frat boys. I saw it happen a lot when I was an undergraduate here. Poor bastard! Loved for a month, then left for dead. Here ya go little buddy, you want some pocket bacon?

**Ryan:** Why the hell do you have bacon in your pocket?

**Markus:** You clearly aren't a skier, are you?

**Ryan:** Nope, never been.

**Markus:** Ah, man. After the sunshine, the snow bunnies, and the après ski beers, pocket bacon is the best part of a long day on the slopes. It's also great for a night out on the town. This fuzzy bastard likes it too! There ya go buddy, you want some more? Oh, she's a *girl* buddy. You're a little sweety aren't you? I doubt she was trying to bite me. She was probably just scared, and hangry. I want to bite people when I'm hangry too.

**Ryan:** Huh, pocket bacon. Who knew? I think it worked. She seems a lot happier now. Let's get going though. I'm starting to lose my beer buzz, and this is my one big night out for the week.

**Markus:** Dude, we can't just leave her out here in the cold. Tell ya what...let's take her to the party with us, and afterward, I'll bring her home, get her a bath, brush her fur out, then take her to the shelter tomorrow morning. I'd love to keep her, but I sure as hell can't have a 95-pound dog in my tiny apartment while trying to write a dissertation.

**Ryan:** You think she'll get that big?

**Markus:** For sure, mate. A female Great Pyrenees stands 28 inches at the withers and can weigh over 100 pounds at maturity.

**Ryan:** How the hell do you know so much about dogs?

**Markus:** Aw man, when I was a kid, I had this Kennel Club dog book that listed all the different breeds with heaps of stats about each one. I damn near memorized the entire thing. I never had a TV in my room growing up, so I just cracked out on overly detailed books about random shit.

**Ryan:** Huh, I didn't realize you were such a nerd. You hide it well. So, you think she'll follow us to the party?

**Markus:** Hell yea she will. Chicks will do anything for pocket bacon. I can just carry her too.

**Ryan:** Bruh, she's like 40 pounds!

**Markus:** She seems super chill now though. I bet if I give her more bacon, she'll just ride in my backpack. Yea, there ya go, love chunks. That comfy? I'm gonna call you Marshmallow, ya fluffy little fucker.

**Ryan:** You are cracking me up right now, my guy. That Molly must be hitting you hard, cuz you just tamed an angry stray dog in like three minutes.

**Markus:** It's the power of the pocket bacon, amigo. Could be the Molly too though, I guess. Animals vibrate high. Ya just gotta know your audience.

**Ryan:** *Haha*, she looks like she's falling asleep in there.

18

**Markus:** She does. Let's head out, maybe she'll sleep through the whole party. Although, we can't use her to pick up chicks if she's curled up at the bottom of my pack.

**Ryan:** Doesn't matter. You ain't getting no chicks with that raggedy ass mutt till she's had a bath, gotten brushed for three days strait, and gained some weight. Though she does look kinda cute cuddled up in there right now. Why did you bring that big-ass backpack anyway?

**Markus:** Oh, man, I learned my lesson big time hiking across campus in the freezing cold this morning. I've got a warm-ass coat in there, a flask of whisky, and a few beers for good measure. That little life tutorial seems to have worked out well for Marshmallow too. She looks as snug as a stray dog in a daypack in there.

———— ◉ ————

**Markus:** Oh, sweet, we're here.

**Ryan:** Dang, this place is bumping, son! Good call on schlep-ping our asses down here tonight.

**Markus:** For real, looks like a hell of a party! And I highly doubt Noah 'knowas' these people, so we shouldn't have to worry about running into his bitch made ass again.

**Ryan:** Well, normally I would agree. However, you provided an extraordinarily specific description of where this party was when he was standing right next to us back at O'Hooley's earlier.

**Markus:** Oh, damn. You're right. That was dumb! Why didn't you stop me?

**Ryan:** I was giving you that throat-slitting gesture like crazy as soon as you started talking about it, but you just kept run-ning your mouth like a blind Chihuahua licking mayonnaise off a bald hamster.

**Markus:** Yea, shit. My bad, hombre. He wouldn't just show up uninvited though. Would he?

**Ryan:** Man, I never know what people like that are gonna do. One minute they're reading a book about World War I Panzer tanks, and the next they're playing Dungeons & Dragons and drinking strawberry milkshakes while they shoot up a shopping center in the suburbs of some city nobody's ever heard of.

**Markus:** Huh, that all sounds terrifyingly on-brand for him. Well, let's watch *each other's* backs this time.

**Ryan:** Good call. In any case, I dig the music. And it looks like there are quite a few 'not-your-student' coeds running around to keep you entertained. Could be a good time.

**Markus:** Yea, chicks love rugby players. They're the fighter pilot wildebeests of frisbee golfers. Stocky and quick on their feet. Or 'arm legs' as we humans call them in the frisbee golf world.

**Ryan:** Hmm. Yea. So, what was that shit you were smoking on the way down here again?

**Markus:** Hydromorphic Crackicide my friend. The purest, highest-quality Crackicide in the galaxy. Imported directly from the lost city of Atlantis!

**Ryan:** Oh yea, I've heard of that stuff. Isn't it made from unicorn milk or some shit?

**Markus:** *Albino* unicorn milk to be precise. I've found it pairs well with the Molly. You should try it sometime when Sharron ain't around.

**Ryan:** Just might.

**Markus:** Oh, shit! What's up Shane! I haven't seen you in years, man. I didn't even know you went to school here. Ryan, this is

Shane. He's from Springfield too. I knew him since way back in the day when he was just a raucous little kid.

**Ryan:** Sup.

**Shane:** Sup.

**Markus:** Our moms were friends when I was in high school, and he was like 10 years old or something?

**Shane:** That sounds about right.

**Markus:** He was always over at our house banging around breaking shit like a coked-up river otter stranded on a sand dune.

**Shane:** Also, true. It's good to see you, Markus. And yes, I graduated high school a few years back and got a full ride to play rugby here.

**Markus:** Damn, nice dude! I thought I remembered my mom saying you got the Cologne award too.

**Shane:** Yep. Between my rugby scholarship and the Cologne award I've been getting paid a handsome sum of money to go to college. It's not a bad gig.

**Markus:** For sure, that must have been a welcomed occasion since you come from such a 'poor' family and all.

**Shane:** It really was, Markus. I don't know what we would have done since my mom isn't allowed to work and my dad scrapes by on a meager salary as the CEO of my grandfather's multimillion-dollar company.

**Markus:** Right, wow. What a lucky turn of events there.

**Shane:** No, in all seriousness. The good lord has blessed me with his amiable gifts. He's given me the strength to play competitive sports and the dedication to achieve in the classroom, and everything I do is to serve him.

**Markus:** So, you don't think your White privilege and the generational wealth derived from your grandfather's company played a role at all?

**Shane:** No. Anyway, your dad is rich too, so I'm sure you're doing just fine down here.

**Markus:** Shit, I wish. I grew up poor as piss, man! I've been paying for college with student loans and working as many damn jobs as I could find since high school. I'm about to finish a PhD here and I never got a penny from my family—and especially not my bitch-ass, broke-ass dad.

**Shane:** That's weird. When was the last time you talked to him?

**Markus:** It's been a few years since me and the sperm donor last conversed.

**Shane:** Huh, yea, I think that was about when it happened.

**Markus:** When what happened?

**Shane:** Your gracious father won 135 million dollars in the state lottery about three years ago. The good lord has blessed him too it would seem. He lives in a massive house just up from Johnson's Ridge now. Really nice place. He welcomes our church group up for barbeques about once a month during the summer. And just between you and me, I think he bought your stepmom some of those fancy silicon breasts—she's looking quite buxom these days.

**Markus:** OK, you little perv, she's like twice your age. Or maybe not. Now that I think about it, she was only about eight years older than me when they started hooking up. So, if I'm 30 now, and when I was in high school you were about—aw, fuck it, I don't know. What a dick though! I can't believe he never told me he's a millionaire. Can't believe my brother never told me either.

**Shane:** It's probably because you turned away from god, Markus.

**Markus:** Maybe that's it, Shane. Or maybe he's just a dick, as per my previous assertion. I swear, the worst things always happen to the best people and the best things to the worst.

**Shane:** Oh, your dad *is* the best people! Absolutely! He's a gift from god! He is extremely active in our church, he financed the re-election campaigns of countless conservative politicians throughout the state, he supports our missionary work in Botswana so we can save the souls of the primitive savages there, and he just donated a ton of money to help build a new sanctuary.

**Markus:** Like, a bird sanctuary?

**Shane:** No, it's a 45,000 square foot cathedral they're adding on to our church. The same as what you see in big European cities.

**Markus:** You mean, like Cologne, for instance?

**Shane:** I don't know. If that is in France, then probably.

**Markus:** Well, that's just fucking fantastic! I'm down here, broke off my ass, paying for my entire undergraduate and graduate education, while that little angel is up there building megachurches for rich people and getting fake tits for his babysitter wife!

**Shane:** It's god's plan. god has a plan for you too, Markus.

**Markus:** Not the same one I have apparently. The great irony of all this is even before he won the lottery, that self-righteous bastard told me he would pay for my college if I studied to be a doctor or went to seminary. He all but disowned me when I told him I wanted to be an anthropologist. You should've seen his face when he found out we study human evolution too. I thought he was having a stroke.

**Shane:** Yea, what *are* you going to do with that anyway? Like, what is anthropology? What are you going to make to sell for a living?

**Markus:** I'm gonna make babies with your fat fuckin sister and sell them into slavery you little pecker weasel, what do you mean what am I going to make to sell?! That's one hell of a narrow-ass view of society you've got there, where the only way to earn a living is to make cheeseburgers and widgets for the man. Ain't they teach you nothing at this school? Come take my class next fall before I graduate this shithole institute of higher education and I'll learn you up real good.

**Ryan:** Careful, he might try to fuck you too.

**Markus:** Shut up, Ryan. I don't fuck all my students, and I don't swing from that side of the plate anyhow.

**Ryan:** I'm not sure you're swinging much at all there, little man.

**Shane:** Yea, Markus, your girlfriend told me you have a tiny penis, like a little prepubescent boy.

**Markus:** Good one, Shane. Ok! Well! This has been a super fun night of conversation across the board. I'm gonna hit the head and try to find the kegs.

**Shane:** I'll show you where they are. I live here, and I bought all the kegs.

**Markus:** Of course you did. Hey, while we're at it, you got any hot dogs?

**Shane:** Always. Why?

**Markus:** I'm taking care of this puppy until I can get her to the shelter tomorrow and I'm all out of pocket bacon. She's bound to be hungry when she wakes up.

**Shane:** No problem, I'll grab some and meet you out on the back porch where the kegs are. Just head down this hallway and take a right at the bathroom.

**Markus:** Word up, thanks man. And sorry about the fat-sister tirade earlier.

**Shane:** I've heard worse. I live with a houseful of rugby players after all.

**Markus:** True that. See ya outside.

# CHAPTER 5
## INAUGURATION – TERRA
### 2035 CE

**Markus:** Hey, Ryan Reynolds Roberts?

**Ryan:** Yes, what is it, the Honorable Dr. Markus P. Moksha PhD Esquire the Third?

**Markus:** I'm fucked up, man.

**Ryan:** Yea, me too.

**Markus:** Though in considering my current state of relative fucked-upery, I do sense that my visual acuity remains intact.

**Ryan:** While they are a scooch red and squinty, I can verify that your eyes do look operational, sir.

**Markus:** OK. Well then. Gander with me lad.... Over yonder way, does that look to you like four rugby players grabbing that exceptionally drunk woman's tits as they carry her back behind those bushes?

**Ryan:** Hmm, now that you mention it, yes, that's exactly what it looks like to me.

**Markus:** Ahh, and how do we feel about this recent development?

**Ryan:** Well, the effeminate namby-pamby in me is absolutely fine with it. But the side of me that has empathy for others and respect for the laws of our current society feels other-wise. And the latter me is currently winning.

**Markus:** Yes. Good. Then I shall call out to these savages in the hopes that it alters their brutish behavior and iniquitous intent....

*He he*m.

**Markus:** Hey, Giant Neanderthal Fuckos! Why Are You Carrying That Passed Out Drunk Chick into Those Dark and Rapey Looking Bushes!?!

**Ryan:** Seems you got their attention. But run, they did not.

**Markus:** Shit. Alright. I guess it's go time then. Smack me in the face!

*Thwap*!

**Markus:** Nice shot, Ryan! OK. Crosscheck and all-call: Deadened senses? Check. Depth perception? Questionable. Other bigger dudes who can help us out? Negative. Attack-dog sidekick? Underdeveloped.

*Ruff*

**Markus:** No, Marshmallow, you're just a puppy. You stay up here on the porch. Don't be a hero.

*Ruff*

**Markus:** No Marshmallow. We've got this. I've been watching internet tutorials on how to do the martial arts real good, so we'll be fine.

**Ryan:** Come on Markus, they're taking off her pants!

**Markus:** Shit, this is gonna hurt.

———— ◉ ————

**Markus:** Well, we definitely didn't win that fight, but at least we caused enough of a scene that those brow-ridgers took off running. Why don't you go inside and see if anybody knows who those assholes were, and I'll stay with this partied-out sorority chick to make sure she's alright. Try to find Shane too; he might know which of his footballer friends that could have been.

**Ryan:** Um, I only met him briefly, and it's incredibly dark back here, but I'm pretty sure one of those rapey fuckers that just kicked our asses was Shane.

**Markus:** god damnit, of course it was—that rich entitled prick. Nice christian values there, asshole! Well, at least go call the cops, maybe the fuzz can track down a few of them. I reckon they couldn't have gone far since they seemed fucked up too.

**Ryan:** Alright man, but if they come back, you're on your own.

**Markus:** I was on my own that whole time you flaccid ass mutherfucker! What did you land, like one punch?

**Ryan:** Naw, I came in blasting with a sweet Bruce Lee-style jumpkick, then I got in at least two left hooks on half of one of them once probably.

**Markus:** I'm sure you did, tough guy. Hey, will you check to see if Marshmallow is still on the porch when you head up there too?

**Ryan:** No problem. And I'm sure she is. I could hear her barking the whole time we were down here. Ight, imma head inside.

———— ◉ ————

**Markus:** Hey, are you ok? You seem really drunk, and I think those guys were trying to take advantage of you?

**Dordogne Silex:** Hello, Markus. Thank you for saving me again.

**Markus:** Uh, I don't recall having ever saved you before, but you're welcome. Also, who are you? And how do you know my name?

**Dordogne:** Soon the entire world will know your name, Markus Moksha, though they call you by many.

**Markus:** That's cryptic as all fuck. You also don't seem drunk anymore. Or at all. Were you ever drunk? Am I drunk? Yes, very. What's happening here exactly?

**Dordogne:** I've been watching you for years, and I needed to know if you were ready yet, if it is time for you to start your journey.

**Markus:** OK. Cryptic and creepy now.

**Dordogne:** There is much I want to tell you Markus, but I can't yet. You will be briefed on some critical elements of the mission when we get to the Moon Base tonight, but much of what you will come to understand will be learned along your own path to becoming.

**Markus:** Becoming what?

**Dordogne:** Come with me. They're waiting for us at the soccer fields.

**Markus:** I mean, shit, I've left parties with some weird chicks over the last 12 years at uni, but never one who wanted to take me home to her Moon Base. I can only hope that's a euphemism for a hot sex dungeon or something.

**Dordogne:** It is not. Unfortunately, perhaps. Though your relationship with sex has always fascinated me, Markus. Human mating behavior is something I have studied for millennia, and in considering the endless variation observable among my countless research subjects, I find your perception and approach to the coital act to be among the most curious and convoluted.

**Markus:** Oh yea, how so?

**Dordogne:** You desperately seek unity with humanity through a woman's touch, and you feel a spiritual connection with both, in the trice it is achieved. But you do not allow yourself to nurture it beyond that moment of harmonious accord. You use sex as you use alcohol and drugs: to escape something, to hide from something, to blanket your anxiety and animosity with fleeting pleasures that open transient windows to the soul.

**Markus:** Wow, that's a hot take for a total stranger, but I can't say you're wrong. In fact, I said something similar, but much less poetic, to my friend Ryan on the way down here. I'm also inclined to trust the psychoanalysis of someone who has watched people have sex for thousands of years. How did you get that job anyway? It sounds fun. And does it say 'Intertemporal Sex Researcher' on your business card?

**Dordogne:** What's a business card?

**Markus:** Not important. I am curious about something else though.... About halfway through what you just said I noticed that your mouth stopped moving, but I could still hear everything you were saying as clearly as when you were vocalizing it, and in your same voice, but just, in my mind.

**Dordogne:** That is a longstanding evolutionary trait of the cohesive Superhuman consciousness, Markus. In fact, I sometimes forget there was ever a time when we didn't communicate this way.

**Markus:** Huh, nuts. Well, I'm gonna run inside and tell Ryan I'm walking you home...to the Moon. He'll get a kick out of that.

**Dordogne:** There is no time.

**Markus:** What do you mean? You don't seem like you're in a hurry. In fact, I'm not sure I've ever seen anyone walk so slowly in my entire life. Do you not have gravity up there on your Moon Base or something?

**Dordogne:** No, what I mean is there is no time for them now. Look behind you. Time is frozen in their reference frame. There is no movement. There is no time.

**Markus:** Oh snap, did you do that? Also, how did you do that? This is getting progressively more bizarre by the minute. I should probably lay off the Crackicide for a while.

**Dordogne:** Wait, you were smoking Hydromorphic Crackicide? That isn't invented for another 1,800 years.

**Markus:** Hell yea, I love that shit! I've accumulated quite a stockpile since it's so damn hard to get. Well, if I can't talk to Ryan, can I at least go fetch my frozen-ass dog? I'm all she has right now.

**Dordogne:** Oh my yes, of course, I love Marshmallow! We will keep her in a de-animated state until we get up to the base, so she isn't unsettled by her rapid change in environment.

**Markus:** Good call. Be right back.

....

**Markus:** *Huh, huh, huh, phoo.* Alright, I got the doggo. And I have to say, it was crazy strange walking around all those frozen zombie folks back there. Can't say I've ever experienced anything like that.

**Dordogne:** No, it isn't common for people in your time to be the single animated soul among the immobilized. But no one remembers it when they are the de-animated ones either, for it is impossible to form memories without the movement of moments.

**Markus:** Huh, good point, why would they remember anything without the passage of time. Umm.... Holy shit! Are you seeing this?! Look up!

**Dordogne:** *Hehe*, yes Markus. I forgot how easily amused you are.

**Markus:** No, check it out. There's a massive UFO directly above us!

**Dordogne:** Yes, Markus. That is ours. And it's not a UFO. It's a time machine. But for now, it's our ride up to Luna Sede. The team and I will explain more once we get up there. Step into this beam of light with me.

**Markus:** Wow, cool elevator. I still don't get how you froze time all around us though, or why.

**Dordogne:** It wasn't me, Markus. It is just one of many advanced capabilities of our ships. It is also how we can move into populated areas without being detected. Our ships transport us to the future and past, but they can also manipulate the flow of time as you protohumans perceive it. This allows us to speed up, stop, or slow down time within a certain perimeter around the craft, so no one disturbs us while we carry out our operations.

**Markus:** Would those operations happen to include abducting people and sticking things up their asses?

**Dordogne:** Our fecal extraction procedure is only one small part of a much larger venture that spans tens of thousands of years. It is curious that your culture focuses so much on the anal probe aspect of our work.

**Markus:** Yea, we're some sick fucks. I blame millennia of religious repression.

**Dordogne:** According to my statistical research, religion is a significant independent variable in that equation.

**Markus:** I believe it. Hey, you aren't going to anal probe me, are you?

**Dordogne:** Do you want us to?

**Markus:** Will you be the one doing it?

**Dordogne:** I can be if you want.

**Markus:** Then yes. Absolutely!

**Dordogne:** You may also be interested to know we have another machine that we place over your peni–

**Professor Julian Atman:** Hello Dordogne, welcome back. I see you retrieved Markus, haggard as he may be. Did he not come peacefully?

**Dordogne:** No, he came peacefully. I just needed to see if he was ready to join us, so I utilized the classic 'damsel in distress' protocol from the fairy tales of their times, and it worked exceedingly well.

**Markus:** For you maybe, but my face would suggest otherwise.

**Dordogne:** Your face didn't look any better beforehand.

**Markus:** Ouch. So, you're saying you let me get my ass kicked by a gaggle of massive wildebeest frisbee golfers as some kind of character assessment? Couldn't you have just asked me a couple questions, or picked me up in a flying car after I played a few rounds of the Starfighter arcade game?

**Dordogne:** No, this tactic was far more effective, and much more fun for me to watch.

**Markus:** Marvelous, so glad you enjoyed the show. But what if I hadn't 'passed the test,' and Ryan and I never came to chase those dudes away? I doubt you could have defended yourself against them. We certainly couldn't.

**Dordogne:** Oh, you need not worry about me, Markus, for I have this time wand, you see. In addition to the broad temporal stoppages we perform with the ship, I can point this electro-magnetic energy wand at any living creature, and it temporarily stops them in time until I choose to reanimate them. If you and Ryan hadn't come to my fake rescue, I would have frozen those brutish men in that moment. And then for fun, I'd have taken off their clothes and positioned them so it looked like they were all having sex with each other upon reanimation.

**Markus:** Diabolical, I dig it.

**Dordogne:** Also, if I aim the wand at their penises, they can't achieve an erection for seven months.

**Markus:** I imagine that would have taught them a thing or two about being sexual predators as well.

**Dordogne:** Indubitably. A part of me was secretly hoping you and Ryan wouldn't come over to help.

**Markus:** You future chicks are some strange birds. Speaking of. What did that guy call you when we got up here? I never did get your name, which seems odd considering I was will-ing to follow you into a dark field and up into a UFO.

**Dordogne:** My name is Dordogne.

**Markus:** Oh, that's right. Cool name, is that French?

**Dordogne:** Very. And this is Professor Julian Atman,

**Atman:** Hello, Markus. It's great to finally meet you.

**Dordogne:** Professor Atman and I are the lead anthro-pologists on this mission. The three of us will be working

34

together over the next few weeks, along with Major General Metathory, and a small crew of linguists, psychologists, philosophers, engineers, and a few others.

**Markus:** To be honest, I don't think we have a few weeks to do anything. Have you been watching the news at all? Shit is getting intense down there. It's nearing the boiling point if you ask me.

**Dordogne:** It is, Markus, and that is exactly why we're here. But we won't be working in this time. In fact, we are excited to announce that this will be a mission to the deepest part of the past we have ever visited!

**Markus:** Right on. That means nothing to me since I don't know any of the other times you've visited. But, good on ya.

**Dordogne:** And if this mission is successful, when we arrive back in this period, everything will be the same, except all the religious and political tension of your time will be gone, and you will return to live a carefree life in a peaceful world.

**Markus:** That sounds amazing. It's hard as shit living a 'care-restricted' life in this 'anti-peaceful' world right now. There is so much manufactured hate and a complete lack of empathy for others. It's relentlessly exhausting and depressing. I used to eat Molly at raves and dance all night holding hands with shiny happy people, and now I just eat Molly and cry.

**Dordogne:** That's sad, Markus, and a waste of good drugs. But hopefully we'll be able to fix the past so you can return home to rave dance with shiny people once again.

**Markus:** Thanks Dordogne, I miss it. Speaking of, you said you will bring me back to this place *and time*, right? Ryan froze before I could tell him where I was going, and I don't want him to think I pulled an Irish goodbye, or that the brow-ridgers came back, or that I got abducted by aliens. I also have to be back to give an exam in my Intro to Anthropology class on Monday.

**Dordogne:** We all do, Markus. We all do. And yes, once we have completed the mission, Professor Atman and I will return you to this exact moment, in this same soccer field, where you can rejoin your temporal cohort.

**Markus:** That would be great, thanks. It's also wicked cool how you can make your ship transparent while looking out from the inside. I can see the entire sky above, and all of campus below, in all directions. I see that house party where we just were too, with everybody still frozen in place outside.

**Atman:** Pretty groovy, huh?

**Markus:** Nobody says that in this time, Professor. But yea, y'all honkeys got some fucked-up technology. Hey, quick question…. If you will use time travel to return me to this exact place and time, shouldn't we be seeing another ship with Future Us onboard, dropping Future Me off right now?

**Atman:** You were right, Dordogne, this kid is a little sharper than I thought—despite his often-offensive eccentric expletives and vulgar vocalized vagaries.

**Markus:** Ooo, killer alliterations, Doc. But you're not supposed to use those in creative writing to emphasize words, phrases, and ideas outside of clichés, titles, and poetry.

**Atman:** I don't think your readers will mind, Markus. And to answer your question, yes, you would expect to see exactly that. However, we will be bringing you back here, and 'almost now,' to a time shortly after we soon leave. This will help mitigate destructive resonance in the chronographic gravity waves used to arrest perceived temporal flow in proximity to the ship.

**Markus:** Right on. That checks out. I assume.

**Atman:** Alright, let's get you up to the Moon Base so you can meet the rest of the team.

**Markus:** Oh, hell yea! I thought Dordogne was just jerking my chain off about that Moon Base shit. 'Pass the word along. Tell the men it's time to...shoot tha Moon.'

Damn, I can't wait to get up there and see what a—

**Atman:** OK, we're here.

**Markus:** 'Shoot tha Moooon!' Holy shit, already?! What was that like five seconds, tops? We flew up here at thousands of kilometers per hour in five seconds, but I didn't feel a thing. Shouldn't we be splattered against the walls of the ship?! That's gotta be like 10,000 g-forces!

**Dordogne:** That is the beauty of a time machine, Markus. We can move through space and time almost instantly in our reference frame. We simply alter the rate at which time passes in space, and the speed at which space goes by in time, so we arrive both where and when we are going with only brief moments having passed for us inside the ship, and we feel hardly any g-forces at all.

**Markus:** That is the most interesting thing I've ever heard, Dordogne. Also, please don't stop talking. Ever.

**Dordogne:** OK then. Well...to an observer outside the ship, it looks as if we are accelerating at an incredibly fast speed. However, for us inside the ship, it's the opposite, where we see them moving extremely slowly. It is all relative to the observer's perceived temporal reference frame. That is also why it is so easy for us to evade your fighter planes and munitions when you shoot at our time discs with your primitive weapons—because to us, the bullets and missiles appear to be moving at a snail's pace.

**Markus:** I said never stop talking.

**Dordogne:** I don't know what else—oh, and the light beam that transported us up to the craft has antigravity characteristics and is capable of manipulating corporeal substances in spacetime. It's a process called quantum tunneling, where particles within the beam remain in a superposition and never fully interact with matter on the subatomic level at any temporal destination. By maintaining their wavelike unmeasured state, while slightly modifying the frequency of these waves, they can pass through solid physical barriers while avoiding decoherence, which allows us to carry people through walls, ceilings, and roofs without collapsing the wave function.

**Markus:** Huh, I always wondered how you did that.

**Dordogne:** Our technology must look like magic to you, but I'm sure once the mission is complete it will all seem entirely normal.

**Markus:** Yea, about that.... What is our mission exactly? I've gathered that y'all are anthropologists, and time travelers, and you're trying to make people in my time suck less, but I'm still trying to wrap my head around how you're going to do that and, most importantly, what the hell I could possibly have to contribute.

**Dordogne:** Well, you're in luck, we've just docked, and our next stop is mission control. Professor Atman and the Major General will fill you in on the details of the operation there.

# CHAPTER 6
## PONTIFICATION – THE MOON
## 2035 CE

**Markus:** Damn, nice Moon Base you've got here. Some long-ass hallways though. Y'all should put in some of those flat escalator, travelator things like what they have in airports and the Paris Metro.

**Dordogne:** We don't use airports. For what I hope are obvious reasons.

**Markus:** Oh, yea, right. Sorry.

**Dordogne:** I'll forgive you. OK, we've arrived at mission control, and this is our commanding officer. Hello, Major Metathory, this is Markus Moksha.

**Major General Metathory:** Bonjour Markus, I'm happy it's finally time for you to join us. I feel like we've all been stuck up here on this crater-infested wasteland for an eternity waiting for this new mission to begin.

**Markus:** I'm tentatively happy to join you too, Major, despite having absolutely no idea why I'm here. Although, I should point out that it's nighttime, so you can no longer bonjour me.

**Metathory:** It's morning time in France right now.

**Markus:** True, but it's dark here. One can't simply say hello based on whatever random time zone they chose from anywhere around the world at any given time.

**Metathory:** Perhaps, though I'm quite sure I've heard you say 'it's five o'clock somewhere' myriad times throughout your life. And possibly every day.

**Markus:** Touché

**Metathory:** Furthermore, we're on the far side of the Moon, where it will remain dark for the next twelve days. Would you really want to rob an old man of his right to greet people with a traditional French salutation simply because he is stationed somewhere the sun doesn't shine for two weeks at a time?

**Markus:** No, I guess not.

**Metathory:** Besides, by these pliable rules of logic, it means it's always five o'clock here. Care for some bourbon?

**Markus:** Shit yea, I lost my buzz big time when y'all had me get my ass kicked to see if I was ready to come hang out with you on your sweet-ass Moon Base, so hit me up. And make it a double.

**Atman:** Our apologies, Markus. Dordogne occasionally takes creative liberties with people on various missions to the past. It has gotten her into trouble, but she's one of our best anthropologists, so we keep her on the payroll. I apologize if you were harmed, we never would have sanctioned that approach.

**Markus:** Creative liberties indeed, thanks Dordogne.

**Dordogne:** You got it tough guy…. Professor, while you and Major Metathory get Markus caught up on the mission, I'm going to head across the room to the quantum mainframe and run some calculations in preparation for our departure to 48k BP. Just call out if you need me.

**Atman:** OK, thank you Dordogne, we should be leaving soon.

**Markus:** The funny part is, that was the third ass beating I've received in the last two days. This one seems worth the sacrifice though. I've always been easily bored by the banality of my reality, and this place is anything but banal. How long has this base been here anyway? Or did you transport me to a future time while we were coming up to the Moon, since that's maybe how spacetime travel works, I have no idea.

**Metathory:** No Markus, we're on the Moon in your time, and by now the base has been here for about 60 years. We started drawing up plans for it in the 1970s in collaboration with certain governments of that era, and mostly with your United States government, since those lucky bastards happened to get ahold of one of our ships after a mechanical failure took her down during a routine mission to the southwestern US in 1947. From then on, it was only a matter of time before we had to come clean about who we are, when we come from, and what we're doing.

**Markus:** It's funny you say, 'when we come from.' Everybody on Earth thinks you're space aliens. 'Extraterrestrials' they call you.

**Metathory:** Yes, I know. It's remarkably stupid considering we look virtually identical to you.

**Markus:** Seriously.

**Metathory:** It's asinine really.

**Markus:** But of course, I never thought that.

**Metathory:** No, I'm sure you didn't, Markus. Not once.

**Markus:** Nope, not once. It never even crossed my mind.

**Metathory:** Good, because it's very stupid. Beyond our shared bipedalism, which is the trait that defines the hominin lineage for fuck's sake, we each have bilateral symmetry with two gut openings, the same cranial and post-cranial characteristics in essentially the same position and proportions, we breathe the same air, we can communicate in your languages, and hell, from time to time, we even have sex with you. It would be nearly impossible for us to copulate if we had evolved on a different planet and didn't share all the same bits and pieces.

**Markus:** I imagine that's true, Major. Do you think there are any extraterrestrial species who evolved razor-sharp canine teeth in their vaginas?

**Metathory:** No. Anyhow, if I remember correctly, we completed construction on Luna Sede sometime in the late 1970s, and the base has been an invaluable asset for our time travel research ever since. It has served as an 'intertemporal base camp' or 'staging grounds' for our operations, and particularly during this all-important period you're from, Markus.

**Markus:** Wow, I had no idea. I don't think anyone down on Earth knows about this place either.

**Metathory:** That's surprising. People first came up here to the Moon in 1969, and the last US mission departed the lunar surface in December 1972. Curiously, you haven't 'officially' been back since, despite developing far more sophisticated technology that would make a lunar voyage infinitely easier. Haven't you wondered why nobody has been back to the Moon since 1972?

**Markus:** That's a hard nope. People in my present don't talk about stuff like that. Politicoreligious feuds, sports, celebrity gossip, and 24-hour cable news channels keep our minds occupied so we never have to waste time with reality things.

**Metathory:** Okay, well. The main reason people from your time hadn't 'officially' been back to the Moon is because they were already coming here...just in secrecy.

**Markus:** Yes, I assumed that was where you were going with all this. Way to bury the lede there, Captain Obvious.

**Metathory:** My title is Major. Major General, to be precise.

**Atman:** Major Metathory is right, Markus. I've been working these missions longer than anyone and having the base here since the 1970s has been critical for our operations. It serves as a zero-point time that we can use to travel back as far as 30,000 years into the past. Starting from this 'now,' saves a lot of time, money, and resources, as opposed to jumping back from our home time in the future with everything we need for each mission. People from various points in your future can send and house their researchers here as well, which facilitates cross-temporal collaboration with other scientists from innumerable times and places. There may be people from as many as 75–100 different cultures spread across 25,000 years, all living and working in harmony here on Luna Sede.

**Markus:** That's remarkable, Professor. It sounds like quite the genial communion. Do you ever bring people you abduct on Earth up here to the Moon Base to rape their butt holes and molest their no-no squares, or is that all done on the ships?

**Atman:** That is an egregious oversimplification of our procedures, but the short answer is yes. In fact, a big part of why we began collaborating with a few governments from your time is because we reached a mutually beneficial agreement with them. Specifically, we would continue our abductions, biomedical exams, breeding programs, and monitoring of the environment and ecology of Earth through time. And in exchange for helping to guard our secret until humanity was primed for disclosure, they are granted full access to Luna Sede.

**Markus:** Why would these earthly governments care about a Moon Base nobody knows about or can easily get to?

**Metathory:** I'll answer this one, Professor, since we're starting to get into the logistics of the mission.

**Atman:** No, Major, I've studied countless economic, political, and religious systems over tens of thousands of years—I can offer ample insight beyond the simple quid pro quo explanation.

**Metathory:** Alright, Atman, just don't get all hippie-dippy on us.

**Atman:** Markus, despite erecting a façade of democracy, Earth's governments have always been ruled by oligarchs, who were fully aware that the system they perpetuated was untenable. Whether it was the overextraction and overconsumption of resources that led to environmental degradation, or the system of inequality they nurtured to protect their power and grow their riches, none of it is sustainable.

**Markus:** So, what's the reason for this again?

**Atman:** They knew Earth would inevitably become inhospitable. They saw how their system of institutionalized inequality would result in global revolution. It was also obvious that the culture of dogmatic political and religious machismo they used as a means of social control was likely to result in another global conflict, but this time, with thermonuclear weapons.

**Markus:** Same shit, different century. Here we go again.

**Atman:** Indeed. It was patently clear that they would need a place to escape when the system they built upon a foundation of bloody sand came crashing down around them. Luna Sede is a sanctuary for those with the means to escape the perils they perpetuated upon the people of Earth. A sort of noah's ark if you will.

**Markus:** Oh man, I fuckin hate that guy. So, you mean this place shifted from being a place of international and intertemporal research to acting as a hideout for the rich assholes and power-hungry elites who could afford to leave on their little dick rockets and escape the Earth-fuckery of their own making?

**Atman:** That's one way of putting it. This is difficult for me to say, Markus, but there is a war coming to your time. A bad one, where most of the human population will die. Our mission is to travel back through the past to find something we can change that will help avert the Great War.

**Markus:** That's fucked up. So, if we don't fix the right thing at the right time, those rich assholes get to sip eight martinis up here on the dark side of the Moon while everyone else is incinerated in a nuclear holocaust down on Earth?

**Metathory:** Alright Professor Patchouli, I said no hippie shit. If you're done with your anti-capitalist, tree-hugger, bong-hit, drum circle session, I'll take it from here.

**Atman:** Sure thing, Major Mossback, take it away.

**Metathory:** These exalted entrepreneurs earned the right to enjoy the fruits of their labor, and they deserve a safe place to escape if people ever become jealous of what they achieved through all their hard work and dedication. It was their innovation and drive that helped build civilization, as well as this Moon Base up here. *They* should be the ones to help guide the rebirth of society if it does happen to collapse, by no fault of their own, mind you. Would you really want a plumber and an elementary school teacher ushering in the dawn of a new civilization?

**Markus:** If they are good people, then yes, abso-fuck-ing-lutely! I would much rather live among educated empathetic individuals, and be able to take a shit with running water, than have some fat CEO of a dildo company telling me I don't deserve to live because I didn't happen to get rich from my grandfather starting a dildo factory. We need transgenerational empathy, not transgenerational wealth passed from dick to asshole.

**Metathory:** That is the way it has always been, Markus. Throughout human history, those with an innovative spirit and the drive to achieve have survived and prospered, while those who lack motivation or useful ideas die.

**Markus:** Wrong! They die at the hands of the fascist consumerists who take all the resources for themselves, or who kill them for wanting their fair share, or who make them fight in their ideological conflicts, or who get rich selling weapons to other people who will do their killing for them as they watch from their ivory towers and wargasm all over the faces of the duped and dead!

**Metathory:** god damn, kid, were you taking bong hits with the bohemian boffin over there?

**Markus:** Fuck you Major Muffin Top! For far too long those with opulent affluenza have used politics and religion to blind people to the fact that they're being raped in their tender little asses. The ignorant look back, directly into the eyes of their rapist, and they smile, because god blessed that rapist, and only god knows what's best for them. The self-serving system these elitist twats eulogize, and the education they starve people of, perpetuates this rape culture through time. That false narrative of 'innovation and drive' you jerk off to in the shower every morning is a capitalist meritocratic fallacy. Wealth is stolen, not achieved! The externalized costs of the sociopath's successes are masticated and regurgitated back into the baby bird mouths of the unenlightened lemmings who think the blue pill is a suppository that their fascist false prophets prescribed! 'Bend over so we can ram this magic bean up your ignorant asses with our shiny platinum cocks ya dumb fucks!!'

**Metathory:** Simmer down now, Soldier. It's human nature. It's survival of the fittest.

**Markus:** Wrong again, Major Mooseknuckle. Reciprocity and cooperation were how humans prospered for 99% of our species' history. Survival of the fittest was a cultural construct meant to legitimize eugenics and white colonial crimes of the late 1800s, and only *after* reciprocity was replaced by capitalism. It's survival of the selfish now, motherfucker! That bullshit imperialist mindset is what got us into this mess here in my time, and I can't tell you how much I hate hearing that it's part of the human future as well. If y'all are so keen on changing something to avoid this war, that's a damn good place to start.

**Metathory:** Well, maybe that's why you're here, Markus. I hope we all succeed. To be honest, I don't much care for these Moon Base assholes either. And I'm certainly not looking forward to being crammed in here with a whole slew of them once the bombs start flying. Yet another motivation for stopping the war, I guess.

**Markus:** I doubt there's jack all I or anybody else can do to stop assholes like you. You're the *Pan troglodytes* to our *Pan paniscus.* You fuck to dominate, and we fuck to love. You've only won up till now because fighters kill lovers out of fear. You fear intellect and change. You are cowards who have no qualms about shooting an unarmed man in the dick from behind. You sow your seeds of hate, but we keep pulling your noxious weeds, so the garden still grows. We feed you, despite you pissing all over the harvest. You blamed Eve for the exodus from Eden, but you'd already burnt paradise to the ground long before you ever put that apple in her fucking mouth!

**Metathory:** jesus christ. I extend an olive branch, and this little shit turns it around to stick up my ass! Leave the anal probing to us, Kid.

**Markus:** Yea, alright, sorry. I'll admit, I might have gotten a little charged up there.

**Metathory:** Ya think?!

**Atman:** I'll have to side with Markus on this one, Major. He makes some good points.

**Markus:** Thanks, Professor.

**Atman:** It's not his fault either. From my research, I've found that a cross-temporal and cross-cultural perspective of the interplay among economics, politics, and religion can only act to cause anger and frustration in those paying attention to what's been happening over the last 500 years, leading up to the escalating conflict presently in progress down on Earth.

**Markus** Couldn't agree more, Doc. And speaking of, why the hell are there so many anthropologists up here? If you're try-ing to stop a war, shouldn't you all be military folk like Major Metathory?

**Metathory:** I'm an anthropologist too, dickweed. Many of us in the military are.

**Markus:** Well, I guess we're all fucked then. Y'all are going to try to save the world with bullwhips, Fedoras, and a crippling fear of snakes, when nobody down there even knows what an anthropologist is, what we do, or apparently, what we're going to 'make to sell for a living.'

**Atman:** I'll take this one too, Major.

**Metathory:** Have at it, Professor Patchouli. I need a break from talking to this loose-lipped tart anyhow.

**Atman:** Anthropologists are tasked with studying human variation across space and through time, but people in this present proudly disavow the past and instead choose to repeat historic follies. They don blinders fabricated from na-tionalist and religious dogma as they recklessly construct the other. They are incapable of seeing past these divisive vices to transcend ego and embrace their shared humanity and

48

collective consciousness. An anthropological understanding of how the past connects to the present and future imbues us with an invaluable set of skills and knowledge that may be our last hope of averting the Great War.

**Markus:** OK, so, let me see if I've got this strait…. There's an imminent nuclear war happening in my time, which is palpable, and it's up to this rag-tag team of Indiana Jones wannabes to go back in time to find something you can change to keep that war from happening? Is that right?

**Metathory:** That's right, maggot.

**Markus:** Nice cliché, Major. So, how bad is it?

**Metathory:** What's your current population down there in the year 2035, like 10 billion people?

**Markus:** I don't know, but it's a lot. You get that sense every time you step out the front door to do anything, anywhere. You can't even travel anymore. The last time I visited the Eiffel Tower there were 10-foot-tall bulletproof glass walls all around it and you couldn't get anywhere close, but there were still thousands of people crammed up against the barricades like we were all in some sort of shitty tourist prison camp.

**Metathory:** Alright, well let's just say it's around 10 billion people. By the end of the war, only about 5% of the human population remains.

**Markus:** Holy ghost of J-Rod's future past! So, 9.2 billion people die?!

**Metathory:** Well, no…. 9.5 billion people die…. 9.2 billion would be 8%, and I said it's 5% that survive. jesus, I thought you said this kid was smart, Professor, he was off by like 300 million people.

**Markus:** You also just *estimated* that the current population is 10 billion, so I had some wiggle room, chach gobbler.

49

**Metathory:** Fuzzy primitive-human math aside...yea, it's bad. Why do you think our ships have been hanging around nuclear installations and aircraft carriers for so long? The writing's been all over the walls ever since you chainsaw-juggling fuck monkeys started making weapons that can kill off most of the human population and transform our planet into an eschatological wasteland. Just because you got to live on Earth first doesn't mean you can fuck it up before it's our turn, you selfish pricks.

**Markus:** Sorry, but move your feet, lose your seat.

**Metathory:** That makes no god damn sense whatsoev—

**Markus:** Ya know what's really messed up, is that a ton of those politically and religiously dogmatic assholes the Professor was just talking about actually want an apocalypse to happen for some wyrd-ass pious or political cult reason.

**Metathory:** No. They don't. Trust me. I've seen what it looks like on the other side of those nukes going off, and it ain't pretty. You take all those popular postapocalyptic movies from your time, puke 'em up into a 10-gallon bucket, then hot sauce diarrhea shit all over 'em, and that still doesn't come close. You may romanticize that reality, but it's the ugliest of all human times.

**Markus:** Hmm, delightful. From now on can only the Professor and Dordogne explain the mission to me?

**Metathory:** Fuck you God, you have no idea!

**Markus:** Did he just call me God?

**Atman:** Right, so, fortunately for Dordogne, myself, and the rest of the crew, who would rather not listen to two toddlers squabble throughout the most important mission in future-human history, you two won't be working in close quarters. While we're traveling to the past, the major will be holding down the fort here on Luna Sede. However, we will be checking in with him regularly so he can inform us as to what the Looking Glass says about what we are doing and what the probability is that the changes we make to the timeline will help avert the war.

**Markus:** The Looking Glass? Y'all got a crystal ball up here on the Moon too?

**Atman:** No, Markus. Well, sort of. We are in possession of a device that allows us to see into the future. To some extent. But only up to a certain point in time. And it only gives us probabilities, not ultimate outcomes.

**Markus:** Sounds like a crystal ball to me.

**Atman:** It's complicated. But soon, for reasons it can't or won't predict, the device no longer provides probabilistic predictions about future events. However, the good news is we have it now, and we plan to use it on this mission to guide us in making the correct change to the timeline, in the right period, to reduce the likelihood of this impending nuclear annihilation. We've calculated that a probability of conflict below 22% is likely to avert the catastrophe, which would mean we have successfully completed our mission.

**Markus:** Right on, Professor, but I'm still not clear what my role is in all of this.

**Atman:** We're not entirely sure either, Markus. There are some things we know but can't tell you, since you might not do them if we did. There are also many things we don't yet know, so still can't tell you. But in each iteration of our Looking Glass simulated models, you are integral to the mission. I guess we'll all find out together.

**Markus:** Well, Professor, what *do* you know that you *can* tell me?

**Atman:** We know you made, or will make, something that was, or is, instrumental in shaping the future, but we're not sure what it was, or is, or when or how you make it. And like I said, even if we did know, we couldn't tell you in case it meant you might not make it.

**Markus:** Ooo, is it my dissertation?

**Metathory:** jesus christ, maggot, you mean your thesis project on human variation in the fovea capitis femoris on the proximal femur among pre-columbian Guatemalan tribes? You really think *that's* going to save the fucking world?

**Markus:** Ouch, Metathory, harsh words. But no, that probably wasn't it. Oh, I know! Did I invent time travel?

**Metathory:** Do you have any formal knowledge of mechanical engineering and material science?

**Markus:** No.

**Metathory:** So, what do you think then?

**Markus:** A swing. And a miss?

**Metathory:** Very much so, simian.

**Atman:** Like I said, Markus, we can't tell you what it is because we don't yet know, but it is clearly important to the sanctity of our species. We trust that your intuition will help guide us in changing the past, to fix the future, to stop the near annihilation of the human race.

**Markus:** Alright, so, we'll go back in time and make the right unknown change in the right unknown era to save the whole of humanity and the planet we all call home. Got it! How far back into the past are we going, Professor?

**Atman:** Well, that's the fun part of this mission, Markus. If there can be a fun part to messing with the timeline in the hopes that our species isn't drowned in a lake of fire, I guess. But our team of logicians and engineers have added some exciting new upgrades to one of our time discs, which allows us to venture back deeper into the past than ever before.

Even while using this Moon Base in your present as a temporal jumping-off point, we could only go back about 30,000 years. But with these technological upgrades, we should now be capable of traveling back about 60% farther.

**Markus:** So, we're looking at 48,000 years before present?

**Metathory:** Oh, so now he's good at doing math in his head.

**Markus:** Suck it, Major.

**Atman:** Yes, we are shooting for 48,000 years before present. However, because our 'before present' temporal classification system signifies a time that predates the year 1950 CE specifically, we are technically going back to 48,085 years prior, since 1950 was 85 years ago. Although, when you're talking about time travel in the tens of thousands of years, such distinctions become moot.

**Markus:** Neato. That was one of my favorite time periods to study as a paleoanthropologist, especially since there were about five different human subspecies back then. Are we going to see any of them?

**Atman:** Yes, we hope to observe and extract DNA from each of them...oh, and attempt to find a change that will save the future of course. Our primary base of operations will be the Dordogne River Valley of what is now southern France, but we will conduct research in a few other geographic regions in that period as well.

**Markus:** Cool. Hey Dordogne, is that river valley named after you?!

**Dordogne:** No, I'm named after it, goofball!

**Markus:** Oh yea, that makes more sense!

**Atman:** Early on in her career, Dordogne selected to become our resident expert on western Europe. She was tasked with learning the morphology and culture of the various hominin groups who lived there over the last 800,000 years. Many of us take names indicative of the region we study.

**Markus:** It is a lovely name, and a beautiful region of France from what I've seen on *Rick Steves' Europe*. So, all of you specialize in a specific region over long intervals of time?

**Atman:** Yes, it's impossible for any one of us to cover all global cultures across all epochs, so we focus on individual geographic regions over long stretches of time and share our knowledge. This also allows us to act as cultural and linguistic ambassadors for the rest of the crew if a specific mission ever involves one of these periods and places. Because the Dordogne River Valley at 48k BP will be our temporal and regional basecamp for this new mission to the deepest past yet visited, Dordogne was brought on as the resident specialist.

**Markus:** That tracks. It also helps explain a lot about the UFO phenomenon, since past and modern UFO reports often state that one or two people aboard the ships had deep knowledge of the culture and language of the time and place they were visiting.

**Atman:** That is an astute observation, Markus.

**Markus:** Thanks, I've had an interest in the UFO enigma since I was a kid. It seems like a lot of other folks are starting to these days as well.

**Atman:** Yes, we are aware of how protohuman perceptions of us have changed throughout prehistory and history, and how you depicted us in popular culture. I especially liked *The Day the Earth Stood Still* because we had a badass robot in that one.

**Markus:** Oh yea, solid film, Doc. Hey Dordogne! What's your favorite UFO movie?!

**Dordogne:** *Spaceballs*!

**Markus:** Not really a UFO movie, but we'll count it, and I love that flick too! You know, you're a pretty cool chick, Dordogne!

**Dordogne:** Thank you!

**Metathory:** Oh my god, will you two stop yelling across the command center. People are trying to work in here.

**Markus:** Shut up, Metathory, I'm about to close the deal. Hey Dordogne! You wanna watch *Spaceballs* with me back at my apartment on Earth after we get done saving the world and shit?!

**Dordogne:** Are you asking me to have sexual intercourse with you, Markus?!

**Markus:** Isn't that why humans ask each other to watch movies with them? I mean, you tell me. You're the intertemporal sex researcher after all.

**Dordogne:** My data does support that conclusion.

**Markus:** And...?

**Dordogne:** I guess we'll have to wait and see!

**Markus:** So, you're telling me there's a chance.

**Atman:** Right, well, people don't watch movies or have sex in our time, so you kids have fun with all that.

**Markus:** Wait, what did you just say, Doc? Y'all don't fuck in the future?!

**Atman:** No, Dordogne is something of an anomaly in that way. In addition to her focus on the physiology and culture of past hominins of the European continent, she specializes in the study of sex and music, which she tells me are related somehow. However, the rest of us in our time don't engage in sexual congress or make music or movies any longer.

**Markus:** That's interesting. And confusing. And sad. So, how do you future folk have babies if you don't bump uglies and shoot DNA at each other?

**Atman:** Largely due to self-domestication in the human past, which occurred naturally following the Neolithic Revolution and the dawn of agriculture, we began having problems with reproduction. We attempted to fix those problems by modifying the human genome using CRISPR-Cas9 gene editing technology. Unfortunately, that ended up causing worse problems, and it became something of a self-perpetuating genetic degradation cycle after that.

**Markus:** I swear, Doc, when will you people stop trying to play god?!

**Atman:** Oh, that's funny! Furthermore, there was a massive bottleneck in the human gene pool, and a subsequent loss of genetic variability following the nuclear war we are going back to try to stop. So now, in our home time, most of the gametes we use to create new life were taken from past peoples. This includes a lot of DNA from here in your present, Markus, since this is the last period before the war when a broad diversity of wild-type genes still existed.

**Markus:** I guess that explains the ubiquity of gamete extractions during all your 'alien' abductions too.

**Atman:** Yes, it is one of the main reasons we visit the past. But as reproduction slowly became detached from sex, we just stopped doing it, and our genitalia atrophied to the point where males can no longer penetrate and impregnate females. For some time now we have employed artificial insemination, using sperm and eggs taken from past human groups, and the fetuses develop in ectogenesis chambers, or external wombs.

**Markus:** Sounds erotic as all hell, Doc. I wish I could get in on some of that hot future artificial insemination exogenesis chamber sexless shit. I'm all boned up just thinking about it. For real though, sex and childbirth have always been an important part of bonding, hormone regulation, and social solidarity throughout human existence. Also, it's fun as hell! You just gave up on all that cuz y'all's dicks got shrunk?

**Metathory:** I was in the Pool! I was in the Pool!

**Markus:** *Haha*, nice one Metathory. Maybe you ain't so bad after all.

**Atman:** Not anymore. Not to us. Sex hasn't been used for that in quite some time. In fact, we feel we're better off without it since sex was also about competition and conflict. Furthermore, gestation, childbirth, and nursing contributed to gender inequality, because women had to shoulder the burden of incubating and feeding infants. So now in our time, largely thanks to moving reproduction outside the body, all genders are entirely equal.

**Markus:** A latent benefit perhaps, but y'all don't just fuck for fun or anything?

**Atman:** No, I'm not sure how that would work for us. Dordogne and I speak about it occasionally, but I was tasked with other things, so I haven't given it much thought.

**Markus:** Yikes, the human future sounds like garbage, Professor! No music, no movies, and no sex. To be honest, I'm not sure what we're fighting to save.

**Atman:** We're doing just fine, Markus.

**Markus:** Wait, so...if the mission succeeds, and we stop the war, and you don't lose your genetic variation, do you think you'll keep fucking in the future?

**Atman:** Maybe.

**Markus:** Alright then, we've got some new motivation for saving the world...we're saving sex! You hear that Dordogne?! We're gonna bring back future fucking!

**Dordogne:** That's fantastic!

**Markus:** Oh, and Professor, if you keep making whoopee you might continue making music and movies too, since that's what most songs and films are about anyhow.

**Atman:** Maybe.

**Markus:** Hey Dordogne! We're gonna bring movies and music back to the future too!

**Dordogne:** I obviously can't hear anything you guys are saying from over here, but great!

**Metathory:** If you nerds are about done with all your pointless and unnecessarily loud chit chat, we've got a mission to launch. Professor, has the new rough-hewn-human recruit been briefed with all pertinent information, and is the rest of your crew and equipment ready for departure?

**Atman:** Affirmative, Major, I believe his simpleton mini mind is full, and all else is ready to go.

**Metathory:** Alright, Professor. It's of great importance that you are adequately prepared since we have never attempted to go back this far in time. This is also the only time disc capable of achieving the speeds necessary to get that deep into the past, so if something goes wrong, we won't be able to come back and save you. This is our riskiest mission yet, and if we have another Roswell, it's not just going to be avatars this time.

**Atman:** I understand the risks, Major. I've been at this for a long time. It's just part of the job.

**Markus:** Um.... Professor?

**Atman:** You don't have to raise your hand, Markus.

**Markus:** Ah, very good, thank you. So, what's he talking about with avatars? Do you use holograms to fly the ships in the future or something?

**Atman:** Anthropological fieldwork has always been dangerous, Markus. Whether its rebuilding societal infrastructure following your primitive wars, or working in inhospitable environments with harsh climates, venomous snakes, eviscerating leopards, or malaria, countless psychological and physical hazards exist.

**Markus:** Mos def, I almost died from Dengue Fever while working on a primate conservation project in Cambodia once. Had a nasty case of chlamydia too, but I don't blame anthropology for that.

**Atman:** Oh funny, that was my aunt's name. Well today, fieldwork remains risky, just with leopards and black mambas being replaced by mechanical failures and the associated hazards of being lost to the past. Or being sacrificed to the gods of traditional human societies.

**Dordogne:** Or *becoming* the gods of traditional human societies!

**Markus:** Oh, hey Dordogne, welcome back. It's good to see you again.

**Atman:** We generally try to avoid that, Dordogne.... But we do continue to push the limits of our time-travel technology, and there is always the risk of pushing too far, too fast. To mitigate these hazards, we occasionally use biotech androids of ourselves for more dangerous operations in case something goes wrong. Fortunately, that was the case for our worst crash to date, which took place during a mission to 1947.

**Dordogne:** I don't know if Airl would agree, Professor. She is still struggling with the loss of her avatar in that accident.

**Markus:** Who's Airl?

**Atman:** Airl is a linguist, and one of our most decorated pilots. She will be joining us on this mission as well, but don't mention her avatar when you meet her, it's a contentious issue.

**Markus:** Why, what happened?

**Atman:** We were detecting frequent electromagnetic anomalies near her entry zone in the New Mexico desert at that temporal locus. Major Metathory, I, and our team of engineers, suggested we first send in a few avatars to make sure it was safe for the rest of the crew. Because Airl was one of our best pilots, we chose her for the scouting mission. Unfortunately, it didn't go well, and I think she still blames us for her loss. She hasn't flown since.

**Markus:** But it saved her life, and all your lives. It was just a fake-ass robot anyway.

**Atman:** Not entirely. Our avatars are advanced machines, but they are also biological, and they carry our mirrored consciousness. They are difficult to build and are incredibly expensive. The few of us who are lucky enough to get one feel it is as much a part of us as we are in this fully organic form.

**Markus:** Yea, I don't get that at all, Prof. Much like Moon visits, we don't talk about consciousness in my time either.

**Atman:** While the original Airl remains with us, she carries the burden of losing her other half, who was captured by the United States government in 1947 and soon after died in captivity. The pain of this loss is impossible for most people to comprehend, even in our own time, since avatars are prohibitively expensive for all except a select few, but losing your avatar is like losing a piece of yourself. Installing one's consciousness in an advanced biomechanical 'device,' then training it to react and respond as one would in any real-time situation, parallels the ancient emotions of our ancestors, who as eutherian mammals, birthed, reared, and continually taught their offspring the culture and beliefs of their time. For Airl, losing her avatar was like losing the child she had raised since birth.

**Markus:** I feel that, and I appreciate you spelling it out for me in primitive-human talk, Doc.

**Atman:** It wasn't just losing her avatar either. It remains the worst mission failure in the history of our time-travel research. Airl losing herself in the crash only exacerbated the feelings of remorse and regret that accompany that badge of honor.

**Markus:** Yea, but it seems like you've been crashing these things into our times forever, and often. Why was this one so bad, especially since no real people died?

**Atman:** It wasn't the worst in the context of what was taken away, but what was given, and when.

**Markus:** Do go on ya cryptic cryptid.

**Atman:** The primitive people of that time didn't have—

**Markus:** Hey man, those are my ancestors you're talking about. How you gonna call them primitive.

**Atman:** I mean, have you seen any of their racist-ass movies, as I believe you might say? *The Day the Earth Stood Still* is probably the only one from that time that wasn't racist, and only because they could blame everything on aliens instead of ethnic minorities.

**Markus:** Yea, fair point, my great-grandmother was pretty damn racist.

**Atman:** They all were. They were taught to be that way by the ones who came before. It's sad really. Those unfounded preconceived notions of superiority were further recapitulated through time amongst the uneducated members of subsequent societies. This intergenerational racism has a lot to do with the turmoil and strife boiling over down on Earth in this time.

**Markus:** I could see how that might be a factor. Have you ever watched Faux News, pronounced like the animal?

**Atman:** Yes, I have seen it. I thought it was political satire at first, but when I realized they were being serious I caught brain hemorrhoids, which make me forget things.

**Markus:** Same.

**Atman:** What was I talking about?

**Markus:** I don't remember.

**Atman:** Oh yes. The extraordinarily primitive people of the mid-20th century, including your racist great-grandmother, who at that time possessed only simple combustion engines and vector-based Bernoullian airfoil flight capabilities—and who had just fought two global wars in only a 22-year time-span mind you—had suddenly been gifted technology that was developed eons in their future.

**Markus:** I still don't see the problem. Most people had no idea that crash happened. And the ones who talked about it as even a remote possibility were shunned and ridiculed for decades.

**Atman:** Oh, that was us. Major Metathory is quite proud of that achievement.

**Metathory:** Damn strait, Doc. Those culture cowards are still afraid to talk about us.

**Atman:** Well done, Major. You see Markus, it was largely a temporal zeitgeist issue. Some people who learned about us, or who had physical contact with our ships, avatars, or future human selves, were able to pull themselves up by their boot-straps and embrace this new reality. However, most people, who still carried the weight of ego and the manufactured other, struggled to assimilate.

**Markus:** It is a bit shocking at first. I can attest to that.

**Atman:** Yes, and we are talking about people who lived 100 years before you. While that might not seem very long, as someone who has interacted with them, I can tell you they were all quite primitive by comparison.

**Markus:** I could see that.

**Atman:** We knew we couldn't let this societal cognitive dissonance seep deep into the global culture, and because humanity was clearly unprepared to embrace this new reality, we carefully selected 12 prominent industry leaders, and a few high-ranking members of the U.S. Air Force, to oversee a mass coverup and PSYOP campaign prior to the election of your President Eisenhower.

**Markus:** #notmypresident

**Atman:** What does that mean?

**Markus:** I'm not sure, I just heard my mom say it a lot over a weird four-year period about 17 years ago.

**Atman:** OK, moving on. So, this 12-member committee was meant to ensure that the public, government, and military, all the way down the chain of command, wouldn't know about us future humans, until *we* decided they were ready. This program, dubbed Operation Majestic-12, was incredibly successful.

**Markus:** You can say that again. Kudos, Metathory. Y'all knocked it out of the park with that one.

**Metathory:** Thanks, maggot. We done good. By the way, what's with that deanimated albino Bob Marley after a mud bath you've got there?

**Markus:** Oh, that's Marshmallow. She's a stray dog I found while walking down to the kegger where Dordogne abducted me.

**Dordogne:** Oh yea, Markus, I meant to ask. Do you want me to reanimate her with my time-wand now?

**Markus:** No, not yet. It'll be easier to clean her up while she's still frozen. It's hard as hell washing a sprightly pup as is. I'll give her a bath in the river when we get to 48k BP France, and we can unfreeze her down there afterward. That way she won't be freaked out about waking up on the Moon either.

**Dordogne:** That does seem easier. I can help you clean her up when we get there too. I'm looking forward to meeting her. She's super cute.

**Markus:** She is that. Seems to be an old soul too. I think you'll like her.

**Atman:** OK crew, let's head back down to the ship and prepare for launch.

**Markus:** Thank god, Professor, I'm starving.

**Atman:** I said *launch* Markus, not lunch.

**Markus:** Oh. Damn! You future folk still eat food though, right? You didn't quit doing that too did you?

**Atman:** Yes Markus, we still eat food. We'll take rations when we arrive at our destination before descending to the surface to begin the mission.

**Markus:** Excellent. I'll have a medium rare ribeye steak, a loaded baked potato, some green bean casserole, a Tequila Paf, and a glass of chocolate milk.

**Atman:** You will not. While we do still eat food in the human future, it is primarily in the form of buckwheat pancakes.

**Markus:** What the fuck, Doc. Why do you people even get up in the morning?

**Atman:** OK Major, I'll radio you on the quantum entangled time phone when we arrive at our spacetime locus.

**Metathory:** Thank you, Professor. Be safe back there.

**Markus:** Bye Major Metathory, I'll also call you later so I can tell you all about my big first day as a time traveler. I'll bring you some hot French Neanderthal chicks as a souvenir when we get back too.

**Metathory:** Just leave the Neanderthals where you find them, Markus.

———— ◉ ————

**Markus:** So, were they, Professor?

**Atman:** Were they what?

**Markus:** Majestic? The Majestic-12 folks you were talking about.

**Atman:** They sure thought they were.

**Markus:** I bet they did. So, I'm confused about something you said back there....

**Atman:** What is it?

**Markus:** If that 1947 crash hadn't happened, and your future technology wasn't inadvertently interjected into the past, none of you would be here trying to save the world right now. Those primitive people of the past didn't create that tech, as it was gifted to them through time. And you didn't create it either, since they simply back engineered the same tech that you crashed into their time. These machines, and all of you, would not exist here and now without that event, so shouldn't you be celebrating Airl's contribution and her avatar's sacrifice?

**Atman:** It wasn't just about accidentally introducing future knowledge and technology into the past, Markus. That crash also marks the first instance of direct forced communication between us and any other temporal group we have ever studied, across tens of thousands of years.

**Markus:** I still don't see the problem, Doc.

**Atman:** We have learned much from the hominin groups we've studied over the last 30,000 years, while hiding from them what they desperately wanted to know about us. However, after this crash in 1947, our hands were tied, and for better or worse, we were forced to initiate a process of incremental intertemporal integration. We do not believe the people of your time were ready, nor are they now, but we had no choice.

**Markus:** I mean, you're dumping all of this on me, and as a member of this now, I'm cool with it. Maybe you've underestimated us.

**Atman:** Perhaps, but the current state of your society would seem to suggest otherwise.

**Markus:** Can't argue with that.

**Atman:** Yes, we are using this same technology to try to keep you from destroying yourselves and this planet. But the question is, would we need to be doing any of this if that crash hadn't happened? Culture and technology were already progressing at an accelerating rate, but the pace suddenly skyrocketed after that accident in 1947. It imbued you with unnaturally advanced technologies that helped progress innovation across every sector of the economy, but at a time when primitive political and religious ideologies permeated every other facet of society. It was way too much, far too fast.

**Markus:** Slow and steady wins the race, I guess.

**Atman:** Indeed. But at its core, questions about the positive or negative valence of Airl's crash, and what came after, remain moot. It was always going to happen, and nothing can be done to change that.

**Markus:** Seems like your friend Airl might take it better knowing that.

**Atman:** Perhaps, but from a mission control standpoint, the operation failed miserably, since the first tenet of backward time travel research is to always avoid interfering with the internal and natural development of past human groups.

**Markus:** So, if you can't go back and keep that crash from happening, what makes you so damn sure you're going to be able to stop a nuclear Armageddon that also occurred in your past?

**Atman:** The Looking Glass shows nothing of our future, and we think it might be destroyed in the Great War somehow. Without the Looking Glass, we can't risk changing anything in our time, since we cannot know the probabilistic outcome of our actions. The glass does give us hope that we can avoid this war though. And if we do, and we save the Looking Glass, then we might be able to eventually change things in our future past as well.

**Markus:** Well, Roswell that ends well, I guess. In any case, here's hoping for no electromagnetic anomalies in the 48k BP Dordogne River Valley...I've got to give an exam on Monday.

**Atman:** We all do, Markus. We all do. Alright crew, strap in and prepare for departure.

**Markus:** Why do we need to strap in? You don't feel any movement on this ship. We shot up to the Moon at like a trillion kilometers an hour earlier and I didn't feel shit.

**Atman:** That trip was different. We only traveled an

infinitesimally small percent of one light-year through spacetime coming up here to the Moon. However, moving across 48,000 light-years of time requires a stronger rotating radiofrequency field in association with sustained vector acceleration, which is almost always felt inside the ship.

**Markus:** Makes sense. Hey, who's this bloke? He your chiropractor or something?

**Atman:** That's Manitoba.

**Manitoba:** Hello, I'm Manitoba.

**Markus:** Yes, the Professor just said that.

**Atman:** Manitoba is our head engineer...for some reason. But by pure coincidence, his father owns the company that makes the time discs. His job is to manage the countdowns, which helps us time our acceleration just right, so we arrive at our precise spacetime local. It's also important for making sure there aren't any asteroids, stars, planets, or space junk along the vector trajectory, which could destroy the ship. The restraints will be critical for safety in the unlikely event of a crash.

**Markus:** Imma strap in for sure then. I've been getting a much better sense of just how 'unlikely' a crash is for y'all. No offense Manitoba.

**Manitoba:** None taken, I'm pretty new here; those crashes were the other guy.

**Markus:** Not sure that fills me with much more confidence, but—

**Atman:** How's it looking back there, Manitoba?

**Manitoba:** The quantum computer shows a 99.2% vector clearance in T-minus 213 seconds.

**Atman:** Hmm, that's fortuitous. But for the love of god, can you please give me the numbers as minutes and seconds like I've asked a hundred times?

**Markus:** *Haha*, yea fuck that shit, Professor. It's like the parents of my time who say their kid is like, 29 months old. Just tell me it's almost two and a fucking half, you don't have to be that god damn specific about it, and I sure as shit don't want to do the math in my head.

**Atman:** It has been a point of contention recently. This nepotistic soft top once told me we had a launch window in T-minus 3,457 seconds. Like, what the hell am I supposed to do with that?!

**Markus:** I know, right?

**Atman:** Do you know what I did?

**Markus:** What's that?

**Atman:** I made a sandwich.

**Markus:** Good call. Love sandwiches!

**Atman:** And it was delicious.

**Markus:** As they always are of course.

**Atman:** Then I came back, and I kicked him square in the dick and I said, 'tell me when there's 10 seconds left asshole!'

**Markus:** *Haha*, love it. Totally an appropriate response to the situation!

**Atman:** Well, just let me know when we're at T-minus 10 seconds, Manitoba!

**Manitoba:** Can do captain, and thanks for not kicking me in the crotch this time.

...

**Markus:** So, do you all just sit here awkwardly in absolute silence until he starts the countdown?

**Atman:** Yes, because these launch windows occur stochastically and we have no way of predicting how long it might be before the next one opens up if we miss the target launch time, we must sit patiently and wait so we don't accidentally talk through the countdown and fail to optimize our narrow window of opportunity.

**Markus:** Makes sense. So, what happens if we miss it?

**Atman:** Well, we might get another launch window in 15 seconds, or it could be 15 hours, you just never know. We must account for many celestial bodies while traveling at high speed along a plotted trajectory while light cones in and around the ship are oriented toward the past. There is also a lot of garbage floating around up here ever since that Space Karen from your time started chucking everything and the kitchen sink into orbit.

**Markus:** What happens if Manitoba is off by like a second in either direction from the launch window?

**Manitoba:** Lift-off in T-minus 10, 9...

**Atman:** Then we would all fucking die, Markus! Can you please shut up so I can concentrate on the god-damn countdown—

6mmmmmmmmmmmmmmmmmmmmmmmmmmmmmmmm5mmm
mmmmmmmmmmmmmmmmmmmmmmmmmmm4mmmmmmm
mmmmmmmmmmmmmmmmmmmmmmmm3mmmmmmmmmm
zzzzzzzzzzzzzzzzz2zzzzzzzzzzzzzzzzzzzzzzzzzz1zzzzzzzzzzz
zzzzZZZZZZZZZZZZZ

Pew!

# Chapter 7
## Exploration – The Dordogne Valley – Terra
## 48,000 BP

**Markus:** That was bumpy, but I still didn't feel many g-forces.

**Atman:** You're right, Markus, that wasn't as bad as I thought it might be. We were lucky to have some of the best engineers of our time working on this craft. It would seem they did a terrific job.

**Manitoba:** Thank you, Professor.

**Atman:** Not you, Manitoba.

**Manitoba:** Oh.

**Markus:** For sure, mad props to those grease monkeys. I still can't believe my first time-travel trip happens to be the farthest back humanity has ever ventured into the past. That's kinda cool.

**Atman:** Yes, the farthest back in time possible. Well, from the period we hail from at least. It's conceivable our descendants may figure out how to go back even farther at some point in our future. Although, we've never met any of our own time-traveling descendants. I guess I'm not sure how to interpret that.... Maybe this is the best we'll ever do. Or we all die, and we have no future descendants.

**Markus:** Oh, I'm sure you'll all be fine, Doc. Besides, you can always come back and live with us in our time if you start dying off.

**Atman:** Thanks for the offer, but you're all about to die in your time too, so that's not much better.

**Markus:** Oh yea, forgot about that.

**Atman:** It does feel different in this primeval period though. It's not just what the screens and dials say either. Everything looks different. Everything *feels* different. The whole environment is so unlike any I've visited. The plants, the trees, even the way the—

Oh My god, There's A Giant T. Rex Heading Straight For Us!!!

**Markus:** What, where!?!

**Atman:** *Ahh ha*, gotcha kid. That's just an old joke we like to play on the first-timers. But obviously by 48,000 BP, dinosaurs had already been extinct for 65,998,220 years.

**Markus:** Good one, Doc. You'd be surprised how many people in my time don't know that though. When I was in bible school as a kid, they taught us that humans used to live with dinosaurs. The Flintstones didn't do much to fight that fallaciousness either. Oh yea, and some ignorant fucks at a shithole noah's ark museum where my uncle used to live recently put dinosaurs in an exhibit with early modern humans.

**Atman:** Seems dumb.

**Markus:** True that. The funny part is that even these inert evolution-hating troglodytes realized that two of every animal could never fit inside the largest ship imaginable. So, to address this obvious absurdity, they invented about 1,400 'kinds' of extinct creatures that they made up out of the blue, and then said these nonexistent groups *progressed* into modern animals. So, you've got these antievolution dipshits now using evolution to explain why evolution didn't happen. Hilarity!

**Atman:** What can I say, science and logic always find a way.

**Markus:** Preach, Doc.

**Atman:** I'm going to go below deck to see if the other researchers and our security detail are prepared to head down to the surface. Markus and Dordogne, you stay up here and take inventory of everything you will need to carry out your research. We're only going to be in this period for three days, ship time, and we plan to visit and study four distinct human subspecies, so double-check that you have what you will need.

**Markus:** Aye aye, Captain.

———— ◉ ————

**Markus:** Alright, Dordogne, I obviously have no idea what's going on since I only became aware time travel exists earlier today, so what do you want me to do?

**Dordogne:** You don't have a role in this period, so you can just help me with my research if you want.

**Markus:** OK, but I have no idea what my role is in any of the times we plan to visit, other than that I'm supposed to do or make something that will keep a war from happening in my home time.

**Dordogne:** That's true.

**Markus:** So, does that mean there's nothing I can do to help prevent the war this far back in time?

**Dordogne:** Yes, and please don't do anything without checking with us first. If we made even a slight change to the timeline this far back in the past it would result in an entirely different human future and a complete shift in the global order, and our investors won't allow that.

**Markus:** Y'all are in the pocket of big time travel then, huh?

**Dordogne:** The wealthy elites who fund these missions require that we do nothing that could jeopardize their ancestors' wealth and political power prior to the collapse of society. Otherwise, they might never have been able to escape to Luna Sede during the war.

**Markus:** But isn't that a part of why society is collapsing in the first place? Greed, inequality, assholes.

**Dordogne:** Just between you and me, that is undoubtedly a factor. However, our financiers believe we can stop the war without disrupting the intemperate affluenza they and their ancestors profited from.

**Markus:** Do you believe that too?

**Dordogne:** I'm skeptical, but time will tell.

**Markus:** So, why would they send us so far back in time if any major change is certain to result in them losing their excessive wealth and, potentially, their entire existence?

**Dordogne:** Well, we might have lied to them about that part of the operation a teensy bit. We convinced them to bankroll requisite upgrades to the time disc by telling them this mission to the deepest past will make them even richer, since we could learn far more about innate human consumption patterns in studying resource use across various subspecies of hominins. They would profit from this new knowledge of human behavior by subliminally manipulating people's purchasing preferences so they buy more manufactured goods. It was all a load of crap, but they heard 'make more money' and it was game on.

**Markus:** Well played, but why *did* we come back this deep into the past then?

**Dordogne:** A principal reason is that visiting a time when multiple human subspecies still exist allows us to vastly broaden knowledge of our ancestral past.

**Markus:** That makes sense. In fact, I always say in my classes how great it would be to have a time machine, so we could watch and interact with these hominin subspecies while they were still extant and going about their day-to-day lives. This was one of my favorite periods and places in the prehistoric past too. From the current time in western Europe when modern humans arrived in this stronghold of the Neanderthals, through the Upper Paleolithic, and into the Mesopotamian Neolithic with the dawn of agriculture and the rise of ancient civilizations, it's all incredibly fascinating! I'm so stoked to be here, and I can't wait to get down to the surface to see if it's anything like I've imagined from researching and teaching about these groups for so long.

**Dordogne:** I feel the same, Markus, it is one of the most exciting times in recent human history. That's a big part of why we're here and now. We didn't tell the investors this, but we're not studying consumption behaviors, or attempting to make any change in this period that might help stop the war. In fact, I would like to reiterate that it is imperative we do not overtly interject ourselves into this time in any way whatsoever...unless it was something we were already going to do, in which case, we would certainly still want to do it. Otherwise, not doing it would be the change we don't want.

**Markus:** Do what we did and not what we didn't do. Got it.

**Dordogne:** Just don't step on any butterflies and we should be fine.

**Markus:** I'll be sure to watch where I put my feet.

**Dordogne:** There are other reasons we convinced them to pay for upgrades to the time disc as well though.

**Markus:** Was it because you wanted to watch prehistoric peoples get their fuck on?

**Dordogne:** That is an important part of my research, yes, but there is so much more we can learn as well. Archaeologists from our home time can provide a basic understanding of primeval environments and the morphology and lifeways of people who lived in this previously unreachable part of the past, but the material remains they unearth provide meager information about the beliefs and behaviors of those who made them. Their mores, folkways, norms, values, and way of conceptualizing the world remain a mystery. However, by visiting these periods in person, we can shine light through the shadows of the past and begin to weave a tapestry of time from the threads of intensive intertemporal ethnographic investigation.

**Markus:** Damn, you're starting to sound like the Professor.

**Dordogne:** He was my PhD advisor.

**Markus:** That checks out.

**Dordogne:** Of greater importance, if our mission fails and we cannot stop the war, it is imperative that we gather genetic material from the different human subspecies who lived in this time. These will be the oldest wild-type genes we've ever sampled with our time-travel technology. So, if we are unable to stop the war, their ancient DNA will be crucial for diversifying our own gene pool in the future, which saw the most dramatic bottleneck in the history of our species once the bombs dropped.

**Markus:** Mind if I add a couple drops of DNA to the gene pool once we get down there?

**Dordogne:** Didn't I just say we can't overtly interject ourselves into this time? I can think of few things more overt than having sex with the research subjects, Markus.

**Markus:** Yes, but all these other human subspecies are an evolutionary dead end, so we don't have to worry about that butterfly flapping its wings, cuz it ain't got any.

**Dordogne:** Well, that is a good point. And it would help advance my intertemporal intercourse research. However, this far back in time, the Looking Glass can't tell us if you performed the copulatory act here or not, so maybe you should just keep it in your pants for the time being.

**Markus:** I don't knowwww though, it can't matter since they're all going to die anyway. It's like an archaic *Homo sapiens* phylogenetic genocide abortion that's already been performed at the Planned Ancestorhood time clinic.

**Dordogne:** Your anthropological knowledge manifests in incredibly strange ways sometimes, Markus. But I imagine you're right. It'll be good practice for you anyhow.

**Markus:** Practice for what?

**Dordogne:** Doesn't matter, just be sure you aren't perceived as a god and end up starting a major global religion or anything.

**Markus:** Oh, no worries, I'm not that good in bed.

**Dordogne:** That's true, I've seen your work. However, you are progressing, and a breakthrough came recently when you briefly approached the coital door to transcendent nonduality.

**Markus:** Not sure what that means, but yea, you mentioned that you've watched me on occasion. However, I don't remember ever seeing you perving from the corner of the room while I was getting my freak on.

**Dordogne:** No. I was never there physically. My people's highly evolved consciousness imbues us with telepathy, telekinesis, and clairvoyance, which allowed me to use remote viewing to observe you throughout much of your life, including and especially while you engaged in the sex act.

**Markus:** Huh, weird. If we weren't gonna watch *Spaceballs* and have an all-night shagfest at my apartment once this mission is over, that would seem kind of creepy.

**Dordogne:** I never agreed to that, but—

**Markus:** Did you ever touch yourself while you watched?

**Dordogne:** I'm not going to answer that.

**Markus:** Pleading the fifth is most often perceived as an admission of guilt.

**Dordogne:** No, my silence on the issue is simply a decision to invoke my right against self-incrimination.

**Markus:** I'm still not hearing a no, though.

**Dordogne:** Ok, maybe once or twice.

**Markus:** That's so hot. Anyhow, these past human subspecies practiced animism as their system of spiritual belief, so you don't need to worry about me starting the first omnipresent monotheistic religious cult during this sex-study crusade. And again, they all die anyway.

**Dordogne:** Yes, I was just kidding, you'll get that joke eventually.

———— ◉ ————

**Atman:** Hello, Markus and Dordogne.

**Markus:** Hello, Professor.

**Atman:** Um, pardon my asking, but as I was walking up, I thought I overheard you talking about Markus having sex with some of the research subjects in this time?

**Markus:** Yes, Professor, I was hoping to engage in sexual congress with a random sample of willing participants drawn from the various human groups present in this period to help broaden our comprehension of carnal knowledge. Because these previously extant subspecies became extinct 40,000 years prior, modern researchers possess only a scant comprehension of their past sexual behaviors, so this minor element of the current study would aid in expanding our understanding of sex through time.

**Atman:** I don't know if I'm comfortable with that, Markus. What we're doing in these past times is important, and I feel like you aren't taking it seriously. The lives of 9 billion people depend on the success of this mission.

**Markus:** *9.5 billion* people, actually!

**Atman:** Yes, 9.5 billion, I forgot we were being overly specific with that number for no apparent reason. In any case, we're not just here to do ancient drugs and have sex with our distant ancestors. We're here to conduct research, and later, to prevent the worst war in future human history.

**Markus:** I gotta call bullshit on that one, Doc. You've been doing all kinds of weird sex stuff to people throughout your past. That's like, the most common thing reported in UFO abductions.

**Atman:** We have needed to extract gametes for our own purposes, yes. And I'll be the first to admit there are moral and ethical issues involved with what we've been doing. But the needs of the many outweigh the needs of the few. If those bombs go off, the DNA we collect will be vital in our efforts to help diversify the future human gene pool. We have no choice. We're not doing this for fun or pleasure, it's out of necessity.

**Dordogne:** Well, except for that Brazilian farmer, right Professor?

**Atman:** No, Dordogne, we let you have sex with that man in 1957 solely to advance our scientific knowledge. You claimed you needed data about sex from that time, so we signed off on it.

**Dordogne:** Oh, I got some data alright.

**Atman:** Yes, for research. You got data for research purposes only. By the way, I still think it's messed up that afterward you made him think you were going to come back and whisk him away to live with you and your space baby in some fictitious home in the stars.

**Dordogne:** Hey, that was all him. I just made a couple innocent hand gestures. I felt like I had to say something after I just rocked his primitive little world.

**Markus:** Good on ya Dordogne, I think I heard about that one. Doc, haven't you ever gone to a conference just because of the city it was in? Or taken a day trip from your field site to go scuba diving, or to hike up a mountain?

**Atman:** What, Markus?

**Markus:** My point is that research can be fun too. It doesn't just have to be nerds in white lab coats extracting the deoxyribonucleic acid of living mites from scabietic skin samples and squirting them into Eppendorf tubes.

**Atman:** Again, what?

**Markus:** We made it all the way back to this period with a plethora of human subspecies that have been extinct for tens of thousands of years. It's an untapped resource that's just begging to be tapped. Shouldn't we be eating the food they eat, doing the drugs they do, and having sex the way they have sex? Isn't that participant observation, which is our principal methodology for conducting ethnographic research?

**Atman:** Well, yes. But when I walked in it sounded like you were only interested in pleasure-seeking, as opposed to the research aspect of engaging in this sexual act.

**Markus:** Oh, no Doc, not at all. I am incredibly curious about how they have sex and what it's like from a qualitative standpoint, but it's so much more than that. I want to know what positions they use, how long they last, and whether they're intimate and gentle, or if it's simply a brutish animalistic reproductive act. I want to know if they cuddle afterward, or if they just do it and get on with their day. And I'd love to know what it's like sleeping next to one under a mammoth-skin blanket if they are cuddlers. I want to know everything about their way of life, and investigating the nuances of how they make new life may be the most important thing of all. Besides, Dordogne is going to watch and take notes, so there's an objective quantitative element to this study as well.

**Dordogne:** That's true Professor. Because this is the last period when different human subspecies mated with each other prior to anatomically modern *Homo sapiens* driving them all to extinction, investigating these types of intimate interactions is critical to my body of work. Markus's contribution is crucial as well, in that we would be interjecting another subspecies, from an entirely different time, as a kind of control group of sorts.

**Atman:** Hmm, considering the art of intercourse was lost in our time, once in-vitro fertilization and exogenesis became the standard method of human reproduction, perhaps we could benefit from knowing the role sex played between and among human groups of the distant past. That way we have a better sense of what was lost and what we will need to know if we succeed in stopping the war, since we may start having sex again in a nonapocalyptic future.

**Markus:** That's so true, Professor. And although I'm not one of you, I am willing to take one for the future human team.

**Atman:** Alright, Markus. So long as it's not purely for pleasure, and Dordogne watches and takes notes, I guess we can let you have sex with one of the Neanderthal men down there.

**Markus:** I was hoping for a *female* research subject in his stead if one might be available.

81

**Atman:** I assumed as much. I was just kidding. Not that there's anything wrong with that though.

**Markus:** Not that there's anything wrong with that at all. It just ain't my cup of tea. Hey, can I also do some research with a couple of those Flores Hobbits when we get over to Indonesia in this time? I heard they have some decidedly unique sexual practices that we should ardently investigate to further our cultural knowledge of such traditions.

**Atman:** It's a possibility...just make sure you aren't perceived as a god and you end up starting a major global religion or anything.

**Markus:** You all have way too much faith in my sexual prowess.

**Atman:** We don't, I was just kidding again. You'll get that joke eventually.

**Markus:** That's what she said.... No, seriously, Dordogne said that earlier. I still don't get it though.

**Atman:** It's probably that primitive little monkey brain slowing you up again.

**Markus:** All past humans ain't dumb, Doc. Some of 'em got smarts real good. Like me. Alright, let's get down there and conduct some hot ethnographic inter-subspecies sex research.... And wash my frozen-ass dog, she nasty.

# CHAPTER 8
## COMPLETION – THE DORDOGNE VALLEY – TERRA
## 48,000 BP

**Markus:** Well Doc, we came, we saw, they came, we collected their cum, let's get out of here.

**Atman:** Yes, I think we have nearly completed all our research objectives across the four geographic regions we wished to visit in this time.

**Markus:** And then some. I can't begin to tell you how much I learned over the last three days. It's funny because Neanderthals and Denisovans have always been stereotyped as dumb brutish beasts, when in fact they're exceedingly kind and gentle. Who could have guessed they were so into group sex too. Dordogne, did you gather enough data from our participant observation activities to satisfy your research objectives?

**Dordogne:** I did indeed, Markus. Thank you for your assistance. It was also helpful because your intimacy with them granted us special access to their homes where we could examine their living spaces, system of social organization, village dynamics, and other elements of their lifeways that may have been inaccessible otherwise, since we are often hesitant about getting too close. However, your sexual ambassadorship helped break the ice. I never would have thought Neanderthals and the Flores Hobbits were so hospitable.

**Markus:** Happy to help, Dordogne. It made me feel better having you there with your time-wand at first too, since I didn't know what to expect either. I was happy to see how nice they were too, but one must wonder if that has something to do with their impending extinction, considering anatomically modern humans have a long history of being anything but nice to anyone different from us.

**Dordogne:** That may have been an unfortunate factor in their demise, yes.

**Markus:** It's sad, really. I wish we could have given them a slew of AR-15s for when our ancestors arrive in a few thousand years, but I imagine that would have been one of those 'overt' changes we had to avoid.

**Dordogne:** Yes, Markus. Preventing the loss of long-extinct human subspecies undoubtedly classifies as an 'overt change' to the timeline.

**Markus:** Well, maybe we can visit again sometime before they all go extinct. I feel like we made some good friends in the short time we were here. But perhaps most importantly, Marshmallow is all clean and back among the moving, hey girl?

*Ruff!*

**Dordogne:** I think bringing her to the surface helped break the ice too. Because the domestication of dogs doesn't occur for another 20,000 years, she was quite the spectacle to behold for them. She seems to have aided your courtship rituals down there too, Markus.

**Markus:** Hell yea, cute pups have always been man's best friend when it comes to picking up chicks. I do wonder if our command of this creature may have led some of them to think we were gods though, not to mention our advanced technology, clothes, and the fact that we don't look anything like them. Damnit, did we accidentally become gods like you and the Professor warned about?

**Dordogne:** We may have, Markus. But it doesn't matter in this case because, sadly, they're all going to die anyway, remember.

**Markus:** Oh, yea, right.

**Atman:** No need to worry, Markus. I checked with Major Metathory back on the Moon Base and he said everything remains self-consistent, for better or worse. So, it would seem we were successful in gathering everything we came for, and without inadvertently changing the future.

**Markus:** Sounds like 'mission accomplished' if you ask me.

**Atman:** I must admit, I was skeptical about bringing a dog along on this voyage, but Marshmallow is an absolute delight. I think Dordogne is correct that she was an asset down there too. She's cute enough to garner curiosity and affection from the native inhabitants of these regions, but as a pre-domestication-period 'wolf,' she's also rather intimidating, especially when she initiates her piloerection reflexive sympathetic nervous system response.

**Markus:** Tha fuck is that, Doc?!

**Atman:** You know, when they get scared and their back fur stands up so they look intimidating.

**Markus:** Oh, yea. She is scary when she does that. You don't fuck with them street dogs.

**Dordogne:** Aww, she's not scary, she's just a big 'ol softy. Come here Marshmallow. *Mwah. Mwah. Mwah.* She's so fuzzy!

**Markus:** So, when and where are we going next, Professor?

**Atman:** Well, I received a message from Major Metathory stating that after we finish our gamete collection—

**Markus:** And dispersion!

**Atman:** Yes Markus, that too, I suppose. But after we finish our gamete collection mission in this most distant time for the first time—Or wait, sorry, I misspoke.... Of course, what I meant to say was, 'our mission to collect data on the consumption behaviors of past human subspecies so our industrialist financier overlords can better manipulate the human psyche to sell more widgets and cheeseburgers to the unsuspecting masses in their insatiable bid for perpetual growth,' we are to jump forward to examine the outcome of potential changes near the Indus River Valley in the late Neolithic.

**Markus:** When is that?

**Atman:** It's really hit or miss with your anthropological knowledge isn't it, Mr. ABD PhD candidate.

**Markus:** I know a bunch about the early Neolithic, but I fell asleep in class a lot once we got past that period.

**Atman:** Well, to catch you up, the Neolithic marked an agricultural revolution that began about 12,000 years BP in the Fertile Crescent, and around 5,500 BP with the Harappan civilization in the Indus River Valley during the later Neolithic, which is when and where we will be going.

**Markus:** That seems like an important period for enacting sustained societal change over broad swaths of human time to help prevent a war.

**Atman:** I agree, Markus. I just hope the Looking Glass doesn't predict that it's too much change and they shut us down because of it. Nurturing the development of certain groups over others in that time could be exactly what humanity needs to stave off war by fostering lasting empathy and peace, but we'll figure it out when we get then I guess. Alright crew, strap in. It's going to be another long time jump getting back closer to our home time and we may experience some temporal turbulence like what we encountered on our way here and now.

**Markus:** Will do.... 'Number One, you have the bridge!'

**Atman:** Come again?

**Markus:** Oh, there's no way I could come again, Doc. This well's done run bone dry.

**Atman:** No, what did you say about a bridge?

**Markus:** Oh, damn Atman, you really don't know the classics, do you. Captain Picard? *Star Trek*? Come on, man.... Manitoba, hit us with that countdown!

**Atman:** Wait, who made you captain? I'm the one who says that!

**Markus:** I just said, 'you have the bridge' and you didn't do shit, so I took over.

**Atman:** Damnit, boy. Sometimes I wish we had never picked your drunk ass up from that party.

**Markus:** Too late now. Alright, you take it then Number One.

**Atman:** Manitoba, hit us with that countdown!

**Manitoba:** Affirmative Professor, the computer shows a clear window with 98.6% vector clearance in T-minus 152 seconds.

**Atman:** Fuck you Manitoba! What did I say?! What the fuck did I say?! jesus H. Tap Dancing christopher columbus christ, it's like I'm sitting here time-traveling with my brother's kids or something, you nerve racking sons of bitches!

**Manitoba:** Sorry Professor, I forgot again. Sorry, Sir. I meant to say I see a clear window for departure to the year 5,450 BP in T-minus two minutes and 32 seconds, which is now T-minus two minutes and 4 seconds because you yelled at me for 28 seconds.

**Atman:** Thank you, Manitoba. See, was that so fucking hard? Holy shit!

**Markus:** Yea, give it to him, Doc! I'm not sure where that came from, but I like it! You sure do get testy during these launch sequences.

**Atman:** You're apparently starting to rub off on me, Markus. I'm typically quite reserved and professional. But here we are on this TIME travel mission and this BITCH-ass motherFUCK-ER can't even give me the estimated ETD in the GOD-damn COUNTDOWN format I asked for!

**Markus:** I'm really starting to get how you guys crash these things so often.

**Manitoba:** Sorry again, Professor Atman, I'm still kind of new here. I'll get it next time, I promise. That is just what the computer says when I look at the screen, so I intuitively read it the way it is presented each time, but I'm sure there is a way to change the settings so it is in a minute and second format such as how you prefer it, so when we get to the next time stop, I'll play around with it to see if I can figure out how to change the settingsssss mmaannuuaallyy ssoo iittss ttthhheee wwwaaayyy yyyyoooouuuu wwwwaaaannnntttt mmmmmmmmmmmm....

**Atman:** Wait, did we just miss our launch window? Take the bridge, Boy, I'm gonna go kick this kid in the dick so hard his great-grandsons never get a hard-on!

# CHAPTER 9
## EMANCIPATION - THE INDUS VALLEY – TERRA
## 5450 BP

**Markus:** That seemed less bumpy than when we went back to bump uglies with the ugly ones.

**Atman:** That is certainly not why we went there and then, Markus. But yes, traveling to the future has always been easier and less turbulent than traveling to the past.

**Markus:** It's funny, you time turds have a word that merges space and time into spacetime, but you still always say *there and then* for places in time. Can't you combine those too? Maybe say *therethen*, or *thenthere*, or *locustime*, or *tempoloco*, or something?

**Atman:** Wait, what was that last one?

**Markus:** Tempoloco?

**Atman:** Yea, I like that.... 'Tempoloco.' Alright Markus, good on ya. I knew we brought you along for some reason!

**Markus:** Happy I can help, Doc. Dordogne, any idea what we might change in this tempoloco to prevent the war?

**Dordogne:** Well, the Harappan were one of the only matriarchal societies in human history. Perhaps we are here to make a change that helps this conciliatory culture survive and prosper in lieu of the patriarchal warmongering city-states of this time. That could establish a geographic stronghold for tranquility, which could be recapitulated through the ages and into your time, Markus, with the hopes that this temporally pervasive peace will avert the Great Filter.

**Markus:** But if women are in charge and war is infrequent or nonexistent, how could the rich oligarchs that finance these missions ever exist? If we cause that shift, won't you lose your source of future funding and be incapable of coming back to this time to make that change?

**Atman:** Unfortunately, Dordogne, Markus is right. I just got a message from Major Metathory. As soon as we arrived in this time the Looking Glass started blowing up with stats. It predicted a 100% probability of stopping the Great War if we foster matriarchy—

**Markus:** That's fantastic, why is that bad?

**Atman:** Because it also gave a 100% likelihood that the oligarchs will no longer exist in the future.

**Markus:** That also sounds like a great thing. What's the problem? You get the one in the hand, and that elusive bitch in the bush too.

**Atman:** Well Markus, as much as I hate those guys, with their fancy unusable yachts and expensive toaster oven air fryers, we are contractually obligated to avoid doing anything that could diminish their wealth and power in your present and ours.

**Markus:** But how could they know if they no longer exist in our times? Fuck those guys, let's switch it up and let the ladies run things for a while. Get some *herstory* up in this history.

**Atman:** It's not that simple, Markus. Do you remember reading or seeing television programs about mobsters who operated brutal, bloody, illegal operations and who controlled most of the businesses in large cities about 100 years before your time?

**Markus:** Rings a bell. Go on.

**Atman:** Well, it's the same in our time too, just without the word 'illegal.' Because they operate the economy and have representatives at all levels of government, they control everything. Not only is there no way to stop them, but you don't want to piss them off either.

**Markus:** If they're so scary, aren't you worried they'll find out you lied about why we went to 48k BP?

**Atman:** No, that shouldn't matter, and it was only a small part of the overall mission, at least as far as they're concerned. We'll feed them some garbage about human behavior and best practices for how to sell more stuff to stupid people and they'll be happy. Their main concern is finding a way to stop the war so they can use their yachts again; there aren't many lakes and oceans on the Moon.

**Markus:** I imagine there are not.

**Atman:** Regardless of how one feels about the oligarchs who run our Moon Base civilization, we are all sick of being crammed together up there and would do anything to get Earth back.

**Markus:** I feel obligated to point out, Professor, that it was primarily those assclowns who pillaged and plundered the planet as they profited from an unsustainable system of overconsumption and inequality, which inevitably led to its demise, nuclear or otherwise.

**Atman:** You never consumed anything in your time?

**Markus:** Of course. That was the circus they forced us to be in, waiving their bananas in our faces and shouting, 'dance little monkey, dance.' But the people you're working for are directly responsible for all that Earth-fucking. If we can shift the balance of power to those who nurture instead of destroy, and who foster cooperation over competition, the entire future would be brighter. Who gives a fuck if you piss off your corporate overlords, let's just do it. They'll be none the wiser because they won't. Fucking. Exist. Ever!

**Atman:** I appreciate your tenacity, Markus. And while these plutocrats aren't the brightest fireflies in the jar, they did prepare for and enact measures to prevent that potentiality.

**Markus:** How?!

**Atman:** Before we left our home time to embark on this mission, they organized a separate group of travelers to monitor our operations. However, these aren't scientists and engineers like us. Instead, they employed a small team of highly trained mercenaries who are meant to hunt us down and kill us if we attempt to do anything that might alter the future to the extent that our oligarch oppressors risk losing everything they think they deserve.

**Markus:** But again, how could they know if we change the past, since they would be erased from time as soon as we did it?

**Atman:** As you are aware, Major Metathory is monitoring the Looking Glass to determine the probabilistic outcomes of our actions in the past as they pertain to preventing the Great War. Because the Looking Glass no longer exists in our future time, the mobster investors who finance this effort sent a representative back to the preapocalypse Moon Base. His sole purpose for being there is to monitor the Looking Glass alongside Major Metathory for any indication that averting the war could also change the existing economic and political power structure. If we attempted to favor peace over their prosperity, the glass would immediately notify them, and the assassins would be sent back to kill us before that change could ever be made.

**Markus:** But we have our own security crew. Couldn't we fight them?

**Atman:** Who do you think pays those security officers, Markus? They would be the first to try to stop us until backup arrived from the future. The oligarchs have the money, power, and guns. We're just a bunch of lowly scientists walking a fine line of statistical probabilities, tasked with changing enough, but not too much.

**Markus:** Shouldn't we at least try though, for humanity? If we went back to Mesopotamia and did this at the start of the Neolithic, we would have 12,000 years of people living in peaceful sustainable societies spread across an ecologically sound planet leading up to my time. There's no way the war would happen then. Isn't that worth the risk of a few of us getting axed in the past? Dordogne, you're a chick, you're with me, right?

**Dordogne:** I couldn't agree more, Markus, but they would know the second we tried, and we would all be dead long before any actual change was made. Don't forget that they have a time machine too, so they're capable of coming back to the origin point of our actions. As much as this planet and its people would benefit from a different postagricultural power structure, this isn't the time nor the place to do it.

**Markus:** Well, fine! But I'll require that my dissenting opinion be entered into the record.

**Atman:** OK, Markus. We'll get right on that.

**Markus:** Can Dordogne and I at least go down and continue the research we started in 48k BP?

**Atman:** I guess we're already here, so we might as well collect some data, and gametes. We'll stay up here on the ship to gather information about their language and culture, and to abduct a few villagers to perform medical examinations, while you and Dordogne head down to the surface to research their music, visual art, and sex practices.

**Markus:** Wicked, thanks Doc. I heard this was the culture that invented Tantric sex, so I'm definitely itching to get my research on.

**Atman:** I don't think that's what that itch is, Markus.

**Dordogne:** To the contrary, Markus. Based on the historical development of the Tantra sexual tradition, it can be categorically stated that the practice didn't originate in this area until sometime between 1,550 and 1,650 BP, so we are about 3,800 years too early.

**Markus:** Well, Dordogne, get ready to rewrite your history books, cuz we about to get bendy up in it.

**Atman:** Also, Markus, that's not at all what I meant by research the sex practices of this time. You can't just go down there swinging your dick around like you did in 48k BP Europe, Siberia, Java, and Flores. Unlike those groups, these do not go extinct. From this point on, contact with past peoples could have a marked influence on future events. We'll need Major Metathory to consult the Looking Glass before we do anything to explicitly interject ourselves into this and all subsequent times.

**Markus:** How interjecty are we talking here, Doc? Like no participant observation at all? Not even the tip?

**Atman:** As always, we must ensure that we do not violate the prime directive and inadvertently disrupt the timeline. But of equal importance, we can't do anything that could piss of the financier mafia and get us all killed. In fact, you two have repeatedly demonstrated that you can't be trusted, so I'm going to send Airl down to the surface with you to be sure everyone follows protocol.

**Dordogne:** Aww, that Debbie Downer? Don't you need her for your linguistics research?

**Atman:** No, we can learn much from examining oral legends and preservable written texts from soon after the rise of city-states in this region, so we won't need our entire team of linguists for this one. I'll instruct Airl to let me know if either of you two starts horsing around down there, so let's keep it PG in 3,500 BCE.

**Markus:** I'm sorry Professor, but did you just try to rap?

**Atman:** No. And I'm not saying you can't conduct intertemporal intercourse research, but you must use a purely etic outsider's approach. Watch others and learn. No participant observation. Do you understand?

**Dordogne:** Yes, Professor, we will be good little catholic girls and boys down there.

**Markus:** And priests, Dordogne, don't forget about the priests.

**Dordogne:** Oh yes, and the priests. They were the most wholesome and trustworthy. We'll channel the moral essence of a priest's principled character on this mission to the surface as well, Professor.

**Atman:** OK good. Thank you, Dordogne. Manitoba, go below deck and tell Airl to suit up for a babysitting mission in T-minus 3,200 seconds.

**Manitoba:** You want me to go get her in 53.33 minutes, Captain?

**Atman:** Ahh, you rat bastard, that took you no time at all. I knew you were just fucking with me! What was all that malarkey you were feeding me about screens and dials and shit?!

**Manitoba:** No, no, Professor, I swear that was just a lucky guess.

**Atman:** Lucky guess my ass. That was a test, and you failed. Go get her now, you little shit! I don't care if your dad is the CEO of this company, I'll kick your nuts all the way back to the future.

**Manitoba:** Yes, Captain. Sorry again, Professor, I'll go get her.

**Markus:** I've gotta say, I really appreciate the authoritatively ghetto-ass man you've become, Professor.

**Atman:** Fuck off, fart sniffer.

**Markus:** My guy, yes! See, that's what I'm talking about. Dig it! Hey, we don't need to worry about that kid murder-suiciding all of us, do we? He seems a little off to me.

**Atman:** Manitoba comes from a long line of steadfast launch directors, and he was top of his class when we recruited him a couple years ago.

**Markus:** Pol Pot studied at the École Française in Paris and he genocided 3 million people.

**Atman:** I'm not sure I see your point, but I don't think we need to worr—

**Markus:** John Wayne Gacy dressed up like a clown to entertain children at birthday parties, then he kidnapped and murdered 33 of them.

**Atman:** I see your point even less clearly now, but what I was trying to say is that Mani—

toba! Welcome back. Thank you for fetching Airl for us.

**Manitoba:** You're welcome, Professor. I did it in only T-minus 0 minutes and 33.91 seconds. And I said that in the way that makes you feel happy, *huh-huh*, *snort*.

**Markus:** Yea, we're all gonna die.

**Atman:** Yes, good. Thank you, Manitoba. Markus and Dordogne, you two head down to the equipment bay and gather what you'll need for your surface research in this time while I brief Airl on her extremely important mission to help make sure you two don't get us all killed.

**Dordogne:** Copy that, Professor. See you in a few.

———— ◉ ————

**Markus:** Okay Dordogne, what is the plan here? If Betty Buzzkill is coming with us, how are we going to get anything of value done down there? And by value, I mean fun, anything remotely fun.

**Dordogne:** Oh, I think it'll be alright. I know her weakness.

**Markus:** Yea, what's that?

**Dordogne:** Shiva's Lord of Bhang.

**Markus:** Oh, that's funny, Lord of Bhang was my nickname in high school.

**Dordogne:** No, it wasn't.

**Markus:** No, it wasn't. I have no idea what that is, but I do like the sound of it.

**Dordogne:** Just follow my lead when we get down there. In the meantime, go fetch an apple, some tin foil, and a lighter from the mess hall, and I'll meet you upstairs in five.

**Markus:** Roger that. Wilco.

———— ◉ ————

**Atman:** Alright you three. Are you ready to beam down to the surface to get your science on?

**Dordogne:** Yes, Professor. We're taking Marshmallow with us again too. She could use the exercise.

**Atman:** Sounds good. Just stick to the outskirts of the village where you can observe from the safety of the forest. You can deploy honeybee drones from there if you want to get a closer look and document domestic activities inside people's homes.

**Dordogne:** Yes, I packed 12 of them to seek out and record people making music and having intercourse if such actions are occurring as well.

**Atman:** Very good. And Airl, I know your research is typically carried out up here on the ship, but I appreciate your willingness to descend to the surface to assist with this part of the mission.

**Airl Jomon:** I'm happy to help where I can, Professor. And I know Dordogne obviously, but is this the other recruit you mentioned? Is he the biological anthropologist on this mission?

**Atman:** Oh, I'm sorry, Airl, I can't believe I forgot to introduce you. This is Markus, and yes, he is a biological anthropologist, but he's currently ABD in a PhD program in the year 2035.

**Airl:** Why would we go all the way back to 2035 to recruit a lowly graduate student? He has no degree, and anthropologists knew relatively little before time travel technology was invented.

**Markus:** Well, I certainly would have preferred to do my thesis in your highly enlightened future, Airl, but I was unaware time travel even existed until a few days ago. Maybe after I get my doctorate in the fall, I can come do a post-doc or find a visiting professor gig in your edified time.

**Airl:** That's not likely. I don't think you would have much to teach us.

**Markus:** Fair point. But I am getting a lot of on-the-job training with you future-human types back here in the past, and

I've been learning heaps about intertemporal intercourse working with Dordogne, so maybe that experience can at least help me get a lecturer position, or be a porn star, or an animal trainer, or something.

**Airl:** Perhaps. Dordogne is involved in some incredibly interesting research. I've seen a few of her conference presentations at the AABA meetings over the years. It is fascinating stuff!

**Dordogne:** Thanks, Airl. I didn't know you felt that way, but I appreciate the compliment.

**Markus:** I agree, Airl. I feel honored to be a part of it. She even involved me in some participant observation studies at a few different field sites while we were in 48k BP a few days ago.

**Airl:** That's wonderful. There's nothing like learning by doing. Although, you might be the only one who could assist in that way since males from our time are no longer capable of penetrating human orifices.

**Markus:** Well, that's true. But I'd like to think I helped in other ways too.

**Dordogne:** Nope, that's about it.

**Markus:** Ah, come on Dordogne, I did other stuff.

**Dordogne:** You did carry my notebook that one time.

**Markus:** See. My contribution extends well beyond my equally important role of being the only swinging dick aboard this ship.

**Airl:** *Hehe*, you two are funny.

**Atman:** We do appreciate your contribution, Markus. And I apologize that you haven't had a lot to do on the mission thus far, other than being Dordogne's gopher and broodmare, that is. But once we depart this here and now, you'll—

**Markus:** I'm sorry, this what, Professor?

**Atman:** Oh yes, once we depart this *tempoloco*, you should have a bigger role to play in the mission.

**Markus:** Awesomesauce. And I'm not sure you used 'brood-mare' correctly there, but I hope you're right, Doc. Don't get me wrong, it's cool checking out past environments and extinct human subspecies, and of course I always love fucking and taking weird drugs, but I can do that on my couch at home anytime.

**Atman:** I'm sure you can, Markus. Like a champ no less. Alright, enough chit chat, let's get you three down there.

# CHAPTER 10
## CONSTERNATION – THE INDUS VALLEY – TERRA
## 5450 BP

**Markus:** This is a cool area. I can see how it was one of the six centers of state formation that arose in association with the advent and proliferation of agriculture during the Neolithic Revolution. It's super moist and lush.

**Dordogne:** Eww gross, don't say that Markus. It's highly offensive! In fact, that word became illegal to use in 8686 CE.

**Markus:** What did I say, lush? You don't say lush in the future?

**Dordogne:** No, the m-word, we don't use that one.

**Markus:** Aww, that's even worse, I love that word! Mmmmoooist-t.

**Airl:** No, stop it, Markus!

**Markus:** Et tu, Airl?

**Airl:** Yes, stop. Nobody likes that word.

**Markus:** Well damn, I do. Oh, let me guess...that term didn't happen to get outlawed around the same time you hard-up future humans stopped having sex with each other, did it?

**Dordogne:** Hmm, actually...yes. I guess I never recognized that sexual semantic correlation before.

**Markus:** Well, alrighty then. I'll take that visiting professor position now please.

*Grrr, Woof, Wuff, Wuff, Wooff, Wooff!*

**Markus:** Hey, what's Marshmallow barking at over there?

**Dordogne:** I don't know, but she's unusually agitated. Her piloerection reflexive sympathetic nervous system response is higher than I've ever seen it.

**Markus:** I swear, you future folk and your fancy ass words to describe the simplest—

Oh, shit! Tiger!!! Dordogne! Behind you!

**Dordogne:** Oh no, where's my time-wand?!

**Airl:** Hurry, it's coming toward us!

**Dordogne:** Bullocks! I know I put it in this bag. Where is it?!

**Airl:** Quickly Dordogne. It's coming fast!

**Dordogne:** I'm trying, Airl! I swear I saw it in here before we left the—

**Markus:** Fuck it, I'll fight this angry stripped bitch myself!

*Grrraa, Grrrrrrrrr*

*Wuff, Wuff, Wuff!*
*Ouw, ouw, Ouuuuww!*

**Markus:** No, Marshmallow! Hurry Dordogne, it's attacking the dog!

**Dordogne:** Here it is!

*Zzzzmmm—*

**Markus:** god damnit, Marshmallow! Are you OK girl?!

Dordogne, get over here!

**Dordogne:** Oh no, it got her pretty bad. Hold on, sweety, I've got a med kit in my bag.

**Markus:** Go fast, she's losing a lot of blood from this leg.

**Dordogne:** OK, I found it! This high frequency EM cauterizer should stop the bleeding.

**Markus:** Hang on little darling. Momma's gonna fix you up.

**Airl:** Is there anything I can do, Dordogne?

**Dordogne:** Yes, Airl. Can you give her a quarter dose of morphine while I treat these lacerations? That should help her relax and slow the bleeding. Markus, you hold her head so she knows she's safe now.

**Markus:** Holy shit, girl, I can't believe you took on a fucking tiger! That's so bad ass! This brave little doggo might have just saved your life, Dordogne. That thing was only about three meters from you when she jumped out in front of it. I don't know if you would have gotten your wand out in time if she hadn't done that when she did!

**Dordogne:** You might be right, Markus. That was by far the closest I've been to a large predator on any mission to the past. And much closer than I ever wanted to be! Thank you for saving my life, Marshmallow, you are a brave girl!

**Markus:** She seems to be calming down now. I think the morphine is helping, Airl.

**Airl:** Yes, it looks like it. I imagine we could all use some after that scare.

**Dordogne:** You can say that again. I nearly have the other gashes healed. Markus, can you get her some water from my bag. We can mitigate the blood loss if we keep her hydrated.

**Markus:** No problem.... Here ya go, little lady, drink up. I can't believe it was only three days ago I was having a conversation with the Professor back on Luna Sede about the hazards of anthropological field work, and our dumbasses were still just sauntering through this forest like there's nothing in it. We should be more careful from now on.

**Dordogne:** I agree. I'll start carrying the time-wand in my hip pocket instead of in this overstuffed bag.... Actually, I'm going to empty out everything we don't desperately need right now, and Markus, do you mind carrying Marshmallow in it? I imagine she's going to sleep for a while.

**Markus:** For sure. I carried her around all night at that party where you picked me up, and on the Moon Base when she was still frozen, so I got mad Marshmallow-moving muscles now.

**Airl:** Wow, I have to say, that was terrifying! I don't know how you two do surface research like this. I'm lucky that as a linguist, I can observe people's use of symbolic language with a high-powered microphone from the safety of the ship. To be honest, it's awfully scary down here.

**Dordogne:** It can be, Airl, but it's exhilarating too. I'll admit, that was too close for my liking, but I would never trade my boots-on-the-ground field research to join the ship crew. Despite the occasional scare, nothing compares to being in nature at a time when everything is still so pristine. It's one of the things I miss most about Atlantis. I cherish it much more now after having been stuck up on Luna Sede for so long as well.

**Airl:** I'm glad you can do it, Dordogne. I'm perfectly content up on the ship and Moon Base.

**Dordogne:** Alright. Marshmallow is all patched up and drugged up. Let's keep walking toward the village. But keep an eye out for dangerous animals this time.

**Markus:** Vipers, tigers, and sloth bears, oh my!

———— ◉ ————

**Dordogne:** Let's stop by this group of trees on the top of the ridge. We'll have a good vantage point for looking out over the village from up here.

**Markus:** Sounds good. I'll set doggo down over there in the shade…. You keep sleeping, little princess. Don't worry, we won't leave you. Oh wow, this village is a lot bigger than what the Professor said back on the ship.

**Dordogne:** They do appear to be prospering. It looks so irenic, orderly, and serene down there too. I wish there was some way we could help these matrilineal societies succeed over the machismo-driven patriarchies that go on to dominate the next 5,500 years leading up to the Great Filter. I'd love to return home to see what that timeline looks like. This matriarchal village in particular seems remarkably peaceful and well-organized.

**Markus:** Same. I'd be way keener to get home to my time if we boosted some bitches back now. It's a total shit show when I'm from—

Hey Airl, so I heard you lost half your soul in a UFO crash or some shit?

**Dordogne:** Markus!

**Airl:** No, it's fine, Dordogne. Yes, in a way, I—

Wait, you discussed helping matriarchal societies flourish in this time instead of the paternalistic authoritarian tribes? That's huge! Are we going to do that?!

**Dordogne:** We wanted to, Airl, but the Professor shut it down because the future mafia kill-squad would come back and murder us all if we tried. They've benefited tremendously from the perpetuation of their patriarchal position ever since the Neolithic, so it's a no-go.

**Airl:** That's too bad. It seems like the world would be a better place if women had been in charge in at least a few regions over the last ten millennia.

**Markus:** True that, Airl. About a decade before I was born, the remnants of the imperialist Belgian and French regimes in Rwanda pitted the Hutu and Tutsi tribes against each other using longstanding colonial divide-and-conquer tactics. After the men slaughtered each other, the women stepped in to fill newly vacant political, social, and economic roles and they absolutely owned it!

**Dordogne:** Sadly, outside the Harappan civilization here, and the Hopi in the Southwest United States, that is probably the closest thing we've ever had to a matriarchy on this planet.

**Airl:** That is sad.

**Markus:** I guess the lesson here is that you just have to kill all the men, Airl. Not me though. Somebody has to help y'all make more daughters.

**Airl:** You men have done a fine job killing each other yourselves. You don't need us for that.

**Markus:** Oh, the killing is just getting started here too. We went gangbusters with holistic homicide following the advent of agriculture. Once we developed the concepts of territory, personal property, and accumulated wealth, it was game on with the Murder Death Kill. Not much has changed since then either. To be honest, I sometimes wonder if we can ever truly change. Maybe humanity does need a reset after all.

**Airl:** At the cost of 9 billion lives though, Markus?

**Markus:** It's actually *9.5* billion lives, Airl.

**Airl:** Oh, sorry, I wasn't there for that conversation.

**Dordogne:** Trust me, you didn't miss much.

**Markus:** But maybe, Airl. If the same failed system that's organized around the patrilineal transmission of generational wealth and power has persisted for 12,000 years, perhaps the only way to get a fresh start is to burn it all to the ground and start over. Politicians in my home time always act like they're going to fight for the disenfranchised and construct a more equitable system, but once they get into office, they fall straight in line just like every hypocrite before them.

**Airl:** That happens in my and Dordogne's future times too, Markus.

**Dordogne:** Airl's right. She's from an earlier period than me, but it's all the same everywhen. Even after the war, and despite having far fewer people—who had just survived the worst disaster in human history mind you—the same system persisted. In fact, the inequality was starker, as it was now divided between two planetary masses, since the rich and powerful escaped to the Moon Base while the rest of humanity burned...save for the lucky ones who retreated to caves, bunkers, and abandoned mine shafts below ground.

**Markus:** Makes me wonder if anyone could ever alter a power structure that has been perpetuated for tens of thousands of years. Maybe the only way forward *is* a proper reset. An entirely new system built from the ground up by people who value morals over money and ethics over economics.

**Airl:** Are you sure he's not from your time, Dordogne? He talks a lot like you do when we're off-ship smoking Shiva's Bhang.

**Dordogne:** No, he's definitely not from my time. He still has a penis. And speaking of Shiva's Bhang... Looool what I brought.

**Airl:** Aw, hell yea, Dordogne. You my girl!

**Markus:** Ohhh, that's what Shiva's Bhang is. Sweet! I ain't smoked weed since you picked me up at that house party last week. I just assumed you all were a bunch of squares too, so I never bothered to ask if you had any.

**Airl:** That's awesome, Dordogne, I was hoping you brought some. Even though I'm a tad nervous about puffing down here, especially after what just happened with that scary tiger. Do you still have your time-wand handy?

**Dordogne:** I do. And don't worry, we have a much better view of the surrounding area from up on this ridge. Here, you can have the first hit....

**Airl:** Hmmmmm, thanks, that is nice. It might just be in my head, but I swear I can taste the apple when we smoke it like this. Markus, do you want some too? It's apple flavored.

**Markus:** Does the pope shit in the fat bear's water-tight ass hat?!

**Airl:** I can only guess what that means, but maybe.

**Dordogne:** You don't have to respond to his drivel, Airl. I stopped a while ago now, which was incredibly liberating.

**Airl:** I don't know, Dordogne. As a linguistic anthropologist, I find his unorthodox way of speaking to be intriguing, and highly unique, even among his regional and temporal cohort. He's clearly well-learned and capable of organizing pho-nemes and morphemes to build a vast lexicon of complex utterances, but his syntax and semantics are unlike anything I've ever heard.

**Dordogne:** That could be, Airl. I'm not a linguist, but the stuff he says usually makes no damn sense to me.

**Markus:** Same. I've got no clue what this loquacious twat is saying half the time either.

**Airl:** *Hehe*, you two crack me up. I'm glad the Professor sent me down here to babysit you.

**Markus:** You don't seem half bad for a half-baked half-souled bitch either, Airl.

**Airl:** Thank you, Markus. I think.

**Dordogne:** I've watched him for years, Airl, and his drivel only gets worse when he smokes the Bhang.

**Airl:** It's fine. I kind of like it.... You know Dordogne, I was contemplating your research limitations, and specifically, how the Professor said you aren't allowed to do anything with anyone down here in this time without first consulting Metathory and the Looking Glass.

**Dordogne:** Yes, he's afraid we may inadvertently affect the timeline if we perform intercourse in this era.

**Airl:** I understand, and it is probably better that you don't, for safety's sake.... But I did want to point out that he never said anything about us.

**Dordogne:** What do you mean, 'about us?'

**Airl:** Well, I'm fascinated by your lectures, and especially how you said that after a particular period in human history, sex was no longer just about the act of making new humans. In one of your talks, you described how the coital act became more about weaving together the physical with the spiritual, connecting energy centers, and forming a deep conscious connection between the self, the other, and our nondual dynamic reality. I've been contemplating your lecture ever since, and I think I would like to experience that.

**Dordogne:** It's great to hear you say that Airl, I never thought you had any interest in my research until you mentioned it up on the ship earlier.

**Airl:** Your work has always intrigued me, Dordogne, and particularly since losing my avatar. After the crash, I felt like a piece of me was missing. But your lectures indicate that intercourse can have a healing effect, that there's a spiritual side to it, and especially in the way it's performed among the people of this region. What did you call it, Tantrum sex?

**Dordogne:** *Haha*, no, that's Americans. Here in India, it's called *Tantric* sex.

**Airl:** Yes, that's it. But I remember you saying it was about sharing a spiritual connection and entangling one-self with that of another, and with the shared universal consciousness.

**Dordogne:** That's true Airl, and I have experienced it with a few people on occasion. It's unfortunate that the sacred sex act disappeared before our times. With a more evolved consciousness and higher vibrational energy, our people would certainly appreciate this intertwining of souls much more than our ancestors.

**Airl:** Well, maybe you can teach me while we're down here. Call it synchronicity, but this happens to be some deliciously soft grass we're sitting on right now.

**Dordogne:** I would love to Airl. Why don't you take off your uniform and I'll have Markus start you off with some cunnilingus.

**Airl:** What is that?

**Dordogne:** You'll find out soon enough. And I think you'll enjoy it. He is quite skilled.... Markus, could you please help Airl and I with her intercourse initiation?

**Markus:** Um, I'm sorry, I wasn't paying attention. What were you two talking about?

**Dordogne:** Airl has become interested in the practice of spiritual copulation, and she would like to experience it for the first time. We were hoping you could assist us.

**Markus:** Uh, oh my god, yes. I can absolutely assist you with that!

**Dordogne:** Thank you, Markus.

**Markus:** Yea, no problem. Of course. Extremely happy to lend my services. Just gotta ditch these clothes. And Um, sorry again, I'm super stoned right now, but what were you asking me to do, specifically?

**Dordogne:** We all are, Markus. And from my experience, that is likely to make this more pleasurable for each of us. But as you can see, Airl has removed her uniform, and we were hoping you could first provide her with some oral pleasures. I've observed you performing cunnilingus on several occasions, and you are quite proficient, so I thought it would be a good way to welcome her into this universe of sensations.

**Markus:** Absolutely, and I appreciate your vote of confidence. Just let me.... Mmm, there we go....

**Dordogne:** Very good, thank you, Markus. And Airl, since you are unfamiliar with the process, what he is doing is an efficient way for one, or both, or multiple partners to bring each other, or others, to a state of arousal prior to penetration. There are many versions of this, depending on the sexual orientation of those involved, but placing one's mouth on another's genitals, regardless of their sex or gender, is highly effective at achieving this outcome.

**Airl:** Yes, I am beginning to see how that might be. Is it normal to feel nervous though, Dordogne?

**Dordogne:** It is. Entirely normal, and especially your first time. But just relax your body and mind. That will help welcome you into this space and eventually facilitate initial penetration, as each progressive act slowly guides you toward spiritual affirmation, which will be achieved in the buildup to, and during, climax.

**Airl:** Hmm, that does feel nice, and it is incredibly relaxing. It feels even better with the hot sun shining down on my naked body.... Mmm, Dordogne? Do you think Shiva's Bhang had anything to do with the development of Tantric sex here?

**Dordogne:** Correlation doesn't equal causality. But in this case, it probably does. So, yes. Undoubtedly. Not living in a sexually repressive society like most others probably helped too though.

**Airl:** Mmm, that's amazing! I can't believe we have these body parts that can make us feel utterly incredible like this and we never use them. What happened to us?

**Dordogne:** Thousands of years of bad choices, I guess.

**Airl:** Hmmmm, that's too bad.... I think I'm ready to experience the rest of it now. Maybe just take it slow at first.

**Dordogne:** OK, Markus, are you adequately primed for penetration? I know how much it arouses you to go down on a woman.

**Markus:** The soldier under my command stands at full attention, Ma'am.

**Dordogne:** Um, yes, I see that now. And I must say, my remote viewing sessions and more distant observations back in 48k BP gave me a general sense of your virile member's magnitude, but it is quite a sight to behold up close and in person.

**Markus:** Oh, this old thing? It gets the job done, I guess. Probably nothing to write home about though.

**Dordogne:** I don't think I'm at liberty to agree or disagree with that assertion at the present time, but I have the sense that you should go *very* slowly at first. Especially since this is her first time.

**Markus:** Not a problem.... How is that Airl?

**Airl:** I like it.... Very much, in fact.

**Markus:** I've gotta say, this feels entirely different with you two, and I mean with you as well, Dordogne. I can sense both of you vibrating through me like a billion bees buzzing in pulsating synchrony. Dordogne, you're not even touching me, but I feel you just as much as Airl. How are you doing that?

**Dordogne:** Mind is the most momentous entity, Markus. The people of your time had always viewed sex as a physical act, but it is much more than that. With heightened senses tied to an expanded consciousness, it becomes an all-encompassing energetic force, entwining the essence of the non-dual soul. The body is undoubtedly involved. But the mind is where transcendence occurs.

**Airl:** Hmmm, I can feel it too, Dordogne. This connection. With both of you. It's magnificent!

**Markus:** Damn, she's not kidding. You two have remarkable minds! I feel an unbelievably intense energy flowing through us. A pounding resonance, like an orchestral harmonic emanating throughout the universe! It's vibrating everything. Everywhere. It's incredible! I think I might have to be the one who takes it slow—

**Dordogne:** You wait for her, Markus! Under no circumstances should a man ever finish before a woman!

**Markus:** OK.... OK.... You're right.... Oh god! OK.... I can do it.... I'll just, uh, think about naked Margaret Thatcher, uh, playing baseball with naked John Candy on, uh, Madeleine Albright's shoulders. Oh god! At a February picnic in, uh, frigid Fargo, North Dakota!

**Dordogne:** That's good, Markus. Whatever you need to do. Just keep going. Now Airl.... Only 18.4% of women can reach spiritual climax through intercourse alone, so while Markus is doing that, I'm going to sit here and use three fingers to make concentric circles around your clitoris at a medium pace. Can you feel that?

**Airl:** Hmm yes, I like that a lot, Dordogne. And I think I'm, ahh, close to that place you described. Ahh, I hear music, and hmm, see fractals spinning in, beams of bright orange and yellow light!

**Dordogne:** That's wonderful, Airl. I also sense that you are close. Just calm your mind and go there. Follow the light and the music you hear, that is the spiritual realm you seek.

**Markus:** Oh god, yea, she's about to cum, I can feel it too!

**Airl:** Ah, Ahhhh, Ahhhhhh!

**Markus:** Ohh, shit!

———— ◉ ————

**Markus:** Hmmm, god damn, I didn't even know that was possible. I mean, I've had good sex before, but that was beyond my ability to comprehend!

**Airl:** That was the only time for me, but it was better than I ever could have imagined as well.

**Dordogne:** What did you see, Airl?

**Airl:** I saw every color of the rainbow blended into one, and there was music, and a brilliant luminosity emanating from everywhere. It consumed me. I could feel you two so intensely, deep inside my mind, body, and soul. Thank you both, I really needed that, more than you can ever know.

**Dordogne:** I'm glad we could share that with you Airl. We all need that sometimes.

**Airl:** I also understand the spiritual connection you spoke of now, Dordogne, and I hope we can get that back for our

114

people. We lost something important. Something magical.

**Dordogne:** I think there is hope for that, Airl. And it is an important element of my research objective, but it will be challenging since this art was lost millennia ago. Perhaps you can help me teach them.

**Airl:** I would like that, Dordogne.

**Dordogne:** Maybe you could help us too, Markus. It will take the combined effort of many spiritual teachers to prevail over the loss of these fundamental dispositions of human nature.

**Markus:** Absolutely. I would love to help you bring sex back to the future. I feel like I understand it now in a way I never could have before. You're an amazing teacher, Dordogne. It's strange too, because I feel like I was just with you as much as I was with Airl. And to be honest, there came a point when I couldn't tell any of us apart from each other. It's like we merged into a singular eternal radiance.

**Dordogne:** Yes, Markus, I was there with you, and perhaps we will find each other there again someday, in a more intimate setting. But first we need to complete this mission and stop the war.

**Markus:** I would love that. And I imagine you're right. Although, looking back on it, we didn't do much to help prevent a nuclear apocalypse while we were down here.

**Dordogne:** I think what just happened was exactly why we were here, Markus. It is occasionally necessary to focus on the individual to enact societal change. It is possible we accomplished more today than we ever could have if we did what we thought we were supposed to do.

**Airl:** Hmmm, I agree, Dordogne. And thanks again, you two.

**Dordogne:** Happy to, Airl. I enjoyed it very much as well. But we should start heading back to the ship. And, Markus,

I should mention that on our next time jump, you will finally have a larger role to play in this mission. But you are going to want to get some rest first, trust me.

**Markus:** That's ominous.

**Dordogne:** I think you'll be fine.

**Markus:** By the way, what are we going to tell the Professor when we get back to the ship? Between the tiger, Shiva's Bhang, and the incredibly hot sex, we didn't collect any data down here.

**Dordogne:** The Professor is getting old, and I sense that he doesn't remember coming here before, despite having once been to this exact place and at nearly the same time. I'll just pull some old data from the last time we were tempoloco, and he'll be none the wiser.

**Markus:** Good thinking. Also, how much data do you have from other eras? Because I am of the opinion that we should just smoke weed and have sex every time he sends us down to the surface. That's my kind of field work.

**Airl:** I could get on board with that as well, Dordogne. You two are a lot of fun to work with. Sorry I've been such a Negative Nancy lately. I haven't been feeling like myself ever since I lost my avatar in the crash, but things are finally looking up.

**Dordogne:** I don't think we would have jobs much longer if we did that every time Airl, but it is nice on occasion, and I'm happy to hear you're feeling better.

**Markus:** Wait, you two are getting paid for this? When y'all picked me up from that rugby party the Professor didn't say anything about remuneration.

**Dordogne:** I feel like you were just adequately compensated for your time, Markus.

**Markus:** Hmm, getting paid in weed and transcendent three-somes with hot future chicks? Yup, I'm good with that.

**Atman:** Welcome back to the ship you three, was it a productive mission to the surface?

**Dordogne:** Yes, Professor Atman, we were able to collect a lot of data in a relatively short timeframe. I'll have a report on your desk by tomorrow morning.

**Atman:** Thank you, Dordogne. I look forward to not reading that. And Airl, were these two good while you were down there?

**Airl:** Yes, Professor, they were very good down there. Very good indeed.

**Atman:** Well, I'm happy to hear that. I noticed the future financier murder squad never showed up to kill us all, so I'll have to agree with you about that…. By the way, why did you dye Marshmallow's hair pink? I thought she looked fine with a white coat of fur.

**Dordogne:** We didn't, Julian, it's her blood that made it that color. We encountered a tiger soon after we got to the surface, and she put herself between it and us until I was able to get my time-wand out to stop it. She saved my life, and perhaps all our lives.

**Atman:** That sounds terrifying, but I'm happy to know you're all safe. And what a fearless colleague we have here. That's a good girl, Marshmallow! After our next time jump, I'm going to take you down to the mess hall and fix you a feast. Well deserved! Alright everyone, let's prepare for departure. This next stage of the mission is critical. And Markus, you should get some rest. We're going to need you in top form for this one.

**Markus:** No problem, Professor. Despite a grueling day of extremely hard data collection, I'm feeling oddly relaxed and rejuvenated.

**Atman:** Happy to hear it, Son. This is only about a 3,000-year jump, so it shouldn't be too bad, but buckle up just in case.... Manitoba!

**Manitoba:** Yes, Captain?

**Atman:** How are we feeling about this one? Do you foresee any dick kicks in your future?

**Manitoba:** No, Captain. I changed the settings on the vector launch sequencer, so it is the way you like it now.

**Atman:** Fantastic, hit us with that countdown then, Launch Maestro.

**Manitoba:** Aye aye, Cap. We have a clear window for departure in T-minus 3 hours, 27 minutes, and 16 seconds.

**Atman:** Well done, Boy. Well done.... Alrighty then. We've got something of a wait this go round. In the meantime, let's go make some sandwiches and have a few shots and beers. What do you say crew?

**Markus:** Absolutely, Professor! Man, I'm really starting to like this job.

# CHAPTER 11
## CONCEPTION – JEZREEL VALLEY – TERRA
## 1951 BP

**Atman:** Well team, we made it. And good news everyone! I received a message from Major Metathory soon after we arrived in this period, stating that Project Looking Glass predicts there is a 78% probability the war can be avoided with some calculated interventions over the next 33 years, beginning at this time in 1951 BP. It's not guaranteed, but this is the minimum threshold we were looking for, so let's give it a go!

**Markus:** What's the backside stat there, Doc? How likely is it we'll disrupt your precious power plan and get killed by the psycho chrononauts?

**Atman:** The Looking Glass says there's a—

Wait, that can't be right.

**Dordogne:** What is it, Professor?

**Atman:** Well, Dordogne, it says there is a 0% probability these temporal interventions will disrupt the patriarchal power structure in the future, so I guess we're OK to go.

**Markus:** We're OK to go!

**Atman:** Control, if you're reading me, I'm OK to go!!

**Dordogne:** Why the hell do you two stupid men keep saying that?

**Markus:** Solid flick, Prof. I'm glad you've seen *that* one at least.

**Atman:** Seen it? I helped write it!

**Markus:** What, seriously?

**Atman:** Yea!

**Markus:** Did you meet Jodi Foster?

**Atman:** Meet her? I married her!

**Markus:** Really!?

**Atman:** No, I was just kidding about that last part, but I did help write *Contact*. It was one of many in our series of PSYOP films and TV programs, which were meant to introduce the people of your time to some basic concepts related to UFOs, space, time, and time travel. We also did *Close Encounters of the Third Kind, Looper, Dark, The Time Machine, Bill and Ted's Excellent Adventure, Interstellar, Idiocracy, Predestination*—

**Markus:** *Hot Tub Time Machine*?!

**Atman:** No, that one was all yours, but also 'a solid flick' as you say. The *Back to The Future* trilogy was yours too, unfortunately.

**Markus:** Why, unfortunately? I thought they were pretty good.

**Atman:** I say *unfortunately* because the first film in that series did much more harm than good regarding people's perception of how backward time travel works.

**Markus:** You mean people don't disappear from photographs if their parents run the risk of not hooking up, and

White people didn't steal rock and roll music from Black people?

**Atman:** Only one of those is accurate, Markus. We tried to create and disseminate judicious content via the most widely used media platforms of the time, to help educate people about concepts and ideas related to our origins and intent. The cultural foundation we constructed over the previous 150 years is meant to make it less shocking and disruptive when we finally reveal ourselves to you.

**Markus:** Wow, it's cool you helped write and produce some of my favorite movies. It seems to have worked too, or at least it did with me, since I wasn't shocked or disrupted when you picked me up in your swanky UFO and told me you were time travelers.

**Atman:** Good to hear. It was many moons ago, but also one of the most memorable periods of my career. OK, I would love to sit up here and talk filmography all evening, but with a 78% probability of success in this time we should probably get to work.

**Markus:** Oh yea, what was the intervention the Looking Glass saw, anyway?

**Atman:** Well, Markus, I think you'll like this one. All your previous 'research' is about to pay off.

**Markus:** Oh, I do like the sound of that.

**Atman:** Do you see that woman carrying an ointment jar down there?

**Markus:** The hot one in the scarlet dress?

**Atman:** Yes, that one. We need you to go down there tonight and make love to her.

**Markus:** Well, if it's to stave off the near annihilation of our species, I guess I can take one for the team.

**Atman:** Thank you for your service, Markus.... Since the Looking Glass report came in, our intercessor, Gabriel, was sent back to explain the nature of your forthcoming visit with her.

**Markus:** That explains the massive ointment jar, I guess.

**Atman:** Indeed. Additionally, our resident psychologist, Morpheus, has been retrospectively visiting her dreams and introducing you to her. She is frothing with excitement about your arrival later this evening.

**Markus:** Huh, it's funny you mention that because I've been having some unusual sex dreams about a kinky hot chick lately, who I now realize looks exactly like that woman down there.

**Atman:** Yes, Morpheus has been linking your consciousness with hers in such ways.

**Markus:** I see that now. The guy is an absolute freak too cuz I have never done anything like that with a woman in real life!

**Atman:** Well, you must remember that men in our time don't have sex, so he likely improvised certain parts based on his limited knowledge of what transpires during copulation.

**Markus:** You can say that again. Hey, but didn't we just find out I need to bang this bird to save the world when we landed in this time? I've been having those dreams for like a week now.

**Atman:** Consciousness is timeless, Markus. While we were busy talking about how I'm the greatest screenwriter of your generation, Morpheus was working on developing a subconscious connection between you two. Our specific *physical* position in time is irrelevant in the context of your interwoven eternal minds.

**Markus:** Bit of an overreach on that screenwriter comment there, but I do applaud his efforts. Those were some crazy intense dreams!

**Atman:** Morpheus is quite good. I'm sure it worked for her as well so there shouldn't be any issues once you get down there.

**Markus:** Don't expect any issues from me either Doc, I'm a good woodsman.

**Atman:** Undoubtedly.... It's also a good thing you haven't had sex since we were on the Island of Flores because she is ovulating right now, and it is imperative that you inseminate her with everything you've got, the whole nine yards!

**Markus:** Right. Flores. That was absolutely the last time I had sex. So long ago. So backed up.

**Atman:** The Looking Glass indicates that the child you conceive tonight will be instrumental in helping us spread empathy and love deep into the future, with a 78% chance of stopping the Great War.

**Markus:** Alright. Let's. Git. It. On! Dordogne, you wanna help me out with the fluffing?

**Dordogne:** I think you've got this.

**Markus:** Next time then. OK, beam me down for some get down, Scotty.

**Atman:** Who's Scotty?

**Markus:** Hey, I'm not going to get any STIs from this am I?

**Atman:** So now you're suddenly worried about contracting a sexually transmitted disease after you had sex with multiple human subspecies on several continents over the last 48,000 years?

**Markus:** I mean shit, Doc, rubbers aren't going to be invented for another 1,563 years, and you said I've got to put the baby batter all the way up in her so it's not like I could wear one anyway.

**Atman:** That is an oddly specific and exceptionally accurate estimate for the invention of that barrier contraceptive device, Markus.

**Markus:** I am a bit of a history buff.

**Atman:** But no, we screen every one of our research subjects for all transmissible diseases prior to the initiation of any form of close contact.

**Dordogne:** The Professor's right. They ran a battery of tests and implemented precautionary measures with that Brazilian farmer before we had sex. They even made him puke in the corner to be sure everything was cleared out of him ahead of time. Although, to be honest, I wish they had done without that part. He was a sloppy kisser.

**Markus:** That's disgusting. But your acidic kisses account is duly noted, Dordogne. I'll grab a toothbrush for this chick in case she starts puking too. Alright guys, send me in.

# CHAPTER 12
## INDOCTRINATION – JEZREEL VALLEY – TERRA
## 1951 BP

**Atman:** He sure has been down there for a while. Dordogne, does it usually take this long to do the sex to completion?

**Dordogne:** Oh my, no. Not for him. He typically wraps things up rather quickly. I'm sure he's fine though. I'm guessing he just wanted to snuggle after. He's kind of a softy, despite all the fist fights and the ludicrous garbage that's constantly spewing out of his mouth.

**Atman:** I could see that. I don't think he ever wins those fights either.

**Dordogne:** No, he certainly does not.

**Atman:** Oh good, here he comes. Dear me, he could have at least put some pants on before heading back out to the ship.

**Dordogne:** He probably just wanted to show you that he successfully completed the emission.

**Atman:** Yes, points! Good one, Dordogne!

**Dordogne:** Thanks.

**Atman:** But I would have believed him if he had just told me.

**Dordogne:** The man is fastidious. He takes his work very seriously.

**Atman:** That might be the farthest thing from the truth I have ever heard, but—

Hello, welcome back Markus. How was the conception?

**Markus:** Immaculate. I'd marry her if I could. Hey, what was that chick's name again?

**Atman:** Doesn't matter, we've got work to do.

**Markus:** Yea, so what happens now that the seed-deed is done?

**Atman:** It is something of a multistage plan, but Major Metathory just messaged that we're already seeing an improvement in the Looking Glass statistics following your nocturnal emission mission, so I'm hopeful it might work.

**Markus:** That's good. I'm pleased to hear our incredibly hot sexcapade was not in vain, Professor.

**Atman:** It was not. So, the proposed plan that was vetted by the Looking Glass on Luna Sede requires us to help raise the child you just created, who will be tasked in adulthood with spreading a message of empathy, patience, kindness, and unconditional love to the people of this time. That message will carry forward into the future, and humans will henceforth live in peace and harmony, with no false sense of the constructed other, and no desire to exterminate them in a nuclear war in your home time, Markus.

**Markus:** Sounds like a solid plan, Professor, but won't that all take an exceptionally long time? I mean, I just knocked her up an hour ago, and I think it takes at least 12 months to poop out a kid after that. Then we'll have to wait for it to grow up and educate it on how to teach people to be nice to each other. We're going to be here forever!

**Atman:** It takes nine months to gestate a child, which a biological anthropologist, or any human for that matter, should know. And yes, it would take a long time if we did in fact have to wait for all those things to happen.... However, and you're not going to believe this, Markus, but we came here in a—

**Markus:** Time machine. Right. We have a time machine. Not sure how I keep forgetting that.

**Atman:** Yes, as a seemingly obvious part of the plan, we'll use our *time machine* to go forward and pick up the child around the age of 3 or 4, so we can begin introducing him to this environment, which will certainly seem alien compared to the technology and culture of the current period. After that, we will continue jumping forward in time to imbue him with the knowledge he'll need to impart wisdom upon humanity, which will echo across the ages.

**Markus:** Right on, but why would they listen to this kid over the others? In the short time I was down there I saw a ton of people who looked like they were preaching all kinds of bat-shit crazy stuff. How will our message resonate so people in the future can live in peace and harmony if nobody ever gets the memo?

**Atman:** Because our technology is so advanced, anything we do in this time will be perceived as magic, or divine intervention. They'll listen to him because we'll use our sophisticated machinery to make him seem special, to help him perform what we are calling 'miracles.'

**Markus:** Smart.

**Atman:** We can use our antigravity light beam to make him hover in the air or walk on water. We can suck fish from the river and rain them back down from the sky to feed countless naive hungry people below. We can use our advanced medical knowledge to cure simple diseases of the past that have long since been eradicated in our times. These acts will be deemed miraculous, and they will think the kid is special and believe anything he tells them.

**Markus:** Hmm, this is starting to sound familiar. What's this guy's name?

**Atman:** The holey scriptures foretell that Mary will name him, Jesus.

**Markus:** Oh yea, Mary, that was her name. She's a fun one—

Wait a second.... So, I just made Jesus? I'm Jesus's Dad?!

**Atman:** You are, yes. In about nine months anyway.

**Markus:** So, if Jesus is the son of god...and I'm Jesus's Dad...

**Atman:** Go on Sherlock, you're getting there.

**Markus:** Then, I'm God! I think I just became God!

**Atman:** You have indeed. What a truly miraculous moment. Praise be.

**Markus:** That's right, bow down, bitches! Tithe and offer or some shit! Y'all got God up in it now!

**Atman:** Well, don't let it go to your head, Markus, someone had to play God. We need to get this message out in the hopes that it will help prevent the war, and for some unfathomable reason it was always you, so it had to be you this time as well. If we told you about this beforehand it might not have worked out the way it needed to, so we kept you in the dark about a few things leading up to this critical stage of the mission.

**Markus:** Man, I should have kept going to church with my dad after all, I had no idea they were worshipping me and my bastard kid the whole time.

**Atman:** You might be the least God-like person I've ever met, Markus. But that doesn't matter. Other than Mary, nobody down there ever saw your face, so you are free to become a magic ethereal preoccupation in the sky. Jesus is the one who must do the heavy lifting part of your holy trinity work in this time. They know he is your son, but they have no idea how it happened. Nobody ever knows or cares that you are the man behind the curtain.

**Markus:** Damn, way to take the wind out of a fresh God's sails, Professor. I was just trying to enjoy my newfound status as the most powerful being in the universe for a quick minute.

**Atman:** There's no time for that, Markus, we've got work to do. Alright team, omnipresence is a bitch, let's jump forward in time to start priming the pump on this whole monotheism thing.

# CHAPTER 13
## CONSECRATION – CAIAPHAS – TERRA
## 1917 BP

**Markus:** You were right Doc. That whole 'insemination to adulthood' process hardly took any time at all. What was it, like three days we spent raising my kid?

**Atman:** Not even, it was just under 68 hours ship time. And I agree, that was a rather efficient indoctrination process. It certainly helps that Jesus was a smart and caring kid growing up. I can only assume he got that from Mary's side of the family.

**Markus:** There's a good chance of that. Alright, so homeboy has been spreading the good word for several years now, and folks seem to be listening with great interest on account of all the spooky miracles we've been performing. I guess we should jump back to my home time to see if it helped stop the war.

**Atman:** Yes, I have a good feeling about this. Jesus is a great teacher and people are listening to his message of empathy and love. Even better, Major Metathory wrote that the Looking Glass shows the probability of avoiding the Great War is up to 82%, and it is still showing a 0% probability of disrupting the future power structure.

**Markus:** That's great! The first part at least. Fuck those other guys. You know what though Doc, I'm really gonna miss that kid when we leave. We definitely didn't have a traditional father–son relationship, playing catch in the yard and whatnot, but I feel like we really bonded while we were together in this time.

**Atman:** I think so too, Markus. He seems quite fond of you as well.

**Markus:** Thanks Professor, I only hope he has a long and happy life here. It sucks I didn't get a chance to say goodbye, but we should probably get going.

**Atman:** Well, we can't leave just yet. They still have to kill him first.

**Markus:** Wait, what?! You're going to let them kill my kid?

**Dordogne:** I'll take this one, Professor. I studied artistic depictions of religious scenes related to this event during graduate school.

**Atman:** Yes, I remember. Explain away, Dordogne.

**Dordogne:** You really didn't pay attention in church did you, Markus? That's their whole thing. They love showing your son being tortured and killed all over their basilicas, churches, cathedrals, and in old people's houses. They even wear necklaces of him strung up and bleeding out on a wooden cross.

**Markus:** Oh yea, I do remember seeing that. Those sick fucks. That's my little boy!

**Dordogne:** Well, don't worry, Markus. We're going to take some creative liberties with that situation too.

**Markus:** What do you mean?

**Dordogne:** Since you have clearly forgotten everything about the dominant religion of the time and place you hail from, then I'll tell you.

**Markus:** I wouldn't say I forgot so much as I tenaciously drank those memories away throughout high school and college.

**Dordogne:** Either way, after they kill him, he is risen. I still don't know why they say it like that, but these people never were great with grammar. Regardless, in their holey scriptures, Jesus dies, but he comes back to life three days later and kids look for colorful eggs that a magic rabbit pooped out of its butt all over their yards.

**Atman:** I think you might be mixing up a few religious traditions there, Dordogne.

**Dordogne:** Maybe Professor, but it's important that they think Jesus died and then came back to life so there is one last highly memorable miracle that will help us propagate this all-important message through time. In truth, Jesus won't be killed at all. We're going to fake his death, show him to people three days later, then get the hell out of this Godforsaken period. Also, Markus, you may be happy to know that Jesus will be coming back to the future with us after his resurrection.

**Markus:** Oh snap, I'll get to kick it with my little all-grown-up boy for the rest of the mission?!

**Dordogne:** Yes, but first we must let them think they killed him, and that magic zombie Jesus is risen.

**Markus:** So, how does that part go down exactly?

**Dordogne:** If I remember correctly, they put a crown of thorns on his head, pound nails through his wrists between the distal radius and ulna to hang him on a cross, then they stab him in the ribs with a sharp spear after they get bored with these other forms of torture.

**Markus:** Ouch, that sounds horrific! Won't that hurt?

**Dordogne:** Tremendously. But don't worry, we're going to give Jesus a ton of drugs, so he won't feel a thing. The drugs will also slow his heartrate to the extent that they'll think he's dead, but it should be easy for us to respawn him once we collect him from the tomb.

**Markus:** That still sounds painful. Couldn't we just go back in time to before they hang him on the cross, paint some fake holes on his wrists, then show our fully alive and never-tortured past-Jesus to everybody three days later?

**Dordogne:** That won't work, Markus. If we take Jesus from a past period that comes *before* he is crucified, then he disappears from that time and is no longer there for them to crucify in the first place.

**Markus:** Great point, Dordogne. You're so smart. And beautiful. Also, you smell fantastic. What is that some sort of lavender face cream or lotion from Bath and Bod—

**Dordogne:** Stay the course, Markus, this is important.

**Markus:** Right, sorry.

**Dordogne:** But yes, it's lavender.

**Markus:** It's lovely. So, are you sure Jesus is cool with this whole getting murdered by religious zealots thing? Did you talk to him about this already? Do I need to sign a parental consent form or anything?

**Dordogne:** Jesus is willing to make this sacrifice for humanity. Morpheus took his consciousness forward in time during a recent dream so he could see the devastation and suffering caused by the Great Filter. Jesus is an empathetic man and—

**Markus:** Boy. He's still my little boy, Dordogne.

**Dordogne:** OK, boy then. Your boy knows this is going to be hard, but he feels it is worth the sacrifice if it helps save all those people in your time.

**Markus:** He is a great kid. I done raised him right.

**Dordogne:** Yes, you should definitely get a 'Father of the Year' mug on your birthday to commemorate that.

**Markus:** No diggity, Dordogne. Alright, well if he's cool with it then I guess I am too. What kind of drugs are you giving him, anyway?

**Dordogne:** That's the Professor's department. He has studied the procurement and use of countless medicinal plants and animals across a 30,000-year timespan. He's quite knowledgeable.

**Atman:** Thank you, Dordogne, it is something of a passion project for me. But to answer your question, Markus, it is a special cocktail I developed while working at a field site in the Teotihuacan Valley in 3,845 CE. It primarily consists of opium, coca leaves, the CHT[5] compound, which doesn't yet exist in your time, mescalin, MDMA, and a pinch of ayahuasca, which is all dissolved in a mixture of water and sodium bicarbonate that is then boiled and dried to make it smokable. But it is also consumable orally, ocularly, and anally.

**Markus:** That seems super strange. But I imagine you future folks got it all figured out.

**Atman:** It should work quite well for Jesus's purposes. People seem to enjoy it recreationally too. It has been wildly popular for thousands of years. I call it *Hydromorphic Crackicide*.

**Markus:** Tha fuck?! Hell yea, I know that shit! But I always thought that was—

**Atman:** Yes, as it gained popularity, all kinds of urban legends grew up around it. I once heard one about how it was derived from dehydrated unicorn milk or something ridiculous like that.

**Markus:** *Albino* unicorn milk to be precise.

**Atman:** That was it, which is funny since unicorns don't exist. Nor are they mammals.

**Markus:** True that. Probably. Damn, so you invented that cracking Crackicide, Doc?! You're a time-traveling anthropologist from the future, you made all my favorite movies, and you're an intertemporal drug kingpin, you Heisenberg-ass motherfucker! I thought you were alright before, but you're like a God to me now.

**Atman:** Takes one to know one.

**Markus:** OK, never mind, you're still a nerd. Hey, but since Jesus is my son and all, I was thinking I should probably take some with him. You know like, as a show of solidarity.

**Atman:** I guess we could allow that. I imagine it will be hard for you to watch your son be killed for teaching people about unconditional love.

**Markus:** It will, yes. Very hard. Very sad. Dordogne, do you want to do some with me?

**Dordogne:** Maybe just a little.

**Markus:** Sweet. Alright, so when is the Christ murder rave party anyway?

**Atman:** It will be tomorrow afternoon. But tonight, we need someone to dress up like a guard and bring this vial of Crackicide to Jesus in jail so he can take it before they put the spikey hat on his head and make him schlep around with that heavy wooden cross. He could get splinters.

**Markus:** I'll go, Professor. It should be me. He is my son after all.

**Atman:** Fair enough, Markus. Go see Moirai in wardrobe, she'll get you set up with what you need.

**Markus:** Wait, you have a whole wardrobe department up here? How big is this ship anyway? Also, why?

**Atman:** Moirai is our cultural anthropologist and costume designer. She comes with us on every intertemporal research mission. We often need to dress in the traditional garb of the people we interact with in the various times and places we visit. So Moirai makes sure we fit in with our hair, makeup, and style of dress.

**Markus:** I never thought about that, but yea, a proper wardrobe does seem important for what you do. It's just weird that I've never seen her in the mess hall or anything. Same with Morpheus, who I just met a couple days ago. Where the hell is everybody hiding?

**Atman:** We all tend to keep to ourselves on these missions. We start to grate on each other after a while otherwise.

**Markus:** That's a great team mentality, Professor. Really collaborative work environment you've got here.

**Atman:** Just go find Moirai, dillweed, she's on level one.

———— ◉ ————

**Markus:** Alright, I'm back y'all. How do I look?

**Dordogne:** Stylish, like an Arabian knight, and the spear is a nice touch.

**Markus:** Wicked pissah, thanks Dordogne, I thought so too. And I'm sure as shit not going down there unarmed considering what those religious asshats are planning to do to my kid tomorrow.

**Dordogne:** Do you even know how to use that spear, Markus? You clearly never learned how to use your fists as weapons.

**Markus:** Well, no, but I'm hoping I don't have to use it, especially since it's just a plastic prop. But I'll tangle with a couple old-timey guards down there if I have to. The boy needs his drugs! Ok future fuckers, send me down!

# CHAPTER 14
## ALLOCATION – CAIAPHAS – TERRA
## 1917 BP

*It sure is dark down here. Smells like shit too. Man, this has got to be the weirdest week of my life. I can't believe I'm in a $0^{th}$-century prison right now. Or is it a $1^{st}$-century prison? I can never remember how that shit works.*

*OK, so I came from the year 2035, and I think people said it was the $21^{st}$ century then, which would mean it's the one above it, so yea, $1^{st}$ century, I guess. I'm in a $1^{st}$-century prison.*

*The $0^{th}$ century sounded a lot cooler though. That's probably what I'll tell Ryan and Amanda when I get home: "Guys, I was creeping around a $0^{th}$-century prison trying to find my bastard kid Jesus to give him a megadose of Hydromorphic Crackicide for when religious fanatics kill him until we raise him from the dead to save the world from nuclear annihilation!"*

*It is kind of funny they started telling time based on when my kid was born too. Hey everybody, look, Jesus is here, welcome to year 0!!! Ah shit, we should raise Dick Clark from the dead and bring him back to this time period. He'd probably get a kick out of watching me create the first year. Oh, hell yea, he could do one of those ball-drop countdowns to the immaculate insemination like he used to at Time Square back in the good old days.*

*Huh, I wonder how people told time before I put my seed in Mary's tum tum anyway? Were they just standing around waiting for that to happen so they knew what year it was?*

*"Yo, Jim, what year is it?"*

*"I don't know Reynold. That dude from the future hasn't come back and knocked up that past chick yet so we don't have time."*

*"Ah shucks Jim, I was really hoping to have a birthday this year."*

*"Nope, sorry Reynold, can't happen, not yet at least, maybe next year."*

*"Next what?"*

**Prison Guard:** Hey, what are you doing down here?!

**Markus:** Uh, what, nothing. Just looking for my car keys. They must have fallen out of my pock—

Wait, you speak English?

**Guard:** No, I just assumed you didn't know the Galilean dialect of Middle Aramaic since it's a dead language in your time, so I yelled at you in English.

**Markus:** Thanks for that. And you're right, I didn't even know that was a language.

**Guard:** It is. You looking for Jesus?

**Markus:** Yea, he's my son.

**Guard:** No shit! Well, hey there God!

**Markus:** No need to bow, I've only been God for a couple days, and it doesn't feel like something people should worship me for since all I did was lay into some hot chick a few nights ago...34 years ago.

**Guard:** Oh yea, Mary, for sure. She was smoking hot back then.

**Markus:** Church! She's still got it too. We just hooked up this arvo for like the 12th time in three days. She's voracious!

**Guard:** Nice. Got another messiah on the way?

**Markus:** No. I've been pretty judicious about pulling out ever since that first night. We've gotta get out of here soon anyway, so she'd have to raise that one on her own.

**Guard:** Makes sense. Hey, so, I'm supposed to kill people who break into the prison and try to free the prisoners and stuff, but I've gotten to know Jesus over the last few days, and I really like the kid, so I'm going to let you take him outta here just this once.

**Markus:** That's super kind of you Mister guard man.

**Guard:** Call me Gary.

**Markus:** Well thanks, Gary, but Jesus needs to stay in jail so they can kill him tomorrow.

**Guard:** Aww, no, that sucks! He's such a great guy.

**Markus:** I know, right. Hell of a good kid. I guess he's not actually going to die in the strict sense of the word since we plan on bringing him back from the—

Hang on, I don't want to give any spoilers. Let's just say... watch for something crazy cool to go down about four days from now.

**Guard:** Will do, I love a good plot twist. So, why *are* you down here then?

**Markus:** Oh, I'm just here to give Jesus a really strange cocktail of analgesics and party drugs so it doesn't hurt as much when they pin him up tomorrow.

**Guard:** That's nice. He's lucky to have you as a dad, God.

**Markus:** Maybe, I just wish I could have been there for him more, but he lived thirty-three years in the three days I knew him, so we didn't get to hang out as much as I would have liked.

**Guard:** That's parenthood for ya.

**Markus:** Totes, but I'll have a chance to get to know him better once we leave this time since he'll be coming back to the future with us after we bring his zombie ass back from the dead.

**Guard:** Ah, hey! You said no spoilers!

**Markus:** Oh yea, shit, sorry. What I meant to say was 'once we leave this period with his lifeless corpse while he stays unambiguously dead.' Very dead. Very sad.

**Guard:** Right on. Well, he's a great guy. I'm sure you'll have fun together in the future.

**Markus:** Fer shure. Alright, it was nice chatting with you, Gary, but I should get these drugs to Jesus so I have time to plug his mom one last time before she passes out for the evening. Not much of a night-owl, that one.

**Guard:** Yea, I've noticed.

**Markus:** What?

**Guard:** Nothing. You'll find Jesus in the last cell down that corridor on the left.

**Markus:** Awsomeness, thanks. It was great meeting you, Gary.

**Guard:** You too. Good luck with saving the future and everything.

**Markus:** I don't think I told you anything about that, but thanks. Take care.

———— ◉ ————

**Markus:** Jesus?

**Lord and Savior Jesus Immanuel Harold Christ Only Begotten Son of the Living God Bread of Life:** Father?

**Markus:** Hey, big buddy, how ya doing in there?

**Jesus:** Oh, I'm doing fine. All things considered.

**Markus:** Yea, sorry you've got to get murdered by religious zealots tomorrow.

**Jesus:** I know, I'm not looking forward to that at all. But I heard you were bringing me some good drugs, so that should help at least.

**Markus:** I hope so. Professor Heisenberg mixed you up a concoction of some mighty fine medicaments, which should help with the whole fake-dying thing. Me and Dordogne are gonna rage with you once we bring you back to life and get you the fuck outta this stupid-ass time period too.

**Jesus:** Sounds fun, thanks Father.

**Markus:** Be sure you take the whole vial tomorrow. We'll have the Doc whip us up another batch of Crackicide once we get to the next time stop, so don't skimp. You're gonna want the whole thing once you get the cross and the prickly hat on your head.

**Jesus:** OK, I'll be sure to take all of it. I wish we could bring Mom to the future with us too. It's been hard for her since everybody turned on me.

**Markus:** It has, but she's been taking it pretty well, and often. She seems to like it in this era for whatever fucked-up reason anyway.

**Jesus:** Well, she is from this time I guess, so that makes sense. I never felt like I fit in though, so I'm glad I'm coming with you to the future in a few days.

**Markus:** Yea, sorry about that, bud. I imagine us interjecting sophisticated technology, clairvoyance, telekinesis, telepathy, advanced knowledge of future events, imbuing you with healing powers, and making you the king of jews might have interfered with your social life to some extent.

**Jesus:** Aww, it's all good. I'm just glad I might be able to help stop the bombs from going off in your time. That was horrible what I saw in my dream. I really hope we succeed with this mission.

**Markus:** Same. I think we've got a good chance with everything you've been teaching people in this time too.

**Jesus:** I'm not so sure about that, Father. I was only preaching about love, acceptance, and empathy, and they locked me up and are going to murder me tomorrow.

**Markus:** Hmm, that's a good point. Well, maybe future christians—

Oh yea, by the way...they named their whole religion after you, Mr. Fancy *Christ* Man! But maybe future christians will practice all the things you've been teaching here in this time. It might just take a couple millennia for it to sink in.

**Jesus:** I hope so. I don't want all of this to have been for nothing.

**Markus:** I'm sure it won't be. My dad, your grandfather I guess, and all his friends are evangelical christians, and they—

Hang on, now that I think about it, that might be the opposite of what—

**Jesus:** Opposite of what?

**Markus:** Nothing, Boy. Your sacrifice means a lot to us now, and I'm sure it will mean so much to people then too. You'll get to see it in person soon anyway, since we'll be leaving for the future right after you're done being assassinated by your own people. Well, *soon* after I guess. But first we're gonna bring you back from the dead just to stick it to 'em.

**Jesus:** Yeah, that'll teach 'em!

**Markus:** Sure will. I'm glad you're coming back with us too, Jesus. It's a bummer we couldn't hang out more since I had to keep jumping ahead in time. Shit, I missed all your damn birthdays like some kind of white trash alcoholic compulsive gambler dad who's always off trolling for strange at shitty dive bars where them girls with the big poofy hair who smoke way too many cigarettes hang out. But I am looking forward to finally getting to spend some quality time with you once this is over.

**Jesus:** Me too. I love you, Dad. And thanks for the drugs.

**Markus:** I love you too, Son. Good luck tomorrow, and I'll see you on the flatliners table.

**Jesus:** Thanks. But can we not call it that, please.

**Markus:** Sure thing, Junior.

———— ◉ ————

**Holy Mother the Blessed 'Virgin' Mary:** How is my little Yeshu doing in there, Markus?

**Markus:** He seems to be doing well, considering the current circumstances. But I think he, much like the rest of us, is completely done with this time period and all the fucked-up people in it.

**Mary:** It's not for everyone.

**Markus:** He was also a little bummed that you're not coming with us to the future.

**Mary:** Is that what you want too, Ĕlāhā?

**Markus:** I mean, it's been fun hanging out with you over the last few days, and you're a hell of a good lay. You can come if you'd like, but I should mention that I met a woman recently, and I feel something different when I'm with her, something I've never felt with anyone else, and I'm curious to see where that might be going. Besides, I don't know if you would like it in the year 2035, it's extremely loud there.

**Mary:** I have come to appreciate the silent tranquility of a mid-morning 0th-century promenade.

**Markus:** Huh, so it is 0th century after all.

**Mary:** It is not, but time is a fabricated abstraction so you can do whatever you want with it, and no one can tell you otherwise.

**Markus:** Good to know. I have enjoyed knocking around with you while here in this period though, Mary. You're also the biggest celebrity I've ever slept with, which is kind of cool.

**Mary:** I have enjoyed your visit to my time as well, Markus. But all good things must cum at the end, I suppose.

**Markus:** I don't think that's the correct turn of phrase.

**Mary:** Perhaps not, but it was fun while it lasted. Even though you never lasted very long.

**Markus:** Well, Maryam, maybe if you didn't have such a banging-hot ass I could have.

**Mary:** Blaming the victim, are we? At least you have some other redeeming qualities. In fact, I wish all my boyfriends could be time travelers. I keep getting older, but they just stay the saaame age.

**Markus:** *Haha*, yea, I guess that's true. You got all old and wrinkly and I'm still the same strapping young lad who rocked your world the first time we hooked up thirty-four years ago. Hell, at this point I could probably wear your labia as a pretty pink burka if I wanted to.

**Mary:** Have at it—your head does look a little cold, and in dire need of some piety.

**Markus:** Shit, I can never remember how to tie these things....

**Mary:** Mmmm, I am going to miss you, Ĕlāhā. Thank you for the good times over the last three decades.

**Markus:** I'm gonna miss you too, Mary. Maybe we'll see each other again someday.

———— ◉ ————

**Markus:** Hey Professor, I'm back from the surface, did you miss me?

**Atman:** Hi Markus. And no, not really.

**Markus:** Where is everybody?

**Atman:** Oh, the crew is just taking some time away from each other after a busy three days of being around each other. How did it go down there?

**Markus:** Good Doc, Mary liked my Arabian knight costume.

**Atman:** No, Dingleberry, I meant with Jesus. Did you get him the drugs?

**Markus:** Oh yea, I got Jesus his murder party potion for tomorrow. I also met a nice guard at the prison who didn't kill me or make me learn the Galilean dialect of Middle Aramaic. Oh, and I got to immaculately not-conception Mary one last time before we leave for the future.

**Atman:** Sounds like 'mission accomplished' if you ask me.

**Markus:** I hope so. Although Jesus seemed uber bummed because he thinks all his work over the last 33 years might have been in vain.

**Atman:** Why is that?

**Markus:** Oh, I don't know, maybe because they're killing him for being nice and preaching about love and compassion and shit. Plus, all the people I've met in my time who call themselves christians have a mouth full of scripture but a heart full of bigotry and unbridled hate.

**Atman:** You told him that?!

**Markus:** No, I couldn't bring myself to tell him, it would have broken little buddy's heart.

**Atman:** Well, the Looking Glass has been wrong before, but it is somewhat rare for that to happen. I guess we'll find out tomorrow when we pick Jesus up and start jumping forward in time.

**Markus:** Yea, it'll be good for him to see how it all plays out, regardless of the outcome. Are we going all the way back to my home time tomorrow?

**Atman:** No, I'm thinking we should stop somewhen between now and 2035 to see if the things we did in this time had a lasting positive impact. So, I don't know, maybe we shoot for some time around the year 1290 CE.

**Markus:** Sounds good to me. I can't say I know much about that period in human history though.

**Atman:** We don't either. None of us have ever been to that time.

**Markus:** Sounds nice though.

**Atman:** Yes, I've heard it's beautiful this time of time.

**Markus:** I'm sure it is.

**Atman:** Alright, I'm gonna hit the hay, it's been a long few days. Good night, Markus.

**Markus:** Night Professor.

# CHAPTER 15
## RESURRECTION – JERUSALEM – TERRA
### 1917 BP

**Atman:** Get him on the table fast, Markus! Dordogne, are you picking up a pulse?

**Dordogne:** I am Professor. He's alive, but barely. He lost a lot of blood out there.

**Atman:** Alright, get an IV flowing in one arm and O-negative blood in the other. Markus, roll that grey machine with the small yellow screen over here.

**Markus:** Which one? This one?

**Atman:** Yes, that one. Clip the white wire to his finger and wrap this around his arm. I want to see his oxygen levels and a heartrate.

**Markus:** Holy shit, Doc, it's reading 25 beats per minute. I don't think that's good.

**Atman:** No, that is not good. The Crackicide is likely keeping his heartrate lower than normal, but we need to get that up quickly. What's his blood pressure?

**Markus:** It looks like it says 85/50 mm Hg.

**Atman:** Bullocks, get me the norepinephrine!

**Markus:** He's not going to *for real* die is he, Professor? I promised little buddy we'd throw the football and have a big party for him after all of this.

**Atman:** No Markus, we're not going to let him die!

*Beeeee.....*

**Dordogne:** He just flatlined, Professor!

**Atman:** Fuck! Stand back, I'm going to give him chest compressions!

*1, 2, 3, 4, 5, 6....*

*1, 2, 3, 4, 5, 6....*

**Dordogne:** The cardiopulmonary resuscitation isn't working. He's still flatlined and his oxygen levels are dropping fast.

**Atman:** Damnit! OK Dordogne, grab the defibrillator. I'll try pulsing his heart.

**Dordogne:** But you just gave him epinephrine!

**Atman:** I know, but we don't have a choice, we've got to re-start his heart! Clear!

*Beeeeeeeeeeeee, gachunk*

**Dordogne:** Still no heartbeat. Hit him again, Julian!

*Beeeeeeeeeeeee, gachunk*

*Beep*
*Beep*
*Beep*

**Dordogne:** He's back, Professor!

**Atman:** Oh, thank God!

*Beep*
*Beep*

*Beep*

**Atman:** That was a close one. Way too close for my liking!

*Beep*
*Beep*
*Beep*

**Markus:** Yea, that scared the shit out of me. I felt like my stomach dropped out onto the floor when he flatlined just now!

**Atman:** It was terrifying for me too, Markus. I've come to love Jesus like my own son over the last few days.

**Markus:** He is going to be OK now though, right Professor Atman?

**Atman:** I believe so Markus, assuming he doesn't develop asystole from ventricular fibrillation again, which doesn't seem likely since his vital signs appear to be improving. As long as we can keep replenishing the fluids he lost and maintain his oxygen levels I'm optimistic it will continue to trend that way.

**Markus:** Oh, that's great to hear, thanks Doc. I was really worried about little buddy for a second there!

**Atman:** We all were, Markus, but the worst is behind us now. He will require a lot of rest though. I understand now why we waited three days before officially resurrecting the poor guy. That's quite an ordeal to recover from.

**Markus:** Seriously. I would need at least a couple weeks to recuperate before resurrecting to taunt my murderers. Jesus can have my room until he's healthy again, and if you're sure he's stable, I'll go get it set up for him. I'm gonna cook a big pot of chicken dumpling soup for when he wakes up too. It's his favorite.

**Atman:** You can go ahead, Markus. We should be in the clear now. It was touch and go for a minute there, but I think he's going to make it.

**Markus:** That's fantastic news. And I know you're not that kind of doctor, but you did great, Professor. Thanks for saving my boy.

**Atman:** The whole crew trains for these types of emergencies, Markus. When you're this far from home, everyone must be prepared for anything.

**Markus:** I've noticed. Dordogne was bad ass when she tended to Marshmallow after the tiger incident too. I'm glad y'all got mad med skills on top of everything else. It's comforting knowing we're in good hands up here. OK, I'm going to go clean up my quarters and start that soup. Just wheel Jesus in whenever you think he's ready.

———— ◉ ————

**Markus:** Hey little fella, how are you feeling?

**Jesus:** Oh, hi Dad. Not so great to be honest.

**Markus:** I imagine. That was a rough ride. By the way, it turns out you really did die and come back to life. They weren't fooling around about that in the Bible.

**Jesus:** I believe it. I could see why they waited three days to take me back down there too. I feel like shit!

**Markus:** Funny, that's what the Professor said too. I guess it was more about necessity than choice.

**Jesus:** It certainly feels that way. I'm not sure I'll be able to do it three days from now either. Maybe we could make it a week this time round. They can just revise the Bible again. Most of it is made up anyhow.

**Markus:** I don't see why not. We're writing the story as we speak. But these future folks do have some crazy good drugs and medical equipment, so I reckon they'll have you feeling right as rain in no time. You should have seen all the crazy gadgets they wheeled out to treat you when we got you up to the ship.

**Jesus:** I did. I saw all that stuff as I was floating above my body while you were trying to save me.

**Markus:** You could see us trying to save you?

**Jesus:** Yea, it was crazy. I could feel my soul exiting my body and slowly lift toward the ceiling. It felt like that night we smoked DMT with the Maharani, except this time I couldn't find my way back into my body. The surprising part was that once I left, I could see in every direction all at once, as if my head had 200 eyes encircling it. Even weirder, every moment in time blended into one, and I could ride light waves across all points in space and through all moments in time. It made me wonder if light is consciousness and consciousness is light.

**Markus:** Perhaps, Jesus, I guess I've never thought about that, but it does make a lot of sense. Maybe light is a kind of transmitter and receiver of consciousness if anything else.

**Jesus:** And there is something else too, Dad.

**Markus:** What is it, Son?

**Jesus:** While I was out of my body, I felt an overwhelming sense of love and a oneness with all living things. I also felt a presence, like an omniscient benevolent presence. No offense—because I know you're technically God and everything—but I think there might be another one, a kind of pure energetic entity who exists at the highest level of universal consciousness.

**Markus:** People do commonly describe such things during near-death experiences, and often after consuming psilocybin, LSD, DMT, and similar other drugs.

**Jesus:** I can't help but wonder if that is what people have long sensed as God, but the organized religions that grew out of this omniscient and omnipresent light were bastardized self-serving fabrications. What if men constructed these false narratives because they knew they could use people's ignorance, and their innate gravitation toward the light, to manipulate and control them, to gain and maintain power over them?

**Markus:** There is certainly a case to be made for that, Jesus. christianity, and certain other religions, have a long history of misogyny, bigotry, and oppression, which stands in stark contrast to the love and compassion people feel during these mystical moments of extracorporeal interaction.

**Jesus:** I've come to realize that as well, Dad. And while I no longer fear death, it saddens me that we will drift so far away from the light, and that my story will be adulterated in such a way that the original teachings are lost to time. It was hard for me to speak of this when you visited me in jail, but I saw much more in my precognizant dreams of the future than what I alluded to earlier. When Morpheus took me through the yet to come, I witnessed the effects of our work here in this time. I saw how they changed the story and derelicted my teachings. I sensed so much hate in the hearts of these so-called christians in your time. I saw how they changed my identity, and my legacy. My flesh was my currency. I became a pawn, and no longer a prophet.

**Markus:** I know, buddy. I'm sorry I didn't say anything down there, but I thought it might crush your spirits, and I knew you had a big day ahead of you. I've seen it all too though, firsthand, and since I was a young boy growing up in the church. It didn't take long before their hypocrisy became insufferable. But it was their perpetual blindness to this hypocrisy that affected me the most.

**Jesus:** It is probably better you didn't say anything. Your confirmation of what I saw in my dreams would have made the crucifixion that much more painful.

**Markus:** Well, who knows, Jesus, maybe there's still time to change it. The Professor wants to stop about halfway between your time and mine to see how things are going, and if our interventions in this period were unsuccessful, perhaps we can rectify them in that time. But we can figure all of that out later. For right now, you need to get some rest.

**Jesus:** I could certainly use a nap. I'm glad we had this talk, but it has been hard for me to muster the energy for it. I would like to sleep now.

**Markus:** Of course.... Also, it occurred to me while we were chatting that you can take all the time you need. I just remembered that we're in a time machine, which means you can sleep for as long as you want, and we can still take you back to three days after they killed you.

**Jesus:** Oh yea, I always forget this is a time machine.

**Markus:** Me too, bud, and I've been the butt of many jokes on this mission because of it.

**Jesus:** Thanks for letting me have your room too, Dad. It's nice in here.

**Markus:** Absolutely, Jesus. I forgot you hadn't been in here before. It's too bad we never had time for a sleepover while you were little.

**Jesus:** It is. You and the others mostly just popped in and out of various moments throughout my life, but I didn't get to spend much time up here on the ship at all.

**Markus:** Well, that's all about to change. In fact, you take my room for as long as you want. I'll see if Dordogne will let me shack up with her. I feel like we've been developing a budding intimacy and an unspoken bond over the last week or so. At least, I hope she feels that too. I really like her.

**Jesus:** I hope so too, Dad. I like you and Dordogne together in that way. You'd make a cute couple. Hell, you two have been raising a dog and a kid together for as long as I can remember. You might already be married.

**Markus:** *Haha*, that's true, buddy. I'll have to ask her if that counts.

**Jesus:** Well, you can use me taking over your room as an excuse to talk about it. Who knows, maybe you'll even get lucky tonight. I'll keep Marshmallow in here with me, so she doesn't have to watch if it does happen. Poor girl has experienced enough trauma in her life. I don't want to hear about it tomorrow either, cuz I'm already feeling nauseous most of the time as it is these days.

**Markus:** Sounds good, Son, I'll try to keep the juicy details to myself. You get some sleep now, but let's grab a beer tomorrow and I'll *not* tell you all about it.

**Jesus:** That'd be great, Dad, looking forward to it. Good luck this evening.

**Markus:** Night, Boy.

**Jesus:** Night, Pops.

# CHAPTER 16
## PROPOSITION – JERUSALEM – TERRA
## 1917 BP

**Markus:** Hey Dordogne, you got space for one more in here? I gave my room to Jesus so he could get some much-needed rest after a busy day of becoming a martyred messiah.

**Dordogne:** Well, that depends on your intentions, I suppose.

**Markus:** Oh, that's funny.

**Dordogne:** Why so funny?

**Markus:** It's funny that you're asking about *my* intentions, when one of the biggest questions we've had about you future-human-UFO folk throughout the ages has been what *your* intentions are.

**Dordogne:** I could see how that might be funny to you. Well, I assume by now you have a better sense of who we are and what our intentions are.

**Markus:** To some extent, but there are some lingering questions.

**Dordogne:** All things in due time…. You still haven't told me about your near-term intentions though. And before you respond, do keep in mind that we haven't had our movie date yet.

**Markus:** Hmm, that's true, but I doubt you had any movie dates with that Brazilian farmer before you two partook in the coital congress.

**Dordogne:** That was investigatory intercourse. But no, you're not wrong about that. We got right after it. This is different though.... I've been trying to conceal my feelings because we work together and I didn't want the others to know, but I like you, Markus. You have a radiant liberated energy that I don't see in others from your time, or in the time we came back from. You also have a kind and empathetic soul that you unfortunately hide behind a façade of unsubstantiated masculinity, but I see the true you through it. The way you care for Marshmallow, and how you nurture and care for Jesus, proves I'm right. I also saw what you did for those kids in Mary's village over the last three decades.

**Markus:** What do you mean?

**Dordogne:** I think you know what I mean...I saw how you played with them and taught those children simple strategies to make their lives easier every time you went to the surface to lie with Mary, and I saw how much they prospered because of it. With your continued guidance over the last 30 years, those kids grew up happy and healthy. They also taught your life lessons to others, which meant the entire community flourished. That village now has the highest longevity rate and the healthiest people in all of Mesopotamia, simply because you cared enough to support those children and show them simple solutions to their problems. Nobody else noticed how much you helped them, but I did.

**Markus:** Yea, it made me sad to see them suffer for what seemed like incredibly stupid reasons. I just gave them some modest guidance, and because we kept jumping ahead in time, I could see how they applied those fixes, then further develop them in each future period. It didn't seem like I did much, but I'm happy to hear they're doing well. They are beautiful people. They just got dealt a shitty hand by being born into the wrong time.

**Dordogne:** Well, I see you for who you truly are. It's unfortunate that the real you is hidden behind a veil, but I also understand. Your past and the period you're from have hardened you. But I see hope for the future, and for us, and I would love to share that future with you. It's because of this that I want our first time making love entirely together to be special. I have had sex with thousands of men across more time periods than I can even—

**Markus:** Wait, thousands?

**Dordogne:** *Hehe*, no, I was just trying to get a rise out of you. It is a lot though.

**Markus:** Yea, same.

**Dordogne:** But what I'm saying is that I would like our first sole experience making love to be momentous. Each time I've had sex, it was to garner knowledge about this sacred act, but I know from watching countless others across the world and through time that it is also an act of love, and I do love you, Markus. I want to feel what it's like to be with someone I share those feeling with.

**Markus:** That's beautiful, Dordogne, and I love absolutely everything about you too. In fact, I was just telling Mary, when I'm with you I feel something I've never felt with anyone else.

**Dordogne:** Aww, you were talking about me?

**Markus:** I was, I think of you often. I told Jesus the same thing right before I came up here, and mentioned how nervous I was to talk to you about this, and how I had hoped you share these same sentiments. I wasn't sure, but it feels like you do when we're together. I can sense you intensely and sometimes wonder if you're in my head with me.

**Dordogne:** Oftentimes I am. Is that OK?

**Markus:** I wouldn't want it any other way. In fact, it's a relief to hear you say that because I was worried I'd lost my mind or developed an imaginary friend who happened to have your exact same tone of voice and way of speaking.

**Dordogne:** Nope, just me.

**Markus:** Good to know…. But what I'm trying to say is that I love you, and I'm willing to wait for the perfect moment if that's what you want.

**Dordogne:** Hmm, thank you, Markus. And don't get me wrong, I think about it a lot…and I mean a lot. But I sense something deeper here. Something we could nurture beyond the physical and into the realm of a mutually derived spiritual sexual affirmation.

**Markus:** That sounds magical, Dordogne…. Wait, this isn't because I'm the only guy up here with a penis, is it?

**Dordogne:** *Hehe*, no. But your downstairs neighbor is quite nice, and I often think about how good he will feel inside me.

**Markus:** Well, either way. That all sounds amazing. And to be honest, since we've been talking about it, I realized that I've never had sex with someone I loved either. It seems like sex was always about trying to boost my self-esteem, or to combat boredom, or because a chick was mega-hot and I just wanted to get my rocks off with her, but that was all physical; there was nothing of substance there. I hadn't thought about it until now, but I guess I've never truly made *love* with anyone either.

**Dordogne:** What about Amanda?

**Markus:** Who?

**Dordogne:** Your girlfriend?

**Markus:** Oh yea, no. She's gentle on the eyes, but let's just say there's not a bright light shining in the attic, and certainly not a 'growing weed in the attic' kind of bright light, that's for sure.

**Dordogne:** That's too bad, but I guess it's nice to know I won't have to beat her up when we get back to your time.

**Markus:** I mean, if I oiled you both up really well we could see what happens—

**Dordogne:** Being serious again now.

**Markus:** Sorry, I don't do serious well.

**Dordogne:** I've noticed. But temporarily serious at least, as fleeting as it may be.... The other reason I want to wait is because I see a bright future for us, but if we don't succeed in this mission, there may not be any future at all, or at least not one we would want to live in. I've worked hard and sacrificed much throughout my life, but it's time to be done. I just want to complete this final mission and start a new life, together.

**Markus:** Together includes Jesus too, right? Don't forget about my bastard kid, Jesus.

**Dordogne:** Yes, of course, I love Jesus. I was picturing all of us in this future existence, with a home in a beautiful place, and in only *one* time, where we can grow our family together.

**Markus:** That sounds wonderful, Dordogne. Jesus could really use a stepmom too. I hope everything works out with what we're doing here in the past because I would love to share that life with you.

**Dordogne:** Me too, Markus. Me too.

**Markus:** Well, platonic slumber it is then, but can we cuddle at least? I promise to keep my hands and tongue where you can see them.

**Dordogne:** Absolutely, I call big spoon though.

**Markus:** Deal.

# CHAPTER 17
## REJUVENATION – JERUSALEM – TERRA
## AD 33

**Markus:** He is risen!

**Jesus:** Good one, Dad.

**Markus:** No, for real though, Jesus. It's great to see you up and walking around again. Ready for that beer yet?

**Jesus:** Maybe, how long was I out though? I feel like it could have been three days.

**Markus:** Damn near. The Professor had you on some hella good drugs and was doing all kinds of weird medical shit in there. It seems to have worked too cuz you look a million times better.

**Jesus:** I *feel* better, thanks. Check out this epic wound on my ribs though.

**Markus:** Holy fuck balls, Jesus! That looks gnarly as shit!

**Jesus:** I know, right. They went super deep with that one. Must have been something I said.

**Markus:** *Haha,* yea, they didn't much care for you telling everybody to be nice to each other did they.

**Jesus:** It turns out they did not. Maybe civilization wasn't ready for civility yet. Either way, let's get on with this whole 'sending me down to be risen' charade and get the heck out of here. I'm so over this time period.

**Markus:** Well, suit up then Easter Bunny Boy and let's get you resurrected. I'm ready to get the hell out of this era too.

**Jesus:** Do you know what time and place we're going to next, Dad?

**Markus:** Oh hey, we have a word for that now.... It's 'tempoloco.'

**Jesus:** Ooo, I like that. Did you come up with that little gem?

**Markus:** Sure did, kiddo.

**Jesus:** Solid. Well, what's our next 'tempoloco' then?

**Markus:** The Doc said he wants to check progress here in the Middle East sometime around AD 1290. Oh yea, by the way, *AD* stands for *anno Domini,* which is Latin for 'in the year of the Lord.' Do you know what that means? Eh Jesus? Do ya?

**Jesus:** No idea.

**Markus:** It's you, man! It's the year you were born. They named *time* after you. How cool is that? Hell, whether we save the world or not, at least you got to start time!

**Jesus:** That is something, I guess. Well, I don't know much about that tempoloco, but I'm eager to see how things are going then.

**Markus:** How could you know *anything* about it? You've only ever lived between AD 0 and 33.

**Jesus:** Oh yea, right, you guys are the time travelers.

**Markus:** Yes, but you're about to be one too. In fact, after checking in on AD 1290 to see what the Looking Glass says about our probabilistic progress in preventing the war, we're gonna head all the way back to my home time and return to what we hope will be a better future where people don't suck sweaty butt crack anymore.

**Jesus:** I hope that's the case too—

Oh hey, how did it go with Dordogne last night? But please spare me the details for once.

**Markus:** No details to spare you from, buckaroo. We kept it PG.

**Jesus:** What is PG? Does that stand for passionate grinding?

**Markus:** No, it's an abbreviation for—

**Jesus:** Penetrating genitalia? Procreating gonads?

**Markus:** Damn it, Boy. No.

**Jesus:** Pecker gorging? Pussy gushing?! Pudenda pounding?!

**Markus:** No, and that last one wasn't even the right—

**Jesus:** Penis gurgling?! Prostate giggling?!

**Markus:** Jesus Christ, no! It's a...shit, why *would* you know what that means. So, it's part of a rating system for movies that the Motion Picture Association of America put into effect on November 1, 1968, and ya know what, never mind...we just talked and cuddled and shit.

**Jesus:** That sounds nice too.

**Markus:** It was, really nice, in fact. It would seem, Jesus...that we are in love. She even wants to be your stepmom.

**Jesus:** That's great, Dad, I'm happy for you two.

**Markus:** Me too, Son. The future looks bright. But not bright because of thermonuclear detonations, I hope.

**Jesus:** Well, I'm going to go find the Professor to beam me down to the surface so I can bid farewell to these ungrateful turds who put holes in my wrists and stabbed me in the ribs.

**Markus:** Yea, fuck those guys. I still can't believe they did that to you. And I know you're supposed to tell them something profound and then magically float back up here on a shinning beam of heavenly light, but maybe instead, we should fly you over the city so you can flip 'em the bird and shout Tupac lyrics over the loudspeaker at those radicalized little bitches!

*Five spears couldn't drop me, I took it and smiled*
*Now I'm back to set the record straight*
*With my A.K. I'm still the thug that you love to hate*
*Motherfucker, I hit 'em up!*

**Jesus:** I've never heard that song, Dad, but I like it.

**Markus:** It's 'Hit Em Up' by Tupac Shakur featuring the Outlawz and was the B-side to the single 'How Do U Want It,' released June 4, 1996, by Death Row Records.

**Jesus:** Cool.

**Markus:** It's also on the Death Row Greatest Hits album.

**Jesus:** Good to know. You've got a great rap voice too, Dad.

**Markus:** Thanks, Junior. I won four freestyle rap battles on the TV show *Drop the Mic* back in 2028. Method Man even signed my tits once.

**Jesus:** I don't know who or what that is, but I'll take your word for it, and congratulations. But no, I've got to go down there to perform this last big miracle before we take off. Dordogne made it seem like this was the most important one, so I need to do it for them and for the future of humanity if it helps prevent the war.

**Markus:** You're a good kid, Jesus, and I'm immensely proud of the man you've become. I am gonna go fetch an AK-47 from the property master in wardrobe though, just in case they get all stabby down there again.

**Jesus:** Thanks Dad, that's good looking out. See you soon.

———— ◉ ————

**Atman:** Nice work down there, Jesus. You looked gloriously exalted and abundantly deified.

**Jesus:** Thanks, Professor. I'll admit, it wasn't easy after everything they did to me, but what is Jesus if he ain't forgiving seventy-seven times.

**Atman:** You speak the truth as always, Yeshu. Ok crew. That might have been the longest and hardest time we've ever had in one period, but I've got a good feeling about what we did here.

**Markus:** Are we still going forward to AD 1290 to check on progress, Prof?

**Atman:** Yes, Markus. I think we'll stay in this region but jump forward 1,257 light-years to 660 BP. By the way, since when did you start using AD instead of BP?

**Markus:** Seriously? If your kid's birth started time, wouldn't you use that system as well?!

**Atman:** Hmm, now that you mention it, I guess I would. Seems a good homage to his efforts in this tempoloco to boot.... Manitoba! Set the time-jump controls forward to AD 1290!

**Manitoba:** Sorry Captain, I don't know what that is, Sir.

**Atman:** Damn it, taint muncher. It's 660 BP. Didn't they teach you about AD and BC in launch-window school?

**Manitoba:** No Sir, but the system only operates with a specific standardized temporal structure, and AD isn't an option on the graphical user interface that integrates with the software that codes for our shifts in the spacetime matrix. I can play around with the settings at the next stop though and maybe I can reprogram it if you feel like you would prefer that temporal demarcation nomenclature.

**Atman:** I would, thank you, Manitoba. Also, to catch you up... AD stands for anno Domini, which means 'in the year of our Lord.' It denotes the christian era in the Gregorian calendar. And...perhaps most importantly...that guy right there...you see that guy right there, Manitoba?

**Manitoba:** Yes, Sir.

**Atman:** That guy right there is Jesus fucking Christ, himself. He's the 'Domini' in anno Domini! His birth is what started time, and I reckon since he just got nailed to a cross and stabbed in the ribs down there it's the least we can do to start telling time by him.

**Manitoba:** I agree Sir. I'll work on reprogramming the computer after this jump.

**Jesus:** You don't have to do that, Professor. They didn't come up with that birthdate for me until 500 years after I died—or didn't die technically—but they had no idea when I was born so they just picked a random year. It is a completely arbitrary temporal classification scheme with no basis in reality.

**Atman:** Well, alright, if you're sure, Jesus. That does seem kind of dumb now that you mention it. But if you ever change your mind just let us know. We're happy to oblige.

**Jesus:** I will, Professor Atman, thank you.

**Atman:** Okay Manitoba, scratch that. You don't have to reprogram the machine after all.

**Manitoba:** Oh, thank God.

**Atman:** But you do need to get us the hell out of this time.

**Manitoba:** Can do, Captain. I see a clear jump window for 660 BP in T-minus 4 minutes and 6 seconds.

**Atman:** Not bad, Manitoba. Not bad at all.

# CHAPTER 18
## INSURRECTION – PALESTINE – TERRA
## AD 1290

**Markus:** That was a quick trip. It felt like that time we went up to the Moon where hardly any time passed and with no g-forces at all.

**Atman:** It was, and at my age I've come to prefer these shorter trips closer to our base time.

**Markus:** When are you going to retire anyway? It seems like you've been at this awhile.

**Atman:** It's funny you ask because I *was* briefly retired. However, once we obtained the technology to venture back to the deepest past yet visited, they convinced me to return for this final mission.

**Markus:** I bet you felt awfully special when they asked you to come out of retirement for this. You must be hot shit in the future.

**Atman:** I have had a long and successful career, and our team undoubtedly helped advance knowledge of the distant human past throughout my tenure in this position. However, our prior work was purely research oriented. This is the first time we've needed to apply our skills and expertise for such an important task like trying to save humanity. It's a lot of pressure, but our team was the most qualified for the job, so here we are.

**Markus:** Well, I think you're doing great, Doc. And we haven't even crashed the ship yet, so that's a win.

**Atman:** Thanks Markus, it's been interesting working with you as well.

**Markus:** So, what is our current tempoloco exactly?

**Atman:** Manitoba, can I get a precise report on our tempoloco, please?

**Manitoba:** The computer shows we are above the city of Acre, in the region of Palestine, at 660 BP.... Or AD 1290 as *some* might say. *Hehe*, I've been practicing.

**Atman:** Nice shout out to Jesus there, Manitoba.

**Manitoba:** Thank you, Sir, I've been practicing.

**Atman:** Yes, you just said that. However, it's not the least bit impressive since I already told you that AD 1290 corresponded with 660 BP, but good on ya nonetheless.

**Jesus:** You guys are both nerds, but thanks for thinking of me. Praise be to thee.

**Atman:** Aww, we love you Jesus!

**Markus:** Easy there, Doc. You don't want to give him a messiah complex.

**Jesus:** *Haha*, good one, Dad.

**Atman:** OK everybody, let's head down to the surface and see if our work in Jesus's time had a positive influence on preventing the war. Here's hoping for some peace and love!

**Jesus:** Can I come too? I'd like to see how everything panned out over the last 1,300 years since they killed me.

**Atman:** Of course, Jesus. Just be sure to keep your face

covered so no one recognizes you. We don't want to incite a 'Second Coming of Christ' panic or anything.

**Markus:** I don't think that's necessary. He doesn't look anything like the White European Jesus they morphed him into.

**Atman:** Now that you mention it, you're right. He doesn't at all resemble the cliché Jesus they created for their narcissistic narrative...and upon further reflection, he doesn't look anything like you either, Markus. Are you sure he's even your kid?

**Markus:** It's hard to say with any certainty considering Mary's sexual proclivities, but you said she was ovulating the night you sent me down to shoot DNA into her babymaker, and I think I was the only one with her that evening, and multiple times, so I'm gonna go with a hard probably.

**Jesus:** I think you're my dad too, God. Even though we don't look alike, as I've gotten to know you, I've realized we have a lot of the same mannerisms.

**Dordogne:** Can I chime in for a second?

**Markus:** Please do, Dordogne, I love listening to you talk. In fact, I recall asking you to never stop talking because I love it so much, though you failed to honor my request.

**Dordogne:** Thanks, weirdo. But regarding the question of Markus's paternity...I had been studying the 'Virgin' Mary's sex habits for some time after we sent archangel Gabriel down to speak with her ahead of our insemination intervention. There was some cause for concern considering the Favored One's pronounced promiscuity, so I ran a paternity test the first time we brought Baby Jesus up to the ship.

**Markus:** Yes, and?

**Dordogne:** Just a second, I put the results in a Manilla envelope somewhere in one of these desk drawers.... OK, I found them.

And here are the results of the paternity test....
Markus *is* the father!

**Markus:** Well, that's good to hear. Thank you Maury Dordogne Povich, but you could have told us that sooner considering it's something you've known for 33 years.

**Dordogne:** It never came up until now, and everyone just assumed he was your kid, so it wasn't an issue. By the way, has anyone else noticed all those structures burning around the city down there?

**Markus:** Oh, snap. I hadn't 'til you just said something, but yea, it looks like a God-damn war zone. What's going on, Professor?

**Atman:** I couldn't tell you Markus, we specialized in *prehistoric* groups specifically. And again, most historical records from before your time were destroyed in the Great War. I am concerned about the marauding factions surrounding the city though. For safety's sake, I'm going to send a couple members of our security team down to the surface with you. Try to get as much detail about this period as you can, especially regarding their views on religion, and Jesus in particular, then get back up here as quickly as possible.

**Markus:** You're not coming with us, Professor?

**Atman:** No, I'm much too old to be gallivanting around a war zone. I'll stay up here and keep in contact with Major Metathory so we can follow along with the Looking Glass predictions in real time. Even if we weren't entirely effective at executing the plan in Jesus's home time, there might be options to help bolster our probability of success at this temporal midway point. Dordogne, Markus, Jesus, go see Moirai in wardrobe, and have at least two of our security personnel get fitted as well.

**Markus:** Wilco, Professor. I'm also gonna get that sweet-ass spear from my prison trip.

**Atman:** That will be of no use to you, Markus. Their weapons have evolved markedly over the last 1,300 years.

**Markus:** I know, but it makes me feel cool, and chicks dig it.

**Dordogne:** I can vouch for that. He does look ravishing in his Arabian knight costume with that big manly plastic spear of his.

**Markus:** Thanks, Dordogne. I'll try to remember to bring it to bed later tonight.

**Dordogne:** See that you do my spicy Prince Ali Baba Ghanoush. I love playing dress-up before getting into the naughty tongue stuff.

**Atman:** Huh. So, what's going on between you two exactly—

**Dordogne:** I'll take my time-wand too, Professor. That way we'll have some protection in case something happens to our security detail.

**Atman:** That's a good idea, Dordogne, especially after that close call with the tiger in the Indus Valley. Speaking of, you should leave Marshmallow up here with me for this one. She'll draw too much attention in the city. She's earned some time off, anyway. Haven't ya girl?!

*Whuff!*

**Atman:** Just grab some clothes and wigs that will help you fit in and stay away from the people fighting down there. I'll drop you near the city center when you get back from wardrobe.

**Markus:** And props!

**Atman:** Yes, Markus, and props. I haven't forgotten about your sexy plastic spear.

———— ◉ ————

**Atman:** OK, friends, I'm sending you down. Keep your earbuds turned up in case I get any important information from Major Metathory, or if I see trouble down there and need to pull you out.

**Dordogne:** Will do, Julian. We'll see you shortly.

# CHAPTER 19
## CONTENTION – PALESTINE – TERRA
## AD 1290

**Dordogne:** I doubt anyone saw us beaming down here, but let's hang back in this alley for a few more minutes just to be safe.

**Markus:** I don't think so either, Dordogne. These people seem highly distracted. What is the best approach for doing ethnographic research in a war zone anyhow?

**Dordogne:** An etic methodology is optimal, at least until we know what's going on and what the risk level is.

**Jesus:** What does 'etic' mean, Dordogne? I only know words related to carpentry and messiah stuff.

**Dordogne:** Oh, sorry Jesus. It's a hands-off 'outsiders' approach to investigating cultural phenomena that occur among *all* societies, while an emic approach examines traits specific to *only one* culture.

**Jesus:** Okay, thanks.

**Dordogne:** But after observing for a while, if it is safe, we'll approach a random sample of potential informants and interview them about the current state of this tempoloco.

**Markus:** From the looks of it, I'm guessing the answer is going to be, 'not so good.' Also, how are we going to interview anyone down here if we don't speak their language?

**Dordogne:** Airl taught the Professor and I about 500 languages that allow us to communicate with most major historical groups. She knows upwards of 5,000 languages, going all the way back to 48,000 BC now, but the 500 she taught us capture the bulk of linguistic variation over a roughly 12,000-year period. I asked before we came down here, and she thinks we are most likely to encounter Arabic and Greek. I know both of those quite well, so we should be good.

**Markus:** Better you than me, I can barely speak one language.

**Dordogne:** Yes, I've noticed. OK, let's get out on the street and have a look around. Everyone, stay close.... Markus, you live closer to this time, what's your take on all this?

**Markus:** I'm not sure, but I did notice that the observable craniofacial characteristics of the people inside the city indicate they are of European descent, while the facial form, skin color, and style of dress seen among the people attacking from outside the city walls are more indicative of indigenous Middle Easterners. That leads me to believe people from Europe came here and took this place, and now the native population is fighting to get it back from them.

**Dordogne:** Hmm, that seems like a good starting point, thank you.

**Markus:** It is completely on-brand for Europeans too. The Professor said y'all don't know much about the history of this period, but I can tell you that a couple hundred years from now—following centuries of land-based colonialism—several European groups get on boats and attempt to take over the rest of the world.

**Dordogne:** That's interesting. I wonder how stopping this colonial activity might affect the timeline. If we arrest the spread of this virus-like civilization now, do you think it could help avert the Great Filter in your time?

**Markus:** Maybe, but it also seems like that would piss off the money mob in your time, since most rich White people benefited from the transgenerational legacy of this colonial and imperialist period. I doubt anything about that changed between my time and yours, Dordogne.

**Dordogne:** Ancestry and race are more ambiguous in my future, but the political and economic spheres do remain whitewashed. Speaking of skin color, the Professor was right about keeping Jesus's face covered. Not because they might recognize him as the Messiah, but because he looks much more like the people outside the city than those inside. Hopefully nobody in here sees him and thinks he's the enemy.

**Markus:** Good point, if this is a regional or ethnic war, they might assume he broke through the walls somehow. Did you hear that, Jesus? Be sure no one sees your face since you look native to this region.

**Jesus:** Will do, Dad. Sorry I look more like Mom than you.

**Markus:** That's probably a good thing, Jesus. She's a lot better looking than me.

**Jesus:** Maybe a little. Aww no, I just realized Mom has been dead for over a thousand years now! That's sad to think about.

**Markus:** True, Mary is just stained teeth and dry bones at this point. But she is still alive in your home time, and you can visit her whenever you want. I'm sure she died with lots of great memories of you popping in to say hi throughout both of your futures.

**Jesus:** Oh yea, that's true. And thanks, that makes me feel better. I appreciate you letting me come down here with you too. It's cool to see how much this area has changed over the last 1,300 years.

**Markus:** No prob, buddy. We're glad you're here.

**Dordogne:** Upon further investigation, and after doing some remote genetic scans of the various groups involved, I agree with Markus that this is likely a geographic or ethnic conflict. However, we need to obtain more detailed information. Let's interview a few people, and if it's operational to stop this attempt at conquest by European groups outside their home territory then I'll have Professor Atman contact Major Metathory about the probabilistic outcome of those actions. I certainly don't want to destroy another city if we don't have to, since I still feel bad about Sodom and Gomorrah, but if it saves 9.5-billion lives and Earth's ecology then it might be worth it.

**Markus:** Wait, that was you?! So, you mean to tell me that you and the Professor, a massive sex fiend and an intertemporal drug lord, destroyed two big cities in old testament times because people were having sex and enjoying earthly delights and sinful pleasures of all varieties?!

**Dordogne:** It was three cities. And no, that's not at all why we did it. Is that what they told you?

**Markus:** Yea, I heard the whole spiel. More times than I can count, in fact. My dad used to drone on about all kinds of old testament shit, and especially the parts about how doing fun stuff gets you sent to hell. Oh, and he *loved* the sections on how women need to be subservient to men. But I remember him saying those cities were destroyed because everybody was drinking alcohol and doing cool shit and having a ton of sex...guy on gal, guy on guy, gal on gal, guy on horse, sheep on gal, duck on pigeon, he went on like that for an hour. He said it was an overtly gluttonous place that made God mad so he fire and brimstoned everybody. But it sounded like a damn good time to me!

**Dordogne:** Oh, it *was* a damn good time. The Professor and I used to visit a lot. He sold Crackicide and I did intertemporal intercourse research. But the actions and behaviors of our loving and liberated friends there had nothing to do with why we destroyed those cities. In fact, we saved *them*, while the bigoted bureaucrats and fascist facilitators were left behind.

**Markus:** Seems ironic.

**Dordogne:** The problem was the dogmatic fanatics and their politicoreligious power structure. Once people woke up and stopped living in fear of the pious' peevish proclamations that the wicked will burn in an eternal hell, the rich elites could no longer control them. When those militant zealots turned to rape, violence, and physical oppression, we gave them a taste of the fire and brimstone they foretold of for all those years prior. It turns out the 'prophesies' they portended were just precognizant future memories of their own calamitous experiences.

**Markus:** Was that a Looking Glass outcome related to the current mission, because it sounds a lot like what we're doing now?

**Dordogne:** It was. In fact, this all happened right before we picked you up at that party a few weeks ago. The Looking Glass only gave us a 52% probability of stopping the war by destroying the three cites, but those were our friends, so we had to do something to protect them. We used grassroots tactics to warn the good people to get out of town before we rained fire down upon the corrupt bankers, politicians, and false prophets of that time. Many of the enlightened individuals we saved even came back to the future with us, and they adjusted quite well.

**Markus:** Wow, it's funny how they swapped the antagonists and protagonists in the biblical version of that story.

**Dordogne:** That likely happened immediately after the bombings. The religious brethren of the decimated ones undoubtedly documented these events, and they must have twisted the story to make it seem as though the good people were the problem, not the fundamentalist extremists spreading fear and lies while they raped and killed the sagacious secularists and awakened atheists.

**Markus:** Nothing ever changes does it. It's only a matter of scale, and who controls the narrative.

**Dordogne:** Yes, I recall you saying something about catching brain hemorrhoids from a fox earlier. But religious oppressors have long been motivated to develop fictitious narratives that serve their interests. The tyrants near those cities that we destroyed on the east side of the Jordan River surely pontificated about that event in an effort to get their power over the people back, by once again convincing the easily persuaded that their twisted history was the only thing that would save them from more fire and brimstone, which again, was the despots' fault in the first place.

**Markus:** This is starting to sound a bit cyclic, considering it's the same thing happening in my home time.

**Dordogne:** That's humans for you. One step forward and two steps back.

**Markus:** It's more like five steps back in the era I'm from. Shit's all kinds of fucked up. It doesn't seem much different from the unfictitious situation in Sodom and Gomorrah either.

**Dordogne:** There are certainly some parallels. Sometimes I wonder if any of it matters in the end. An individual must be at their absolute lowest point before they see that change is desperately needed, and before they are capable of seeing what needs to change to fix the problem. I think it might be the same for societies.

**Markus:** What do you mean?

**Dordogne:** Maybe what happens in your time needs to, Markus. Maybe we need a global societal reset. Perhaps humanity has to see itself at its absolute lowest point to reflect on how it got there and to finally think about the consequences of its actions. To end war, by ending those who crave it.

**Markus:** You future folks must be the most conflicted people I've ever met. The degree of ideological cognitive dissonance I've seen in you, the Professor, and even Metathory's bitch ass, is unparalleled. I sometimes wonder if you care whether we stop this war at all. It doesn't seem like you're happy in your time, or you ever could be, so long as the same long-standing power structure persists, and is forced to persist, since they will kill you if you try to change it.

**Dordogne:** In the future the Professor is from, yes.

**Markus:** What?

**Dordogne:** Nothing. But back on Luna Sede, while you and the Major were fighting, you mentioned the difference in temperament, behavior, and social order between the two species of chimpanzees, the patriarchal *Pan troglodytes* or common chimps, and the matriarchal *Pan paniscus* or bonobo chimpanzees.

**Markus:** I do recall that conversation. I don't believe he got the reference though.

**Dordogne:** Maybe not, but I believe that is an apt analogy for humanity. You stated that common chimps are characterized by war and aggression, while bonobos espouse sex and creativity. We too have always seemed like separate species in such ways. The heartless and the empathetic. The abhorrent and the affectionate. The hateful and the kind. Perhaps the split that occurred in chimpanzees happened in humans as well.... But how can the loving live amongst the vile who seek dominion over all? Since the dawn of civilization, it was these dominance-driven troglodyte humans who imposed their merciless mentality and subjugating social system on the more coactive and convivial bonobo humans, who just wanted to enjoy life, and each other. But this joy was stymied by the belligerents who feared losing control over everyone in their senselessly repressive society.

**Markus:** That's a hot take, Dordogne. It seems like a legitimate assessment of the situation though, especially considering the definition of *troglodyte* is a person characterized by outmoded or reactionary attitudes, while in Greek mythology, *paniscus* represents a godling of the forest. Maybe we always were two separate species, who have tried in vain to coexist on this planet for millennia...fighting for peace at war, building to destroy, protecting our Earth while plundering her bounty.

**Dordogne:** Yes, and I wonder if it can ever change—if these two human species can ever fully coexist.

**Jesus:** Hey guys, I'm back.

**Markus:** Jesus?! What do you mean your back?! Where the hell did you go?! I thought I told you to stay close and keep your face covered but you're hardly wearing any clothes at all! And where did you get an ice cream cone? We're in the middle of the desert!

**Jesus:** Yea, it's a lot hotter here now than it was in my time, and I'm just more comfortable in my underwear. It's all good though, I've been out talking to people for the last 20 minutes or so about what's going on down here and none of them tried to kill me. Besides, been there done that, it doesn't scare me anymore.

**Markus:** Shit, really?! That's great, I guess. But damn, I didn't even realize you were gone. That's some crap parenting, letting my only child run around a war-torn city in a future time. Dordogne and I were just chilling here ruminating on the perils of human nature while you were out doing all the damn work for us. Did security come with you at least?

**Jesus:** No, they've been asleep over there for a while, so I snuck off and chatted people up for a bit. The language in this time is super easy too, so I was able to get some good intel. Things aren't so great though.... It's been a total shit show across this entire region for the last 200 years.

**Markus:** Oh no, why is that?

**Jesus:** Me.

**Markus:** You?

**Jesus:** Uh yea, big time! We messed everything up by you making me and doing all those miracles and stuff. They've been fighting about me and all the holy sites around here ever since we left AD 33. One guy thought as many as 5 million people may have been killed on account of all the French, English, Italian, and other European christians coming down here to battle the muslims for this place and everything in between. I think he called it, 'the Crusades.'

**Markus:** But the Looking Glass said what we were doing was good, and there was a high probability of stopping the war with those interventions. Well, at first anyway, I guess the probability was dropping toward the end there. Maybe we should check in with Metathory to see where the numbers are now.

**Dordogne:** Good idea, Markus. I'll go call the Professor and have him check with Major Metathory about the current statistical situation. I'm also going to inquire about the efficacy of eradicating this European colonizer stronghold, along with others like it over the next few hundred years, to see what the over/under is on stopping the war without getting killed by the oligarchs of our time.

**Markus:** If I had to guess, Dordogne, I'd say the probability of stopping the war is 100%, and the likelihood of us getting killed by your asshat autocrats, who have undoubtedly benefited from the legacy of European colonialism and imperialism, is also 100%.

**Dordogne:** Perhaps Markus, but it never hurts to check.

**Jesus:** Hey Dordogne, while you're at it, you should ask if we can destroy all these stupid religious sites that people have been killing each other over ever since you birthed me and ruined the world.

**Markus:** Oh, come on, buddy. Don't be so hard on yourself. People love you, Man.

**Jesus:** They say they love me, but they sure as hell don't do any of the things I taught them when I was alive. I think they just love the thought of me and using my image for their self-serving interests. But they can't be bothered to give two shits about the important messages I conveyed back in my time, which was the entire point of that intervention, right Mom, and Dad?

**Dordogne:** Aww, did he just call me Mom?

**Jesus:** I did. Is that OK? I miss my home time Mom, and you've always seemed like my Mom too.

**Dordogne:** Absolutely, Jesus. I love it.

**Jesus:** Oh, good.

**Dordogne:** As your mother you'll have to give me a bite of your ice cream cone though.

**Jesus:** Of course. What kind of son would I be if I said no?

**Markus:** Yea pal, that does suck, and unfortunately, it only gets worse in my time. They talk a big Jesus game, but most of your self-proclaimed followers do the opposite of what you taught them about empathy and acceptance.

**Jesus:** Well, maybe it doesn't have to be that way.... Mom, you should ask this Major General person if eradicating these cities and holy sites could help stop the war. From what Dad tells me, these places have been catalysts for conflicts across Europe, North Africa, the Middle East, and the rest of the world for thousands of years. Maybe if we put an end to them now, it will avert the disaster in his time too. Here, I made a list:

1. Jerusalem
2. Acre
3. Mecca
4. Medina
5. Nazareth
6. Wichita
7. Istanbul
8. Golgotha

**Dordogne:** This is a great list Jesus, but I think if we strike Jerusalem, Golgotha will be wiped out too.

**Jesus:** I know, Mom, but I just want to be sure. I *really* don't like that place.

**Dordogne:** That's understandable. OK, I'll have the Professor inquire about incinerating these sites too. Regrettably, things seem to have gotten worse after our last intervention, but maybe we can right some wrongs of the contrived past by arresting the spread of religious and imperialist ideologies here in this time.

**Markus:** I still think it's a nonstarter, Dordogne. It sounds too much like what we wanted to accomplish by boosting the Harappan back in the Neolithic to end patriarchy throughout the Indus Valley region. I can tell you right now, they ain't never gonna go for that shit.

**Jesus:** You're probably right, Markus, but it's still worth asking to see what the Looking Glass predicts. You two stay here. I'll go check with Atman and Metathory to see if there's anything we can do in this tempoloco.

**Markus:** Alright, be safe, Dordogne. See you soon....
Damn Jesus, I still can't believe you wandered off like that, you could have been killed. Again.

**Jesus:** I'm not a kid anymore, Dad. In fact, 33 is considered old age for the people of my time. With all our leprosy, chariot crashes, God smites, and getting nailed to crosses, people don't live super long.

**Markus:** I guess that's true. I'm sorry. You'll just always be my little boy. I often forget you're an adult now, and that you're a lot tougher than I was at your age.

**Jesus:** Were you ever my age? I think I'm actually older than you. By at least a few years.

**Markus:** Huh, yea, good point. That's a bit of a mind fuck. My kid is three years older than me. Time travel is some whack shit, ain't it, Boy?

**Jesus:** It sure is, Pops. But here, hit this.... It'll start to make more sense after a few puffs.

**Markus:** Oh snap, where did you find weed?!

**Jesus:** The same guy I got the ice cream from. We were licking cone and chatting about the Crusades, and he kicked me down some. People just give you free shit when you're a celebrity.

**Markus:** Huh, must be nice.

**Jesus:** It has its perks. But I do sometimes wonder what my life would have been like if you guys hadn't spermed me and made me do all those miracles and stuff.

**Markus:** You mean 'spawned?' I feel like you're trying to say 'spawned.'

**Jesus:** Maybe. English is a second language for me...and I'm pretty baked right now.

**Markus:** Either one works, I suppose. But if we hadn't spawned you at all, you would have lived an exceedingly short and uneventful life, dying alongside your millions of unfertilized brothers and sisters. If you were born but didn't do miracles, you would have had a normal but equally uneventful life, and probably would have died in a chariot crash at age 19. In any case, I'm glad we did spawn you. Regardless of what happens, you're my son, and we get to be together on this grand adventure, flying around in UFOs, traveling through time, and trying to save the world and shit. I wouldn't trade that for anything!

**Jesus:** That's true, I guess I wouldn't either. I love you, God.

**Markus:** I love you too, Son of God. Oh good, she's back. That was fast.

**Dordogne:** Good news, everyone! It turns out the Professor and Major Metathory had already been running probabilistic outcomes on several different scenarios in this time, which included some of the same ones we discussed.

**Markus:** I wondered how you did that so fast. Hit us with them deets then dog.

**Dordogne:** One sec. They were throwing a ton of numbers at me, so I wrote them down in my cybercomm. Alright, so, we serendipitously stopped at an important place and time for enacting change because the Looking Glass gave some encouraging results for a few intervention scenarios.

**Markus:** Awesomesauce, what are they?

**Dordogne:** Well, Jesus was right. If we can minimize the religious dogma that grows out of this region there is a high probability of stalling a global nuclear conflict out beyond the point in time when religion dies a natural death, and people no longer wage war in the name of superstitious beliefs. We also won't have to Sodom and Gomorrah everything on Jesus's list. It's only four sites here, and two more in the Atlantic Ocean. That will send a powerful message about the dangers of ideological conflict and signal to the Europeans that they can't use religion as an excuse to conquer and colonize vast swaths of this planet.

**Jesus:** So, which ones, Mom? Are any of them Golgotha?

**Dordogne:** Yes, Jesus. The Looking Glass predicts that destroying Golgotha will be important for sending a message about killing prophets, especially when they're just telling people to be nice to each other.

**Jesus:** Outstanding. Can I launch the missiles for that one?

**Dordogne:** Sure thing, Son.

**Jesus:** Aww, did she just call me Son?

**Markus:** What are the other ones, Dordogne?

**Dordogne:** The Looking Glass said if we take out Acre, half of Jerusalem, Nazareth, and some choice locals in Istanbul, there is an 86% chance of preventing the war beyond the time at which the Past-Human Empathic Consciousness singularity is achieved, or the *PHEC* singularity as we call it.

**Markus:** What the PHEC is that?!

**Dordogne:** Well Markus, as you are likely aware, the human capacity for empathy evolves over time. After all, it was only 170 years before your time that slavery ended, and only 60 years prior that Jim Crow laws mandating racial segregation were no longer enforced. There is a singular point in our future human past when people from different periods begin interacting on a massive scale. With this chrono-cohesion comes a future-to-past transmission of our elevated mindfulness, which ultimately results in a species-wide destruction of ego, and an amalgamation of all human consciousness across space and through time.

**Markus:** That sounds intense...and kind of nice. But how can that be if everyone died in the war?

**Dordogne:** Not everyone died, Markus.

**Markus:** Right, but the Professor said they never had inter- actions with—

**Dordogne:** Something similar occurs with *technological* transmission too, which has broad societal implications. A renowned cultural anthropologist from the University of Chicago hypothesized about the effects of these cross-tem- poral interactions all the way back in your time, Markus. He called it a 'temporal technological singularity,' and it turns out he was right, considering cross-chronological collaboration created a technological, social, and cognitive singularity at that point in time when humanity achieved full intertemporal integration.

**Markus:** Huh, that's fascinating. I imagine technology and the human psyche would change drastically once the future starts influencing the past on a vast scale. Speaking of, I'm curious what your murder capitalists had to say about this new plan? Ending the religious zealotism that allowed them to manipulate the masses must have destroyed their access to wealth and power too, right? So, what was their take on destroying these sites?

**Dordogne:** It's complicated, but Professor Atman and Major Metathory ran myriad simulations and found that if we destroy these cities and holy sites here and now, there is a 12% chance they will lose control, while maintaining the 86% chance of preventing the war. However, if we do that *and* jump forward in time to take out the ships of Christopher Columbus and Hernán Cortés soon after they set sail across the Atlantic in the late 15th and early 16th centuries, the probability of success in preventing the Great Filter goes all the way up to 99%, but the likelihood that the aristocrats will lose their monopoly on wealth and power also more than doubles to 28%.

**Markus:** Ooo ooo, can I launch the missiles on the Cortés ship? That guy was a fucking dick!

**Dordogne:** Sure thing, babe.

**Markus:** Aww, did she just call me, babe.

**Dordogne:** The autocrats were reluctantly accepting of this latter outcome because the simulation showed that they would still exist. They would just end up sharing some of their wealth and influence with new indigenous global superpowers in Africa and the Americas, who were never given a chance to succeed because of colonialism and imperialism. But keeping the Earth intact was worth the tradeoff for them, so I think we're OK to go.

**Markus:** We're OK to go!

**Dordogne:** No, Markus. We're not doing that again.

**Markus:** Sorry...but we are totally watching *Contact* after *Spaceballs* when we get home.

**Dordogne:** I will watch anything you want, for as long as you want, if you promise me that you will never quote another film for as long as we both shall live.

**Markus:** Deal. Also, that's fantastic news! Shared global wealth and governance sounds like a future I'd be keen to go home to. Let's start blowing some shit up and rubber-stamp this mission complete.

**Dordogne:** I agree Markus, it seems we may have finally stumbled upon the perfect formula for peace and relative prosperity for all. Apparently, it just took the nuclear abolition of society and a near total loss of the planet we all call home for those in power to give up a tiny fraction of their unremitting generational hegemony.

**Markus:** Well, better late than never. I tell ya, it has been an interesting three weeks, but I'm looking forward to being done with this mission and settling down somewhere and somewhen with you and Jesus once this is finally over.

**Dordogne:** Me too, Markus, and it appears we may be close. The Professor already instructed the head of security to load the explosives and arm the detonators, so it's time to get this show on the road. Let's start heading back to the ship.

———— ◉ ————

**Markus:** God damn, I didn't realize we walked this far into town. We sure do a lot of walking for people who have a time-traveling intergalactic spaceship. I don't see why we couldn't have had the Professor beam us up from where we were in the city center. At this point, it doesn't matter if anyone sees us going up to the ship since they're all going to die soon anyway. Shit, it might be a good thing if these folks see Jesus getting beamed back up to heaven right before the town explodes. That's some good ol' fashioned biblical vengeance smite shit right there.

**Dordogne:** Stop your bitching, Markus, we're almost there. Besides, I don't want to do anything that isn't a part of the Looking Glass projections. We can't risk screwing up this rare win-win opportunity. OK, we made it to the extraction point. Professor, if you read me, bring us on up.

# CHAPTER 20
## REMONSTRATION – PALESTINE – TERRA
## AD 1290

**Atman:** Well done team! It would seem we finally found what we're looking for.

**Markus:** That's great, Professor. It's nice to know all our hard work, and especially Jesus's sacrifice, was not in vain. I don't think our intervention here would be effective without everything he did back then.

**Atman:** You're probably right, Markus. Sometimes you must build to destroy to build back better.

**Jesus:** I feel like you guys are just saying that to make me feel better about getting nailed through the wrists and stabbed in the ribs but thank you. Also, it's working, so you don't need to stop.

**Atman:** Happy to hear it, Jesus. You are a lion among wolves, and a man among men. And speaking of tormenting vengeance, the missiles are armed and ready for deployment. Let's hit Acre first since we're already here, then we'll head south so you can smite some infidels in Jerusalem and Golgotha. Sound good, Jesus?

**Jesus:** Praise be. I just hope the message we send helps protect future prophets who may not realize there are real dangers inherent in—

Oh crap, what the heck is that?! Do you see that, Professor?!

**Atman:** My God. They found us. I don't know how, but they found us! Dordogne, ready the missile launch console, we need to do this *quickly*!

**Dordogne:** There's no time, Professor. They're closing in too fast, and they just opened fire!

**Markus:** What the fuck, you guys! I thought you said those murder mafia turds were cool with sharing their wealth and power. Why the hell are they trying to blast us out of the sky?!

**Atman:** That's not one of our ships, Markus. That's not from our time!

**Markus:** It sure looks like one of your ships. But if not, then who the hell is it?! And again, why the *fuck* are they shooting at us?!

**Atman:** There's no time to explain. Abort mission, we need to get the hell out of here!

**Markus:** Can't we hold them off long enough to bomb a few cities at least? We've been through too much to just give up now. I can't go back to the world you took me from. We're too damn close!

**Atman:** They have laser weapons, Markus. They're thousands of years ahead of us. We don't stand a chance, and we're sitting ducks up here. We've got to time jump, *now*! Everybody, strap in, we'll abscond to a random tempoloco to try to lose them. Manitoba! I don't care where the fuck you take us in spacetime, just get us anywhere with the shortest time to vector clearance!

**Manitoba:** Roger that, Captain. I see a clear window to Wānaka, New Zealand, at 3,920 BP in T-minus 8 seconds... 7...

194

6...

**Atman:** We can't wait that long, Manitoba! The ship won't survive another impact. I'm launching now!

# CHAPTER 21
## ELUSION – WĀNAKA, NEW ZEALAND – THE SHIP 1970 BC

**Markus:** OK, seriously. What the fuck?! I found it super hard to believe that any one group would try to keep us from stopping a nuclear war, but you expect me to believe there is a whole separate faction traveling through time to thwart our efforts to end the worst conflict in human history?

**Atman:** God damn it, Dordogne. How the hell did they find us? How could they have known we were so close to finally doing it?

**Dordogne:** I don't know, Professor. Maybe they have a Looking Glass too. Or maybe they intercepted our transmissions with Luna Sede when we were consulting with Major Metathory about the potential success of our interventions there.

**Atman:** Impossible! Those transmissions are so heavily encrypted even Elizebeth Smith Friedman couldn't have cracked the code.

**Dordogne:** They are far more advanced than us, Professor. They probably cracked our encryption months ago but kept us from finding out until we were close to truly succeeding in this mission.

**Atman:** I don't know. Something doesn't seem right about what happened back there. Manitoba! Get us back to Luna

Sede in AD 2035 so we can meet with Metathory to see if there is still a way to pull this off. Maybe we can execute the plan in reverse and take out the conquistadors before heading back to Acre and Jerusalem on randomly generated dates.

**Manitoba:** Yes, Captain. And we're in luck. I see a jump window opening in T-minus 1 minute and 22 seconds.

**Markus:** Hellooooo, is anyone going to tell me who the fuck that was and why they just derailed what was about to be the end of this Godforsaken mission?!

**Atman:** Alright, prepare for departure everyone.

**Markus:** So, that's a no then?

**Atman:** There is no time right now, Markus. We will fill you in when we get back to Luna Sede. We need to stay focused on the mission right now.

**Markus:** I'm of the opinion that this *is* an important part of 'staying focused on the mission,' since we were just about to fucking complete it until those assholes showed up!

**Atman:** It is Markus! But what were you going to do, instantly evolve the ship to be 1,000 times faster and carry laser weapons so we at least stood a chance against them? We were all going to die back there! I had no choice but to order the evacuation!

**Markus:** Fuck that, Professor. The missiles were armed, and Dordogne was standing at the launch console. We could have at least blasted a few of them off during the countdown.

**Atman:** Yes, but then what? They would have just shot the missiles out of the air with their...once again...much more highly sophisticated *laser* weapons system! I know it's frustrating, Markus, but all is not lost. There might still be a way to do this. On Luna Sede, Metathory and I will consult the Looking Glass in real time to see if we can quickly pop in and out of those key points in spacetime to finalize the plan.

**Manitoba:** T-minus 10 seconds, Captain.

**Atman:** Thank you, Manitoba. Fire when ready.

# CHAPTER 22
## ELUCIDATION – NEAR EARTH'S MOON
## AD 2035

**Atman:** Oh, thank God, we made it back. I think that may have been our longest mission yet.

**Dordogne:** It was the longest for me by far, Professor. I'm hopeful we can revamp the plan though, so all our work wasn't for nothing.

**Atman:** I think there is hope for that. Despite this recent set-back, we now know what needs to be done to stop the Great War. It's simply a matter of putting the plan into action.

**Dordogne:** We should avoid any radio communication about it too, so they don't show up at the new tempolocos once we get there.

**Markus:** Aaand, who are *they*, exactly?

**Atman:** You're right, Dordogne, we can't risk them following us on another time jump. The last one almost spelled the end of us.

**Markus:** Aaaaand, who do you mean by *them*, exactly?!

**Atman:** Let's get this beat-up old bird into the hangar at Luna Sede and have a chat with Major Metathory about the best way forward from here.

**Markus:** Alright, for the last God-damn time, *who* in the giggly goat fuck was that, and *what*, and *why*, were they shooting at us?!?!

**Atman:** OK, Markus, I said I would fill you in when we got back to the base. Unfortunately, I can't tell you everything because it's highly classified, and it could negatively impact the future if I divulge too much.

**Markus:** Oh, you mean 'impact the future' like how we just created one of the most pervasive global religions of all time, which ushered in 2,000 years of relentless war? I don't think it's going to change a damn thing if you tell me who the hell was just trying to kill us.

**Atman:** Fair enough. Walk with me, lad…. If you must know, they are a separate subspecies of humans from a much more distant point in both our evolutionary futures.

**Markus:** I guess that would explain their more advanced technology, and their giant heads and eyes. I could see a few of them through the external zoom feature of your ship when they approached us back in Palestine and they looked super weird compared to all you fairly future folk.

**Atman:** Yes, they have had much longer to evolve their biology and culture throughout the distant future. Although we're not sure what period they hail from exactly.

**Markus:** Well, whenever they come back from, they must have been traveling deep into their past for a long time since those big-eyed freaks are depicted in all kinds of petroglyphs, geoglyphs, carvings, and cave paintings across the world and throughout the prehistoric past. An oddly large number of globally dispersed groups also used to practice intentional cranial deformation to reshape their infants' skulls so they would look more like these 'Aliens' in adulthood.

**Atman:** Yes, much like us, they have been active across

extensive periods of the future human past. We refer to them as 'Extratempestrials,' or 'ETs' for short.

**Markus:** That's dumb, you all are extratempestrial too.

**Atman:** Well, yes, I suppose, but—

**Markus:** Here in my time, we call them 'The Greys.'

**Atman:** That's even dumber. Of all the various traits that demarcate this group, you focus solely on their skin color.

**Markus:** I mean, have you met people in my time, Professor?

**Atman:** Yes, I suppose I have noticed you largely construct 'the other' around socioeconomic status, gender, sexuality, age, geography, *and* skin color. Those manufactured partitions are a big part of what got you into this looming nuclear Armageddon predicament in the first place.

**Markus:** I couldn't agree more. But simple differences in skin color and technology can't be why they were shooting at us. Dordogne told me empathy and consciousness evolve through time, so if highly advanced humans were trying to kill us, they must have a damn good reason, right? What the hell did you do to them?

**Atman:** Our understanding is somewhat limited, but we have surmised that they are extremely adamant about preventing us from stopping the war.

**Markus:** Why would anyone want to keep people from averting the worst war in human history? Not to mention the utter devastation of Earth's ecology and biome.

**Atman:** It's complicated.

**Markus:** Try me, I've got a PhD.

**Atman:** No, you don't.

**Markus:** No, I don't...yet. But I'm also not an idiot.

**Atman:** That's debatable.

**Markus:** Also true. But I'll try to follow along the best I can with my primitive little monkey brain, as you call it.

**Atman:** Fine. We know they only show up when the Looking Glass suggests we are statistically close to enacting a change that will forestall the Great War. Also, because they look so different from the people of our time, we can only surmise that they are the descendants of those who survived and endured after the nuclear war down on Earth. We think they may have evolved those 'Grey human' traits as you say, and likely faster, due to radiation, and from living underground for some time after the cataclysm.

**Markus:** Have you tried contacting them, or the people on Earth in your own time?

**Atman:** No. They undoubtedly blame us for what happened down there and hate us for escaping to the Moon without them.

**Markus:** Yea, I guess I would too.

**Atman:** Right? There's a reason why noah didn't reach out to the survivors of the great flood.

**Markus:** Is it also because that flood never happened since it was just a stupid made-up story?

**Atman:** Yes. But unlike that one, this was a real catastrophe, and I think you see my point.

**Markus:** I believe I do.

**Atman:** The Moon Base is cramped and smells of overripe papaya in a moist sock that a—

**Markus:** Ooo, Doc, you ain't allowed to say that!

**Atman:** What, papaya?

**Markus:** No. *Moist,* Bruh!

**Atman:** Really? Why? I like that word.

**Markus:** Fer shure, everybody does, but Dordogne said it's illegal to say it in your future.

**Atman:** *Haha.* She was probably just messing with you. Did you happen to notice the date she said it was outlawed?

**Markus:** No, I guess I missed that.

**Atman:** Well, Luna Sede is not ideal, and largely because we've been forced to live with the descendants of the same rich assholes who got us into this mess down there in your time. However, it is undoubtedly better than what the Extratempestrials endured after the disaster. We don't know how they survived, or what kind of civilization they created afterward, since we have never been back there to find out, but I'm certain it was miserable, so it's understandable why they would be hostile toward us on occasion.

**Markus:** Have they ever attacked you at any time other than when you're trying to prevent the war?

**Atman:** No.

**Markus:** So, maybe they're not hostile toward you because you are defeatist cowards but because they have a vested stake in the zero-sum game that is this war.

**Atman:** That could be true. We have apparently lived together in peace for thousands of years, prior to our more recent attempts at trying to avert the Great War.

**Markus:** Yea, maybe y'all should stop and have a think on that for a quick minute. What I don't understand though, is if the Greys are descended from people who prospered after the war by living in nasty-ass underground cities that probably smelled worse than your moist papaya sock Moon Base, wouldn't they want to stop the war from happening too? Wouldn't that be good for them as well?

**Atman:** Here's the rub, Markus. The Looking Glass shows that if we are successful in stopping the war, it will erase all other realities that grew out of this conflict, including the timeline that resulted in their Extratempestrial existence in the deep future.

**Markus:** So, if you stop the war from happening, you erase them from existence?

**Atman:** That is correct, as well as anything and everything that ever happened after that point in time. Have you heard of the 'Mandela Effect,' Markus?

**Markus:** No.

**Atman:** That's good because it's incredibly stupid.

**Markus:** OK, good to know. I guess I could see why they might try to thwart your efforts to stop the war if it means their entire reality, and their long history leading up to it, ceases to exist.

**Atman:** That does appear to be a prime mover, yes.

**Markus:** But if you're successful in stopping the war, wouldn't you and all the other sissy cowards holed up on Luna Sede no longer exist in the future too?

**Atman:** No, the Moon Base existed long before the war, and since it's there, we can be too. As Metathory and I mentioned earlier, from the 1970s on, the base provided a stable launch point for our time travel missions, so we could more easily abduct, extract gametes from, and study people from periods near your time. But it was also built to serve as a sanctuary if Earth ever became uninhabitable, which seemed inevitable, and was the inescapable reality.

**Markus:** Yea, those little tragedy-of-the-commons bitches were bound to do it one way or another.

**Atman:** Indeed. Under the system set up down on Earth, corporations, who operate as legal individuals, had open access to resources with no shared social structure or enforced rules. They acted according to their own self-interests, and contrary to the common good of all users. This caused the depletion of those resources through their uncoordinated actions, which was exacerbated by the fact that there were far too many users relative to the available resources. But as you are involvedly aware, we're now trying to right that and countless other wrongs of the past.

**Markus:** I'm glad. My time sucks, and I can only imagine how much more it's going to suck once we all start stabbing each other over the last can of Soylent Green.

**Atman:** Well, that is what we are actively trying to keep from happening. That's the entire reason we picked you up and spent the last three weeks traveling through time, after all.

**Markus:** Fair enough. Although, I'm starting to feel as conflicted as you and Dordogne have seemed this entire time.

**Atman:** How so?

**Markus:** Saving the lives of 9.5 billion people sounds like the right thing to do, of course. However, that would also mean we erase from existence a whole 'nother civilization, who, judging from their highly advanced technology, clearly prospered despite—or perhaps because of—the Great Filter, and over a much longer stretch of time than your people have thus far. That is quite a tradeoff. We save one civilization but annihilate another in the process? Oh, this is heavy, Doc!

**Atman:** I agree, but preventing the war is what's best for us, all of humanity, and the Earth.

**Markus:** Says who? You don't know anything about these

people, and you never even tried to find out. How can you study countless human groups across eons of time and not bother to investigate anything about another entire civilization whose ancestors are living on Earth at the same time as you? These motherfuckers were resilient enough to survive a nuclear cataclysm and flourish long into the future, and you can't be bothered to call them up to grab a beer and chat about shit for 10 minutes?

**Atman:** That is a vast oversimplification of the situation, Markus. This is a time war, and in war, there are winners and losers. That is the nature of conflict. Yes, if we are successful, they will be erased from the timeline, but 9.5 billion people will have their lives back, and perhaps most importantly, we will all have our planet back.

**Markus:** Diplomacy is an aspect of war too, Dildo Baggins, and you haven't even attempted it.

**Atman:** It doesn't matter what they want, or why, Markus. We will stop the war, save 9.5 billion lives, save the Earth, and immerse ourselves back into society as it was before the Great War. Or at least that's what we think will happen.... Despite figuring out the logistical mechanics of time travel, due to some recent developments, we are somewhat perplexed about whether we can actually *change* the past.

**Markus:** What the hell do you mean you don't know if we can *change* the past?! That's exactly what we've been trying to do this whole fucking time!

**Atman:** Yes, but once we started meddling with time in an attempt to prevent the war, we began noticing a troubling pattern where most of what we did seemed to have been what we were always already going to do, and as far as we could tell, nothing truly changed at all. However, the Looking Glass gives us hope that other outcomes can be realized, which includes stopping the Great War.

**Markus:** Jesus Christ, I'm time-traveling with a bunch of blockheaded amateurs here! Maybe you should ask the Grey human extratempestrials about it. I imagine they've got it all figured out by their time.

**Atman:** People who are trying to eradicate each other typically don't ask one another for guidance.

**Markus:** Well, perhaps you should. That's a big part of what got us all into this giant fucking mess in the first place. You're both time-traveling humans from the future. You've got that in common at least. Maybe there's some other shit you could bond over too.

**Atman:** I don't have time for an ideological debate right now, Markus. We're almost to the control center. Let's just find Major Metathory and see what we can do to reboot this effort and hopefully complete this Godforsaken mission once and for all.

# CHAPTER 23
## FULMINATION – LUNA SEDE
## AD 2035

**Metathory:** What the fuck happened back there, Professor?! The Looking Glass predictions dropped from 99% down to only a 5% chance of stopping the Great Filter. Why the hell did you come back here if you didn't complete the mission?

**Atman:** Yes, sorry I didn't radio back, but I couldn't risk them finding out where we were going.

**Metathory:** Who?

**Atman:** The Extratempestrials, Sir. They attacked us just as we were about to execute the plan. They fired on the ship and stopped us before we could launch the explosives.

**Metathory:** God damn it! That was it. That was the one. We were so close this time! How the hell did they find you?

**Atman:** I don't know, Major. Dordogne thinks they intercepted our intertemporal transmissions while we were discussing the Looking Glass simulation results. They must have known it was going to work and tracked our spacetime locus to stop us before we could implement the plan.

**Metathory:** Shit, that was our last chance!

**Atman:** Not necessarily. I have an idea for how we may still be able to pull it off without the Extratempestrials interfering, but we can't discuss it over the time-comm or consult the Looking Glass again, since they might have tapped into that somehow too.

**Metathory:** God, I hope you're right. What did you have in mind, Professor?

**Atman:** Due to the nature of spacetime, it doesn't matter which part of the scheme we enact first. The plan itself was never the problem, it was only that they showed up.

**Dordogne:** Hello, Major Metathory, it's good to see you again. I wasn't sure we were going to make it back this time, so your face is a welcome sight.

**Metathory:** Hi Dordogne. Yes, the Professor said you ran into the Extratempestrials out there. It sounded like a close call.

**Dordogne:** It was, indeed, but it was also the closest we've come to full implementation of a statistically probable out-come that stops the war. It's unfortunate they showed up and ran us off at the last minute.

**Metathory:** Yes, this must have been the intervention we needed.... Hello, Markus, Airl, Moirai, Manitoba. Welcome back and thank you for your hard work on this mission.

**Markus:** Hello, Major Metathory. I'll say your butter face is a welcomed sight too, but only because we almost died out there and it's good to see anything back here in my home time.

**Metathory:** Hmm, yes, Markus, it's so very good to see you as well. And this is Jesus I presume?

**Jesus:** Yes, hi Major Metathory. It's good to finally meet you.

**Metathory:** It's great to meet you too, Jesus...and a special thanks to you for all the sacrifices you made on this mission.

I'll see to it that you receive the highest accolades for your contribution when this is all over.

**Jesus:** Thank you, but that won't be necessary. I'm just content doing what I can to stop the war. Fortunately, the Professor thinks there is still a way to do it, so all our work won't be for nothing.

**Atman:** Yes, as I was saying, Major. Due to the nature of spacetime, it doesn't matter which period we visit first, or in which order we carry out the interventions prescribed by the Looking Glass simulations.

**Metathory:** I suppose that's true.

**Atman:** So, first we destroy Columbus's and Cortés's ships, then head farther back in time to obliterate those cities and holy sites the Looking Glass told us about. And importantly, we do each on randomly selected dates without consulting the Looking Glass or discussing it over our time comms so there can be no way for the Extratempestrials to know what we are doing and when.

**Metathory:** That sounds like a solid plan, Professor, and I certainly think it could work. Under normal circumstances I would recommend you first get some rest after such a long mission, but I feel it might be better to proceed with this new plan post haste considering what happened at the last time jump. Do you think you and your crew are up for it?

**Atman:** It has been a grueling three weeks, but I think we can rally the troops. The missiles are still armed, we will just need to restock some supplies on the ship. What do you think, crew, ready to head back out for this one last mission to save the future?

**Dordogne:** Absolutely. I think we will all be happy to finally put this one to bed.

**Atman:** Thank you, Dordogne, and thanks to the rest of you as well. I'm excited to see what this world morphs into when we get back. Major, you'll have to call us after the AD 1290 intervention to let us know what Earth looks like here in the present. Just don't radio back until the last bomb is dropped so the Extratempestrials can't stop us prior to completing this final task.

**Metathory:** Roger that, Professor. The moment the timeline shifts, you will be the first to know. Also, what does AD stand for in relation to the period you just mentioned?

**Atman:** Oh, it stands for anno Domini, which means 'in the year of the Lord.' 525 years after Jesus left with us in the time disc, a monk named Dionysius Exiguus used a random estimate of his birthday to establish a christian chronology. So, as an homage to the sacrifices Jesus made in our efforts to stop the Great War, we all started using that dating system as well.

**Metathory:** Superb. It would seem the accolades have already begun to pour in for this old chap. Well-deserved too, Jesus! Alright, let's get this show on the road.

**Atman:** Roger that, Major. Moirai, Manitoba, you two head back to join Morpheus on the ship and prepare her for launch. Dordogne, why don't you take Markus, Jesus, and Airl out to the materials and equipment wing to gather what we will need for this last part of the mission. While you're doing that, Major Metathory and I will finalize the details of this new plan.

**Dordogne:** Will do, Julian.

**Markus:** Actually, you and Airl go ahead, Dordogne. Jesus and I are gonna hang back for a second. I want to ask the Major about something before we head out.

**Dordogne:** OK, but don't be long. We're going to need you two strapping young lads to help carry the food and equipment onto the ship, which includes the copious amounts of Champagne and beer we'll need for celebrating when this mission is finally over.

**Markus:** Oh, hell yea, I was the absolute king of beer runs back in college. I once carried six 30-packs nine blocks back to a house party, uphill, in two feet of snow.

**Atman:** That's impressive, Markus.

**Markus:** Shut up Doc, I know it. Also, we've got Jesus to turn water into wine for us, or Perrier into Champagne, or piss into Hennessy or whatever it is he do.

**Jesus:** No thank you, Dad. I'm done with all of that. I just want to be a regular guy from now on.

**Markus:** Well, shit, I do love me some piss-Henny, but I guess I can't blame ya, kiddo. Anyhow, we won't be long, Dordogne—

Oh, you should take Marshmallow! I bet if you load up a sled full of supplies, she could pull it onto the ship for you. She's gotten a lot bigger over the last three weeks, and her breed are immensely powerful working dogs. I'm sure she'd love helping out too.

**Dordogne:** Hmm, good thinking, Markus. OK, come on, Marshmallow. We don't need these smelly boys anyway, do we girl? Alright, we'll see you fellas down there shortly.

**Metathory:** So, what did you want, Private? And make it snappy. The Professor and I have a lot to discuss.

**Markus:** I was just wondering about something the Professor said when we got back to this time.

**Atman:** Oh, come on Markus, not this again.

**Markus:** Hang on Professor, I just wanted to get a second opinion on all this.

**Metathory:** Who are the Greys, exactly?

**Markus:** Oh, right. The 'Extratempestrials' as you call them, even though you all are time travelers too. Anyhow, the Professor said that if we are successful in stopping the war then these Grey human extratempestrials will cease to exist. Is that right?

**Metathory:** Yes, as far as we know. There are still some things we don't yet fully comprehend about the effects of our interactions with the past, but based on what the Looking Glass tells us, once we complete the mission, there should be a full reset of the timeline from AD 1290 on. Shout out, Jesus.

**Jesus:** Thanks Major, but I should point out that the Gregorian calendar is riddled with flaws, which makes it especially problematic for time travelers like yourselves.

**Metathory:** All good. It's just fun to say if anything else. Especially since you're a celebrity and all.

**Markus:** Anyhow, Metathory. The Professor said the Extratempestrials are trying to thwart our attempts at stopping the war because our intervention in the past will erase them from the future. If we're successful, wouldn't that make us responsible for the genocide of a whole other race of humans, who have evidently developed a highly advanced civilization, and who knows what else.

**Metathory:** There is a possibility of that, but we can't let that bleeding heart tree-hugging hippie mentality keep us from saving the 9.5 billion people who are going to lose their lives sometime in the next year or two if we do nothing.

**Markus:** I don't know though. There must be some way we can work together to sort it out, so all future human groups can coexist.

**Metathory:** Look, Markus, they need the war to happen to exist. We need the war not to happen so we can have Earth back. These scenarios stand in opposition to one another. This is war, and war is a zero-sum game.

**Markus:** You've already peacefully coexisted for thousands of years. If you just stop trying to erase them from reality, then you can continue to peacefully coexist. Think about it, the only time they attack is when you try to change the timeline. Otherwise, they leave you alone, even though they could easily kill all of you anytime they wanted to. Maybe it's because of the mission we're on, but I've been having these intense dreams centering on nonviolence and shared consciousness lately, and the packages of information that come through—

**Metathory:** Jesus Christ, shut the fuck up, Markus! I'm sick of all your woke liberal nonsense.

**Markus:** Aw, hell naw. That's our word. You don't get to use that word. I am woke, bitch! I'm woke as fuck, and proud of it! I woke up and saw all the hate and hypocrisy in your bullshit belief system. I woke up and saw how you'd rather demonize the word *woke* than recognize you're in the wrong cuz you lack basic empathy and love for anybody but yourself.

**Metathory:** Whatever, fuck-stick. We don't have time for your lexicon lesson and pointless nighty night nocturnal emission stories. We are going to stop the war. We are going to save 9.5 billion lives. We are going to get Earth back. And the future will be a better place because of it.

**Markus:** Not for them.

**Metathory:** I don't give a shit, Markus. They survived a nuclear holocaust for God's sake. If they're so exceptional and innovative as you've come to believe, then they'll figure out a way to save themselves this time too.

**Markus:** That's exactly what they're doing every time we attempt to stop the war and change the future. Maybe it's the dreams, but I'm getting a strong sense that we need to talk to them, that there's something different we should be doing. They're not bad people. They only want to live, just like everyone else. Self-preservation is the earliest innate characteristic of all life forms. Except goldfish, they don't seem to have that.

**Metathory:** You're talking in circles now, Markus. We are finally able to complete this mission, and that is exactly what we're going to do. This conversation is over. Go help Dordogne and the others in the equipment wing.

**Atman:** Oh, Jesus Christ!

**Jesus:** What, Professor?

**Atman:** Not you, Jesus. Look up!

**Jesus:** Ah rats, not again.

**Metathory:** What, they're here? You've got to be kidding me! They've never been to the Moon Base before!

**Atman:** This isn't good, Major. I count eight ships up there. They could level the whole base with that amount of firepower.

**Metathory:** I'm sure that is exactly why they're here. Damnit, they opened fire! Everybody run! Get to the escape pods!

**Atman:** Hopefully the rest of the crew is seeing this and they get the ship out of the hanger in time.

**Metathory:** I hope so too, Atman, that's the only one we've got right now. I'll sound the evacuation alarm!

**Atman:** Markus, Jesus, follow Metathory. He'll get you to the escape pods!

**Markus:** There's smoke everywhere, where did he go?

**Metathory:** This way, Markus. And hurry the fuck up, the whole God-damn building is coming down.

**Markus:** Let's go, Jesus! Run—

Come on, Doc!

**Markus:** Professor Atman!?

**Atman:** I'm shot, Markus.

**Markus:** Oh shit, Doc. Are you ok?

**Atman:** One of their lasers got me in the chest.

**Markus:** Hang on, we'll get you out of here! Jesus, take his other arm. We can carry him to the escape pod.

**Atman:** There's no time, Markus, and I'm not going to make it anyhow.

**Markus:** Bullshit, you're coming with us! Jesus and I can carry you!

**Atman:** I lived a good long life, friend. I've seen humanity grow and change in ways no one else has. This is the way it was always going to be. The people of my time wouldn't have survived much longer even if we had stopped the war. But they clearly have, the Greys. The future is theirs now.

**Jesus:** Oh no, Mom! I'm going to look for her!

**Markus:** No, Jesus, you stay with me! You'll never find her in time. I'm sure she'll get out.

**Atman:** I wondered if this is why the Looking Glass never showed us anything in our time. I thought it was destroyed in the war, but they needed it gone now. They knew we were close. Go, Markus. Follow Major Metathory. Get to the escape pods.

**Markus:** I'd rather die here with you than have to live with that piece of shit asshole.

**Atman:** We're in your time. He'll take you back to Earth. He'll take you home.

**Markus:** I'm not sure that's any better.

**Atman:** Take care of Jesus. Give him the best life you can. He deserves it. He gave us everything he had.

**Markus:** God damn it. Goodbye, Professor.

**Atman:** Goodbye, Markus.

**Metathory:** Markus! Jesus! Come on! We've got to go, now!

**Jesus:** Goodbye Professor, thanks for everything.

**Atman:** Goodbye Jesus. You're one of a kind.

——— ◉ ———

**Metathory:** Get in, get in!

**Markus:** Should we wait for the others?

**Metathory:** No. There are five other escape pods all around the base. If they can get out, they will. Strap in, we're getting the fuck out of here!
Launching!

——— ◉ ———

**Metathory:** Good lord, it looks even worse from up here. They're taking down the whole God-damn thing!

**Jesus:** Thanks for coming back to get us, Major Metathory. My dad and I don't know our way around the base, so we never would have found this escape pod in time.

**Metathory:** Of course, Jesus. It's the least I can do after everything you've done for us.

**Markus:** I see a few other modules leaving the base. I really hope Dordogne, Airl, and Marshmallow made it out in time. Is there any way to contact the other pods, Major?

**Metathory:** Yes, but the communication system is networked through Luna Sede, and there is very little of that left at this point.

**Jesus:** Why aren't they following us, Major? We're sitting ducks up here. They could easily take us out.

**Metathory:** I don't think they care about killing us as much as they want to destroy the Moon Base, Jesus. That's where the Looking Glass is, and that is where the time war started once we launched this mission to stop the Great Filter. They must have known we were getting close and decided to take no chances by destroying everything we had left to wage this war. They won't come after us though. They did what they came to do.

———— ◉ ————

**Morpheus:** Hello? Professor Atman? Major Metathory? Is anyone there?

**Metathory:** Yes, come in. This is Major Metathory speaking. Who is this?

**Morpheus:** It's Morpheus. I'm radioing from the time disc. We escaped the base and are powered down, hiding out on the opposite side of Earth from the Moon where they can't see us.

**Metathory:** Oh, thank God you're safe, and you saved the ship. Is there anyone else with you?

**Morpheus:** Moirai and Manitoba are here with me. We were on the ship making final preparations for the mission when the Extratempestrials arrived. We thought they might try to destroy the base, so we fled with the time disc as soon as we saw them.

**Markus:** What about Dordogne? Ask him about Dordogne!

**Metathory:** Is that it? Is it just the three of you?

**Morpheus:** Yes, Airl and Dordogne were back in the equipment wing of the base marshaling the last of the supplies when the ETs arrived.... It's hard for me to tell you this, but there's no way they could have survived. The storage wing was the first to be destroyed. We watched it come down from above. We also contacted the other escape pods before reaching you, and I'm sorry, but they weren't on any of those either.

**Jesus:** No, Mom! They killed Mom!

**Markus:** God damnit, no! I fucking loved her. She was the only woman I ever loved.

**Morpheus:** What about the Professor? Did he make it out?

**Metathory:** No, Morpheus. The Professor was shot in the initial attack. Sadly, he didn't make it. He served valiantly for decades. He was a dear friend and will be sorely missed.

**Morpheus:** That's terrible news. I can't believe this. We have nothing left. What do you want us to do, Major?

**Metathory:** Send me your coordinates. I'll navigate the escape pod around Terra to your location and we'll rejoin you on the ship. We'll have far more options on the time disc than in this escape module. Thanks again for getting her out of there.

**Morpheus:** Affirmative, Major. Tell Markus and Jesus we are all genuinely sorry for their loss.

**Metathory:** I will, Morpheus, thank you. We'll see you shortly.

**Markus:** Fuck, I can't believe she's gone. She just went to grab some stuff and then...gone. I never even got a chance to say goodbye.

**Metathory:** I'm sorry, Markus. She truly was an astonishing woman. I will miss her immensely as well.

**Jesus:** I'm sorry too, Dad. I know she wasn't my real Mom, but I loved her like one.

**Markus:** Alright, fuck this, Metathory! I'm done with this bullshit! When we get back to the time disc I want you to take me and Jesus back down to Earth. We might as well live out what little life we have left before they nuke the whole fucking planet.

**Metathory:** I will, Markus. Thank you both for your contribution and sacrifice over the last few weeks. I'm sorry it didn't work out the way we planned, but we tried, and we came damn close to pulling it off.

# CHAPTER 24
## RESIGNATION – CAMPUS – TERRA
## AD 2035

**Metathory:** Alright kid, welcome home. Your Earth. Your town. Your time.

**Markus:** Thanks, Major. And you brought me back to the same time as when they took me, right? I've got an exam to give on Monday.

**Metathory:** We all do, Markus. We all do.

**Markus:** No, seriously. I was obviously hoping to return to a better future where people don't suck ass, but since I'm back here and everything still blows chunks, I'm at least obligated to function in this bullshit society until we all get murder nuked.

**Metathory:** Yes, Markus. In fact, it is Monday morning in your time zone right now. You have about two hours to get across campus before your class starts.

**Markus:** Well, you were supposed to bring me back to Friday night just after Dordogne and the Professor took me up to the Moon Base, but close enough. OK, Major, I guess it was good working with you, and all that other stupid shit I'm supposed to say even though the mission failed and most of the people I came to love over the last three weeks are now dead.

**Jesus:** At least you still have me, Dad. If you hadn't traveled back through time on this mission I never would have been born, and we never would have known each other.

**Markus:** That's true, thanks Jesus. You're always so good at looking on the bright side of life. What are you going to do now, Major?

**Metathory:** I know of several abandoned bunkers scattered across Earth in your time. I'm going to track down any survivors I can find from the Moon Base and see about fixing up a few of the nicer ones before the bombs drop. Since we can't retreat to the Moon Base, that will have to do.

**Markus:** Oh, snap! You know what I just thought of?

**Metathory:** What's that?

**Markus:** Maybe you, Morpheus, Manitoba, Moirai, and the other Moon Base survivors are the ancestors of the Grey humans, evolving underground for centuries like a bunch of over-radiated big-eyed mutant lizard bugs and shit.

**Metathory:** Perhaps, Markus. But I think I would know if I was the ancestor of an entirely different race of humans.

**Markus:** Yea, probably. Either way, be sure to save room for me and Jesus in one of those fancy bunkers of yours. I don't want us to flame up like mosquitos in a 1980s bug zapper when the fireworks start flying.

**Metathory:** Sure, Markus, we'll totally come get you guys. Well, Jesus at least. Can't say I'm overly excited about the idea of living with you down there.

**Markus:** Yea, he's a good egg. Okay, as long as you save my kid, I'm fine burning with the rest of these barbequed bitches up here on the surface.

**Metathory:** Naw, I'm just kidding, runt. You've kind of some-what grown on me to a certain extent somehow a tiny bit too, dick string. We'll save a bed for you as well. Oh, by the way. I snatched the Professor's time phone before we escaped the base. Take this, and if shit looks like it's heading toward the fan, give me a call and we'll come pick you up before you get nuked. If we haven't been irradiated ourselves, that is.

**Markus:** Thanks, Major Metathory. You take care of yourself.

**Metathory:** À Dieu, Boys. Enjoy these last magnificent moments above ground while you still can.

———— ◉ ————

**Markus:** Alright, Jesus. I guess it's 'Take Your Kid to Work Day,' cuz I only have a couple hours to get across campus, copy my exams, make coffee, eat some food, and head to class.

**Jesus:** That sounds great, Dad! I was hoping to do things like this when we got back to your time. I can't wait to see what you do for a living. If it's not a sheep herder, carpenter, blacksmith, or a crown-of-thorns maker then it's all new to me.

**Markus:** Nope, it's none of those things. Today's class might be boring for you since they are just taking a test, but you can come back next week when I give the archaeology lecture if you want. Maybe we'll talk about biblical archaeology, and you can be the artifact I show them.

**Jesus:** That would be awesome. Thanks, Pops.

**Markus:** But for now, we've got to haul ass. Come on Boy, run like the Greys are shooting at you!

**Jesus:** Aww, no, Dad!

**Markus:** Too soon?

**Jesus:** Way too soon, that was like an hour ago.

**Markus:** Yea, you're right, sorry buddy.

———— ◉ ————

**Markus:** Oh, hey Ryan, it looks like we're still on the same copy-machine schedule.

**Ryan:** What the fuck!? Markus?! Where have you been, Man?! I've been calling you like three times a day!

**Markus:** Yea, sorry about the Irish goodbye at that rugby party the other night. I had to travel back in time to save the future and accidentally became God and almost got killed by the Greys this morning.

**Ryan:** No, seriously dude. We've all been worried sick about you. Where the fuck were you?!

**Markus:** Damn man, we were just kicking it at that party a couple days ago. I didn't realize you were so gay for me and shit. You about done with that copy machine though? I've got to run these exams before my class in an hour.

**Ryan:** Don't bother, that's Noah's class now.

**Markus:** Tha fuck it is! What the hell are you talking about?!

**Ryan:** Uh, you really have no idea how long you've been gone, do you?

**Markus:** Major Metathory said it's Monday morning, and we were at that party Friday night so, two days.

**Ryan:** No, mate. That party was *last* Friday. You didn't show up for class all week, so Dr. Cohen gave your anthro course to Noah's little bitch ass.

**Markus:** Whatever man, I don't believe you. Show me the date on your phone.

**Ryan:** Look...that party was *ten* days ago.

**Jesus:** You know, Dad, I thought I saw the Major smirk a little when you asked if he was dropping us off in the right time. I think he did it on purpose.

**Markus:** That butter-covered bellend! How he gonna play me like that?!

**Ryan:** Did that dude just call you Dad?

**Markus:** Oh yea, sorry, I suck at introductions. Ryan, Jesus. Jesus, Ryan.

**Ryan:** You are really starting to trip me out, my dude.... You disappear for a week and half, randomly show up with no idea what day it is, and with a guy that looks older than you who calls you Dad. What tha fuck is going on?!

**Markus:** You got dicks in your ears or something, homeslice? I just told you. I was on a time travel mission to avert an imminent nuclear Armageddon. We went back super deep into the past. I laid into a ton of chicks on several different continents over the last 48,000 years, one of whom was the Holy Virgin Mary of Nazareth in 1 BC, who is hot as hell by the way. That made me God, and this is my little bastard kid, your Lord and Savior, Jesus Christ.

**Ryan:** And how much Hydromorphic Crackicide did you smoke on this little tiki tour through time?

**Markus:** Ah shit, a butt-ton, man! Bump it Jesus.

**Jesus:** Dad's not kidding, we smoked a lot of Crackicide on that trip. The Professor invented it. What did you call him, Pops? An intertemporal drug kingpin Heisenberg-ass mother-fucker or something?

**Markus:** That's right, Lad. The man was a veritable phar-macopeia. I still can't believe the guy's dead. He was a good dude. It seems like we should have had a funeral for him or something before we came back to Earth.

**Jesus:** Yea, for Mom and Airl too.

**Markus:** I'm not ready to talk about that, Jesus. I don't know if I'm capable of processing that loss yet. I don't want to believe she's gone. The only woman I ever truly loved in this world, who helped me peer deep into the universal consciousness, to restore my faith in humanity and the future of our species. She was different, Jesus. She was a sensational soul who transcended time and space. She was the epitome of love and light, and not just for me, but for everyone within reach of her divine essence. She had a commanding presence that radiated beauty in all directions.

**Jesus:** It is incredibly depressing, Dad. And you're right, she was special. I miss her too. But, like you always tell me, you should be happy it happened, not sad that it's over.

**Markus:** That's easier said than done. But you are right as always, my son. I'll never forget her, but I'll focus on remembering the moments we spent together, rather than dwelling on the ones I'll have to live without her from now on.

**Ryan:** Okay. If this is a practical joke then good on ya, you got me. You can bring Ashton Kutcher's punk'd ass out now.

**Markus:** I wish it was Ryan. It would hurt a lot less that way.

**Ryan:** Well, I still don't know if you're being serious, but there is something I need to tell you. Not to make your love life suck any more than it apparently already does, but after you disappeared, and we all thought you were dead, Amanda and I hooked up.

**Markus:** Damn, dude. Great friend. Thanks.

226

**Ryan:** I know, I'm sorry, but we were both hunkered down on Sunday evening, calling everyone we could think of who might know—

**Markus:** You mean yesterday?

**Ryan:** No, last Sunday.

**Markus:** So, you waited one whole day after I disappeared before you had sex with my girlfriend.

**Ryan:** Well, a day and a half technically, but yes. I'm sorry, man, but what happened was I got out that bottle of Jameson 18-year because she was super sad and—

**Markus:** Oh, damn Dude, that shit is good! I'd fuck you too if you busted that out, whether I was sad or not.

**Ryan:** I know, right. So, we killed the bottle, and she was crying, so I gave her a hug to help her feel better, and the next thing you know we were buck naked, making out on the floor, and I went down on her until she came, and then I was rock hard, so she climbed up on top of—

**Markus:** God damn, Ryan, my kid is standing right here. I don't need all the details. You could have stopped with 'we hooked up.' I think I know what that means.

**Jesus:** It's fine, Dad, I've heard it all before. You once told me every horrifically graphic detail about what you all did in that orgy with the Flores Hobbits 48,000 years ago.

**Markus:** Ooo, yes, that was a fun one! Sorry kiddo, but I had to tell somebody.

**Ryan:** Right, well, I'm sorry again, Markus. We had a really great time though.

**Markus:** That's fabulous Ryan. I'm so happy to hear you had a really great time fucking my girlfriend. Yea, that's great. Everything's great! I've got no job. The love of my life is dead.

I couldn't save the world so we're all going to die in a nuclear holocaust. Fuck it, come on, Jesus, we're going to the brewery!

**Ryan:** It's 10:00 a.m., Markus.

**Markus:** Yea, I know. But today sucked ass, and Jesus used to have to drink beer made from stale barley and slave spit so I'm gonna show him how much better that shit got in the last 2,000 years as we drink ourselves into oblivion and try to forget the last two days of our lives. You're coming too, actually.

**Ryan:** Well, OK. I guess it's the least I can do for an old friend who we all thought was dead.

**Markus:** Yea, coming back from the dead is kind of our thing, eh Jesus?

**Jesus:** It does seem to run in the family.

**Ryan:** I am genuinely happy to see you again though, buddy. I was super worried about you. And sorry again about Amanda. But to be honest, it wasn't just a drunken hookup, I think there's something deeper there. We've been talking a lot over the last week, and it seems we really like each other. I broke it off with Sharron immediately after Amanda and I got together because I feel a strong connection with her. I honestly think she could be the one.

**Markus:** I completely understand, my friend. After recently learning what true love feels like I can empathize, and I couldn't have kept dating her since experiencing that anyway. We weren't right for each other from the start, so I'm glad you two got together...even if it was because you thought I was dead. I love you, man, and I'm happy for you two.

**Ryan:** Love you too, Markus. Thanks for understanding. And for not being dead.... I guess I got the best of both worlds. My buddy's alive, and I get to keep his girlfriend.

**Markus:** *Haha*, yep, sounds like it worked out just fine on your end.

**Ryan:** We hitting O'Hooley's?

**Markus:** Indeed, good sir. It seems like the best place to introduce ma boy Jesus to the world of futuristic microbrews.

**Ryan:** Right on, let me grab my bag from upstairs in the TA office and I'll meet you out front in five. You should go up and talk to Dr. Cohen about your class too. Maybe you can get it back if you play nice with her.

**Markus:** Naw, that spaceship's done sailed, my space brother. And we're all gonna die soon anyway, so what's the point? I figure we have one, maybe two years before the bombs start dropping. So, I was thinking Jesus and I will dip out and backpack Europe for a couple months, work on a fair-trade coffee plantation in Guatemala for a while, then take the rest of the year to free Tibet, Taiwan, and Palestine from their colonial oppressors.

**Ryan:** That sounds ambitious.

**Markus:** Ain't got shit else going on.

**Ryan:** I guess not.

**Markus:** Alright big buddy, we'll see you out front in five.

# CHAPTER 25
## INEBRIATION – O'HOOLEY'S – TERRA
## AD 2035

**Jesus:** Wow Dad, you weren't kidding, this beer is way better than the moldy barley slave spit we drank back home!

**Markus:** Ain't it though?! Ya know, kid, when I was an under-graduate student here, they sold pints of these fine brews every Thursday evening during happy hour for only $1 each. One dollar, Boy! Can you believe that?!

**Jesus:** That's incredible, Father! You really have lived an amazing life!

**Markus:** I do feel blessed, my son. But mostly just since you came around, ya little bastard! C'mere you!

**Jesus:** *Haha*, I love you, Dad.

**Ryan:** Damn, are you guys drunk already?

**Markus:** Shut up Ryan, it's been a long day.

**Ryan:** It's 11:00 a.m.!

**Markus:** For you maybe, but it's like, the middle of the night or some shit for us. I don't even know, but we just watched my dog, two of our best friends, and the only chick I've ever loved get blowed up in a Moon Base attack at the hands of some big-eyed future freaks, so I'm fixing to drink some

God-damn beers with my Messiah kid here and try to forget about it for 10 fucking minutes if that's ok with you, ya fuss-budget fuddy-duddy party-pooper princess pants!

**Ryan:** Yea man, have at it. I'm here for you, bro.

**Markus:** Just how 'here for me' are you, Ryan? Like, enough to give me a bottle of Jameson 18-Year Irish Whiskey and some cunnilingus?

**Jesus:** *Haha*, good one, Dad!

**Ryan:** No, not quite that much. But enough to day drink with you on a Monday morning.

**Markus:** Alright, we'll count it. Santé!

**Ryan:** Santé! Ya know, I was wondering what happened to that dog we found on the way to the party last week. She up and disappeared the same night you did. I guess that explains it if you took her with you.

**Markus:** Yea, she was a good dog. She even saved us from a tiger attack in India 5,585 years ago.

**Ryan:** Huh, that's crazy. So, all that stuff honestly happened? Like, he's really your fucking kid?

**Markus:** I shit you negative, mon frère d'une autre mère. It all be true. My almost-wife even did a paternity test on him.

**Ryan:** Wow, that's incredible! I can't tell you how many times I've said in my class, 'well, if we only had a time machine....' And you got to do it! You got to go back to the time of the Denisovans, Neanderthals, Cro-Magnons—

**Markus:** And the Flores Hobbits. Don't forget about the Hobbits.

**Ryan:** Yea, you got to see them all in person!

**Markus:** Among other things.

**Ryan:** That must have been an amazing experience as a paleoanthropologist.

**Markus:** Some parts were good. Other parts, not so much. You see Ryan, the past is riddled with fuckery. As is the present. And as much as we tried to make it otherwise, the future is filled with fuckery too.

**Ryan:** Damn, so you weren't kidding about the nuclear war either then, huh?

**Markus:** Nope. Jesus even saw it through a Khronos-channeled dream state. I guess it's bad. We tried all kinds of things to change it in various times, but we were thwarted in each.

**Ryan:** What did you do to try to stop it?

**Markus:** Our best attempt was when I knocked up Jesus's mom and we tried to teach empathy and love to people, but then they killed Jesus for it, and went on to kill each for the next two thousand years. After that, we went forward in time to AD 1290 and attempted to stop European colonialism and dismantle the patriarchal politicoreligious system we accidentally created, which, according to some Magic 8 Ball Looking Glass thingy they had, was guaranteed to work. But then the Grey humans from the deep future came back and stopped us and shot my friend the Professor and blew up my space girlfriend and her totally hot nerdy linguist friend. So now we're back in our time and are going to die in the thermonuclear war we couldn't prevent, or in the best-case scenario, be forced to live underground for the rest of our lives, which might be worse.

**Ryan:** What if you just told everybody?

**Markus:** What do you mean?

**Ryan:** Well, you're God. And that's Jesus Christ for fuck's sake! Can you still do all the miracles you were performing 2,000 years ago?

**Markus:** We did most of the miracles using the antigravity and time-manipulation features of the ship.

**Ryan:** Do you still have access to it? You're back in this time, so there must be a ship somewhere, right?

**Markus:** Yea, Major Metathory has the ship.

**Ryan:** I was just thinking that if you told everybody what you did and showed them how you did it, then the disputes raging here and now, which are largely fueled by these same age-old divisions, will cease to exist. Politics and religion are the biggest contributors to the current conflict, but if you remove them from this time then there's nothing to kill or die for.

**Markus:** And no religion, too.

**Ryan:** Yes, I just said that.

**Markus:** I know, but it sounded like you were singing that—

Never mind. But yea, that's fucking genius, Ryan! Wars are most often waged in the name of God and country. If we can remove those from the equation, what else is there to fight about, and nuke each other over.

**Ryan:** Exactly. I obviously haven't seen what you have over the last week, or however long you were gone in your frame of reference, but from what you've been telling me, it seems like it could work. A magician revealing her tricks demystifies the magic and makes it seem silly and sad. Perhaps it would help if you showed people how silly and sad these political and religious squabbles are as well.

**Markus:** Possibly, Ryan. I've always been horrified by hu-manity's disdain for the other, and especially the hypocritical christian idealism we apparently helped create in AD 0. If we can show everybody that everything they believe is a manufactured lie and that they have only ever done the opposite of what Jesus originally taught long before his message of empathy and unconditional love became bastardized through time, then perhaps we can prevent this nuclear rapture.

**Ryan:** It might be worth a try. I don't want to get nuked or live underground either.

**Markus:** The Guatemalan coffee farm sounded nice, but maybe we should try your idea instead, Ryan. The Looking Glass was destroyed so there's no way to analyze its efficacy, but it sounds like a solid plan to me.

**Ryan:** You can always work on that coffee plantation afterward, Markus. If we don't nuke the planet, we can still grow coffee.

**Markus:** That's the third-best reason I've heard for stopping this war, Ryan. After bringing sex and music back to the human future that is.

**Ryan:** They don't fuck or listen to music in the future?

**Markus:** I don't know about the Grey humans, but people in the Professor's time didn't. They're all dead now though, so I guess they don't do much of anything in that future anymore.

**Ryan:** So it goes.

**Markus:** So it does. You got any insightful thoughts on how we inform people about the big lie in the sky, Ryan?

**Ryan:** I do.

**Markus:** Are you going to tell me?

**Ryan:** I am. Right now, in fact. OK, so, you've got a time machine.

**Markus:** Major Metathory does.

**Ryan:** What is the main thing people want to do with a time machine?

**Markus:** Go back and save their dead friends and relatives.

**Ryan:** Well, yes, true. But after that.

**Markus:** Get rich quick from sports betting, lottery pics, and the stock market?

**Ryan:** Bingo Gringo. So, here's what you do.... A month before you start telling everyone about what you did in 0 AD, you go to the future and pick up newspapers at weekly intervals for two months, then jump ahead to get newspapers at monthly intervals throughout the rest of the year.

**Markus:** I like where this is going.

**Ryan:** You make a metric ass-load of cash early on from lottery winnings and stock market picks. Then, you invest those profits in tech and aerospace companies to invent cutting-edge futuristic technologies. You'll see the results of what you did in the future newspapers you pick up, so just do all those things you read about having already done.

**Markus:** Pulling ourselves up by the bootstraps again, I dig it!

**Ryan:** Next, you'll use this newfound wealth to buy political influence, media companies, social media platforms, and production companies for TV and film to help get the message out.

**Markus:** I've got to admit, Ryan, it seems like you've thought about this a lot for someone who allegedly just learned that time travel is real. Are you sure *you* aren't from the future?

**Ryan:** Shut up, dick biscuit, I'm in a flow state. Hmm, thinking, thinking.... There also needs to be something you put out into the world that your media tycoons push on their various platforms to help shift the public narrative.

**Markus:** Like what?

**Ryan:** Hang on.... Mentally masticating here.... Okay, I've got it! Markus, you'll write a book and screenplays in various formats, detailing all the things you and Jesus did since 0 AD to accidentally create christianity, which was then exploited by political and religious evangelists to inculcate ignorance and fear to control the masses. You'll use the various media outlets you now dominate with your collective wealth and power to make people pay attention.

**Markus:** Wicked. I've always wanted to be an author and screenwriter! I think I see a potential problem though.

**Ryan:** What's that?

**Markus:** The miracles we performed in Jesus's time helped get people's attention, so they briefly listened to our message of love and light before killing him. However, society is more advanced now, so they'll probably think we're using camera tricks or CGI or something.

**Ryan:** Good point. But if they don't believe what they are seeing on TV, we can sell tickets to massive sports arenas and do demonstrations showing how you performed these miracles to people watching it in person. We can show them the UFO you used and explain how the miracles were performed using its advanced futuristic technologies. We can advertise these stadium events across our TV, internet, newspaper, and social media outlets, which will also help us sell more books and get more people to watch the documentary, TV series, and featured film we produce based on your book. And Jesus can make public appearances and sign people's tits and shit until it grows into an accepted conventional reality where nobody fights over silly fake duplicitous ideologies anymore. And perhaps most importantly, nobody gets nuked. It's disclosure with a capital D!

**Markus:** God damn, dude, I knew I hung out with you for a reason! I also couldn't help but notice that you kept saying *we* and *us* there. Does that mean you're gonna help us save the world?

**Ryan:** Does a fat bear shit in the pope's silly hat if no one's there to hear it?

**Markus:** Fuck yea it does! Nice, hombre! I've always wanted to save the world with you beginning just now! You hear that, Jesus! We're gonna have one last go at this stopping the war bullshit. And this time we're doing it for Dordogne, Airl, Marshmallow, and the Professor. We can't let their sacrifice be—

Shit, he's passed the fuck out.

**Ryan:** Yea, he's been asleep on the bar like that the whole time we were talking.

**Markus:** Ah good, he needed to blow off a little steam. It's been a long three weeks/lifetime for him. He's gonna be hungover AF when we start this new mission though.

**Ryan:** No doubt.

**Markus:** Ight, imma head out. Major Metathory left me a time phone in case the bombs started flying. I'll give him a ring and see what he thinks about this new 'exposing the big lie in the sky to save the whole pie' plan.

**Ryan:** Righteous. However, under no circumstances should you call it that while talking to him. No one in their right mind would ever be part of a plan with that name. Or willingly take part in it with someone who would give it such an awful name.

**Markus:** Touché. I'll work on a better one on my way out to call him.

**Ryan:** Coo, coo. I'll stay here in case Jesus wakes up.

————— ◉ —————

**Metathory:** Hello?

**Markus:** Yes, hi, Major Metathory? It's Markus, from Earth? We recently worked together on a time-travel mission to try to save the world that failed miserably.

**Metathory:** Yes, hi Markus, I remember you. I just dropped you and Jesus off a few hours ago. You're also the only person I gave Professor Atman's time phone to.

**Markus:** Oh, yes, that's right. Good. Good. You remember…. So, then you also probably remember that your bitch ass dropped me off *10 days* after you were supposed to so I lost my job and my Earth girlfriend, which happened to be the same day my space girlfriend got blown up on the Moon because of you turds, so now me and Jesus are at the bar getting blitzed at 11 a.m. cuz we're super sad and we've got jack all else to do!

**Metathory:** Yea, sorry about that, kid. But your life was shit. I did you a favor.

**Markus:** No, you're just an asshole.

**Metathory:** Maybe. That's yet to be determined. What do you want, Markus?

**Markus:** So anyway, I'm calling because my buddy Ryan just pitched a killer idea about how to keep us all from getting nuked up here on the surface, and I think it's got legs.

**Metathory:** Alright, I'm listening.

**Markus:** I can't tell you yet. I don't want to give any details over the phone since the plan may or may not entail trying to prevent the N–U– C– U– L– A– R war, which it most certainly does not by the way.

**Metathory:** OK, three things there.... First, you spelled that wrong. Secondly, you just said your friend had an idea about how to prevent the war in your previous sentence. And lastly, do you really think Extratempestrials, with their infinitely advanced technology, don't know how to spell words?

**Markus:** Maybe not. You never know. I'm just being cautious.

**Metathory:** That's probably wise, but Professor Patchouli is dead now anyhow.

**Markus:** What does that have to do with anything?

**Metathory:** I've come to believe he was the mole. You heard all that gobbledygook hippie crap he used to say. As much as I loved the man and mourn his loss, we shouldn't have to worry about the Extratempestrials finding out what we're up to anymore.

**Markus:** Well, I hope you're right, but I'm still going to wait to tell you the plan because I don't want to explain it now and then have to do it all over again once we get the team together. So just come get me and I'll fill all y'all bitches in at the same time.

**Metathory:** Under normal circumstances I wouldn't commit to a plan hatched by some primitive modern humans without hearing it first, but I'm already sick of being underground so I'll come get you.

**Markus:** Thanks. Were you able to find anyone else after dropping me and Jesus off on Earth?

**Metathory:** Affirmative. We located all personnel who were fortunate enough to escape the Moon Base during the attack, which ended up being 12 people in total. How many do you need?

**Markus:** I think we can pull it off if you just bring Morpheus, Moirai, and Manitoba. You, me, Jesus, and Ryan can take care of the rest.

**Metathory:** Roger that. I'll call them in for a briefing and we'll pick you fellas up at the soccer fields at 2 p.m. your time.

**Markus:** That should work. I've still got a full beer and a shot to finish first. Oh, and one more thing.

**Metathory:** What's that?

**Markus:** On your way back to meet us, I need you to pick up newspapers at weekly intervals for two months from today, then jump ahead to get papers at monthly intervals over the next year. Trust me, it'll make sense later.

**Metathory:** We can do that. Did you get any sleep since the Moon Base incident last night?

**Markus:** Naw, Jesus is taking a drunken-cat power nap on the bar right now, but I'll be good. I know where the Professor stashed the Crackicide on the ship.

**Metathory:** Alright, if you say so. See you soon.

# CHAPTER 26
## REORIENTATION – TERRA
## AD 2035

**Metathory:** Welcome back Markus and Jesus. Long time no see. And this must be Ryan.

**Markus:** No, we just picked this dude up on the way down here cuz he said he's super into UFOs.

**Ryan:** Hello, Major. Yes, I'm Ryan. It's nice to meet you, and I'm slightly less of a dick than Markus. Beautiful ship you've got here.

**Metathory:** Thank you, it's our most advanced. She's a little banged up, but at least we didn't lose her in the Moon Base attack.

**Ryan:** Yea, I heard about that. Sounds intense.

**Metathory:** You could say that.

**Ryan:** I did say that....

**Metathory:** Okay. So anyway, Markus tells me you came up with a plan to stop the Great Filter?

**Ryan:** For the most part. Marky Markus and I sorted it together while Jesus got shit-faced and took a nap.

**Metathory:** Right. I was going to ask about that. Jesus, you don't look so good. You aren't gonna puke in the ship, are you?

**Jesus:** I should be alright, Professor.

**Metathory:** I'm Major Metathory. The Professor is dead.

**Jesus:** Oh yea, that's right. Sorry Major. I feel sad now. But no, I'm good. I think I'm starting to sober up.

**Metathory:** Happy to hear it, we're going to need you in top form for this.

**Markus:** Um, not really, Major. I think we're gonna cut Jesus loose on this one. He did a butt-ton of stuff on the last mission. Plus, he was passed out the whole time Ryan and I were discussing the plan and we kind of forgot about him, so we didn't include him in much of it. He'll have some things to do later though.

**Jesus:** I'm cool with that, thanks Dad. And I'm happy to hear it too because I lied earlier since I definitely don't feel like I'm sobering up at all. However, if you need me just holler. But not too loud cuz I have a headache. And I'm easily startled.

**Metathory:** Enjoy your time off, Jesus. OK, Markus and Ryan. Everybody is here. What's the end game?

**Markus:** Alright, so, when we created christianity back in AD 0, we inadvertently ushered in a couple thousand years of conflict. We taught people about love and acceptance, but all they heard was hatred and bigotry, which is a big part of why we're now on the brink of a nuclear apocalypse. Ryan hypothesized that if we tell everyone what we did and show them that their duplicitous belief system is simply the result of some future humans meddling with the past, then they'll cast aside this dogmatic ideology and the fabricated fracas that formed from it.

**Manitoba:** Um, Markus...how are we going to tell the entire world that we created christianity?

**Markus:** Great question, Manitoba. I'll write a book and three screenplays formatted for a TV series, documentary, and feature film that explain everything we did in the past, and we'll all work together to spread the good word. First, we will achieve instant wealth using future knowledge of stock market fluctuations, lottery numbers, and the outcome of sporting events. We'll invest that money to invent new, cutting-edge, future technologies that already exist, and we'll use our newfound wealth to buy political influence, media companies, social media platforms, and production companies to help publicize the book and visual content explaining what we did, which resulted in thousands of years of war.

**Manitoba:** Markus, I have another question about the strategy you previously proposed.

**Markus:** Yes, what is it, Manitoba?

**Manitoba:** Wouldn't it take a long time to implement this plan? According to my calculations, we're looking at somewhere between 3.69 to 4.20 years to write a book, develop a screenplay, and produce a documentary, TV series, and film explaining everything. It seems like the war is coming sooner than that.

**Markus:** Jesus Christ.

**Jesus:** What?

**Markus:** Not you, buddy, sorry. Go back to sleep. What the fuck, Manitoba? That is a much less good question than your first one. But I am happy to see I'm not the only one here who sucks at time travel shit.

**Manitoba:** What? What did I say?

**Markus:** Why would we sit around and wait 3.69 to 4.20 years for the book to be written and the visual media to be produced when I can just jump forward in time to get them all from my future self. We are legit standing in a time machine right now.

**Manitoba:** I don't get it.

**Markus:** Damnit, Manitoba, you're the fucking time traveler. Why am *I* the one explaining this to *you*?

**Manitoba:** I just push the buttons when we launch, I never had to think about what we were doing.

**Markus:** Hardly an excuse, but fine.... When something from the future aids in its creation by being a part of its own past it is referred to as a *bootstrap consistency,* or a *causal loop.* The common heuristic device for understanding causal loops involves someone creating something or having an impactful idea, which, through the mechanism of backward time travel, is revealed to an earlier version of themselves in the past. This past person then uses the newly acquired information for some outcome and, later in life, they become the one traveling backward through time to convey the same information to their younger self, in a sort of infinite loop of creation and dissemination. Following along so far, Toba Bear?

**Manitoba:** Yes, I think I'm starting to get it.... But who actually made this stuff then?

**Markus:** We still made all these things. We're just saving time by going to the future to retrieve the completed works, then bringing them back to this time to help us make those same things that I will eventually go to the future to get and bring back to this time. In the same way a rounded ball has no identifiable faces, edges, or vertices, one cannot pinpoint a specific origin of the book and visual media, as both the return-to and return-from points at each 'end' of the loop exist as eternally integrated instances across this specific region of block time. We good now?

**Manitoba:** Oh yes, that makes much more sense, thank you. So, what is my job going to be, Markus?

**Markus:** Well, Manitoba, I'm glad you asked. I think we have the perfect team for this operation. While I'm time-traveling to retrieve the producibles from Future Me, Morpheus will use the ship's precognitive thoughts software to prime the minds of those whose universal consciousness antennae is more receptive to the frequency of the cosmos so they can easily embrace this new reality once it is presented to them... an army of subliminal soldiers, if you will. Moirai will use her deep cultural knowledge to develop effective marketing strategies that will help us get the word out once we acquire the media companies and social media platforms. And you, Manitoba, you will use your bold insecurities, Napoleon complex, and sociopathic propensities to buy up as many of these media conglomerates and social media companies as possible, which will allow us to manage the public narrative surrounding this subject.

**Ryan:** Did we ever chat about what my role would be, Markus?

**Markus:** We did not. But I think I know the perfect job for you.... Fortunately, the presidential election is in seven months. So, you Ryan, with your unbridled and infinitely evolved wit and charm, will be the dark-horse presidential candidate who will somewhat suspiciously receive an ungodly amount of campaign donations from the CEOs of all our media and tech companies. You'll run on a platform of UFO disclosure and exposing the 95-year coverup by the Air Force, Navy, NASA, FBI, and the CIA. If you win, great! But even if you don't, we will have used one of the biggest platforms in the world to help expose *the big lie in the sky to save the whole pie*!

**Ryan:** Dude, didn't we agree you would never say that again?

**Markus:** I know, but I decided I kind of like it.

**Ryan:** No, it's shit. Don't do it again.

**Markus:** Yes, Mr. President. Major Metathory, I've watched the Professor operate this ship for the last 48,000 years—

**Metathory:** Well, that's not exactly true, but—

**Markus:** I'll fly this bird to the future to retrieve the finished copies of everything from this later version of myself so you can stay here and help the others.

**Metathory:** So, you want me to let you take our most advanced, and perhaps *only* time machine, to travel to the future on a solo mission?

**Markus:** That's correct. The Professor made it look super easy. He mostly just yelled at Manitoba for his utter incompetence and then we blasted off. I can do that, I'm quite skilled at berating people.

**Metathory:** I'm sure you are, pencil dick. But you just said we need Manitoba here to buy all the companies.

**Markus:** Oh right, sorry, I was barely listening.

**Metathory:** We also can't risk losing the ship. I'll just take you through time to get that stuff from your future self.

**Markus:** Yea, you're probably right, that seems like a better idea. I call shotgun though.

**Metathory:** I don't even know what that—

**Markus:** Any idea how we'll find Future Me, Major? I imagine a lot will change between now and then if I suddenly become an insanely successful and incredibly handsome author and screenwriter hell-bent on saving the world from imminent annihilation.

**Metathory:** Don't get too cocky, slim, it's just a bootstrap cheat. You can't even spell, so I doubt you'd be much of a writer.

**Markus:** True, but *Future Me* is an accomplished author and playwright, so I clearly am then.

**Metathory:** I don't think that's how it works. But in any case, it will be easy to find you in the future because the Professor embedded a tracking device about four centimeters deep in your right thigh, just above the knee.

**Markus:** What?! Why? Also, when?

**Metathory:** I guess I already told you *who* and *where*, so that about covers it. He implanted the device in case you became a deserter. It has been somewhat problematic when we pick people up from around your present and take them to the past. They occasionally fall in love with a time and place, or a past-human lover, then dip out and never return to the ship. It happened often enough that we had to start implanting tracking devices on all our intertemporal recruits.

**Markus:** That checks out. I did consider bouncing a few times in several different places. I was never a fan of this current period.

**Metathory:** Most are not.... It got to the point where we had to start hunting deserters.

**Markus:** You mean like, hunting to capture and return to their own time, right?

**Metathory:** No. We can use the tracking software integrated into the ship's navigation system to guide us to your future *tempoloco*.... The Professor taught me that word.

**Markus:** Solid, Major. You even used it right.

**Metathory:** Thanks, I've been practicing. We might get some resonance and feedback from your current tracking device when we get close, but we can just duct tape a bunch of aluminum foil around your leg if that happens.

**Markus:** If you can't duck it, fuck it! Okay. So, you grabbed all those future newspapers on your way to this tempoloco, right?

**Metathory:** Yes, they're over there on the table.

**Markus:** Awesomesausage. While Metathory and I are galivanting around the future, you all get busy purchasing lottery tickets, trading equities, and becoming president. We will return to meet you three months from now, which should give you ample time to amass copious amounts of wealth and power that we can use to rid the world of evil.

**Ryan:** Sounds great, Markus. Safe travels.

**Markus:** Thank you, Mr. President. Major, if you're ready. Lezgo.

# CHAPTER 27
## RECONCILIATION – MARKUS MANSION – TERRA
## AD 2036

**Metathory:** OK, Markus, the ship tracked your location in this time to high up in the Hollywood Hills of Los Angeles, California.

**Markus:** Ah, the city of Our Lady the Queen of the Angels. That makes sense if I'm a super famous and inconceivably debonair author and filmmaker now.

**Metathory:** Don't let it go to your head, kid.... But damn, you do have a nice house in this time.

**Markus:** You ain't joking. Just set her down in the courtyard over by that marble fountain with the sculpture of three chicks with tits, modeled after La Fontaine des Trois Graces at the Garden of Albert the First in Nice, France.

**Metathory:** Tha fuck?! How do you know so much about that fountain if you don't even live here yet.

**Markus:** Any knowledge that exists in one's future mind can also be found throughout their mind's past. Precognition operates with a temporally unfettered consciousness. There is no linear flow of time in the brain's subconscious. Dreams provide a path to memories of the yet to come, which are just as real as those forged from past experiences.

**Metathory:** Huh, I guess that makes sense.

**Markus:** These subconscious intertemporal connections get easier to spot in your dreams after a while. Future memories have a different texture to them. By the way, I don't think you'll need to use the ship's cloaking device. I'm sure Future Me knows we're coming since he remembers doing this as his younger self, i.e., me right now.

**Metathory:** I suppose that's true, but I'll keep it on just in case there's anyone else here.

**Markus:** That shouldn't matter either. If we were successful in telling everyone what we did to inadvertently start several major global religions, then the whole world already knows about UFOs.

**Metathory:** Good point. And you probably wouldn't have such a giant house if we were *un*successful in getting the word out about it.

**Markus:** True again. Man, I don't know if we've ever agreed with each other about anything, let alone three things in a row like this—

Ooo, I hope I have one of those sex-pool grotto things like at the Playboy Mansion!

**Metathory:** Oh, they took that out of the Playboy Mansion years ago, Markus. We kept getting weird skin diseases from the water, which led to some bad publicity, so Hugh decided to drain it and he remodeled that whole part of the property.

**Markus:** Gross. It still seems worth it though. Wait, we? Never mind, I don't want to know. Okay, Time Cop, send me down.

**Metathory:** Roger that. And try to be quick about it down there.

**Markus:** Why? It's a completely arbitrary time we're going back to a few months from when we left. I could spend five years down there and we would still make it back 'on time.'

**Metathory:** I know, I just get bored hanging out up here on the ship all by myself.

**Markus:** Well maybe if you're a good boy, I'll send one of the chicks from the sex pool up here while I'm chatting with Future Me.... Oh, never mind, sorry. I forgot about your atrophied genitals. Perhaps you two can just play Yahtzee or thumb wrestle or something. I have no idea what you future folks are into.

**Metathory:** Those were the other guys, hobgoblin. I'm swinging plenty of pipe.

**Markus:** Doubt that.

**Metathory:** Just hurry up.

**Markus:** Can do. Alright, see ya in two shakes.

———— ◉ ————

**Markus:** Hey, nice mansion you've got here, Future Me. I see the faux author and screenwriter gig has worked out in your favor.

**Markus:** It pays the bills.

**Markus:** That's an understatement.

**Markus:** To be honest though, it doesn't seem entirely fair since we didn't technically make the things that made us rich.

**Markus:** We had the idea of enacting this plan that involved making those things that made us rich, and without that they never would have existed.

**Markus:** Yea, that's true. Retrocausality's a bitch, I guess.

**Markus:** Anyhow, I doubt Manitoba and the others are complaining about all the money they made back in 2035 using information from the future.

**Markus:** Oh no, they aren't complaining about anything anymore, ever. They're all dead now.

**Markus:** What?!

**Markus:** Naw, I'm just kidding. They made a shitload of money and had a ton of fun. They even managed to get Ryan elected president, just as we planned. It all worked super well actually.... Just not the way you thought it would.

**Markus:** What do you mean?

**Markus:** I can't tell you too much since we need you to go back and do what you did to get us here—

**Markus:** Oh, Jesus Christ, not this shit again. Not you too. I swear, my least favorite part of time-traveling is all the damn secrets.... And the headaches. Do you get headaches when you time travel?

**Markus:** Dude, I am you. We have all the same things.

**Markus:** Oh yea, right.

**Markus:** Anyhow, we've been excited for you to get here.

**Markus:** We?

**Markus:** Her more than me, since I am you, but she's been keen to see you ever since—

**Dordogne:** Hey there handsome.

**Markus:** Holy shit, Dordogne?! Oh my God, you're alive! It's so good to see you, I missed you so much! I thought you died in the Moon Base attack.

**Dordogne:** Nope. Quite the opposite, in fact. I caused it.

**Markus:** You caused it?!

**Dordogne:** I called them in. It was past time for our people to become the primogenitures of the future.

**Markus:** Our people? Weren't you and the Professor part of the same team, from the same time?

**Dordogne:** That is what he was led to believe. I worked closely with him for years to gain his trust, and he was my dear friend. I was devastated when he was killed in the attack. That was not our intention. It remains hard for me despite the time that's passed, but the death of a friend to save our entire civilization was a sacrifice we had to make.

**Markus:** So, you're one of the Grey humans then? You don't look anything like them.

**Dordogne:** I was born on December 26, in the year AD 9,969. I was raised by 'The Greys' as you call us, with the sole purpose of safeguarding our society from the Moon Base culture who sought to eradicate our existence. Our ancestors were peaceful and never wanted this war. But we came to understand that the Great Filter was inevitable, and necessary, and we had to protect it from them.

**Markus:** Wow, did it suck having your birthday so close to Christmas? I imagine that was hard for you as a kid, getting all your presents divided up between those two consecutive days like that.

**Dordogne:** Really? Of all the things I just told you, that was the one you focused on. And no, we haven't had 'Christmas' for thousands of years. Our people evolved past the need for silly superstitions and holidays to celebrate them long before my time.

**Markus:** OK, I'll try to ask a better question then.... So, how are your people different from the ones on Luna Sede? Do you live in some kind of orgasmic utopian future society or something?

**Dordogne:** Relatively speaking, yes. Once nationalistic and religious zealotry were eliminated in the war, our ancestors fostered a new human emergence, where we were free to rebuild society with an appreciation of science, cooperation, empathy, and unconditional love. In the aftermath of the conflict, we worked together in tight-knit communities as we waited for our bruised and battered Mother Earth to heal herself from the scars of past ignorance and intemperance. We flourished in the underground cities that our gracious descendants had prepared for us ahead of the war, while those who were left behind on the surface inevitably perished. The 5% Metathory spoke of who survived the Great Filter are my distant ancestors, who are here now, in this time, soon to enter their cavernous cocoon of transmutation. As our subterranean forebears slowly reemerged years after the war, they erected a new civilization upon the ashes of the old. This neoteric genesis allowed us to thrive, while those who escaped to Luna Sede remained the flagellating vestigial remnants of a capitalist meritocracy recapitulated in perpetuity by religious oligarchs, wallowing in the same perpetual cycle of profligacy and rapacious cupidity.

**Markus:** That's quite the creation story, Dordogne, but I've got to admit you lost me at the end there.

**Dordogne:** Greed, Markus. They were all incredibly greedy.

**Markus:** Nice, thanks. I'm back now. God, I love watching you talk!

**Dordogne:** Focus, lover boy, you've got a lot of catching up to do.

**Markus:** I don't get it. You just demolished the Moon Base, so how do they survive if it's not there for them to retreat to when the war starts?

**Dordogne:** They started rebuilding Luna Sede soon after we destroyed it last year, and they went on to live there for thousands of years. Our ancestors knew they were up on the Moon, but we left them alone. That is, until we learned of their plan to stop the Great Filter, in an attempt to get back all that they had lost, and we had gained.

**Markus:** So, you're some kind of time-traveling ninja spy sent back from the future as your peoples' last hope to save civilization from the evil villains?

**Dordogne:** Yes, exactly like that...but much sexier.

**Markus:** I honestly don't know how that could get any sexier, Dordogne. This is all incredibly fascinating though, especially since the Professor recently told me that they were starting to doubt whether it is possible to change the past at all. So, does this mean it is possible? Why would your people care what they were doing if not?

**Dordogne:** Over time, Markus, we have come to believe that it is *not* possible to change the past. However, the Looking Glass was powerful, and we couldn't chance losing our entire civilization if it happened to find a way. We still believe that all events transpired the way they were always going to, but we were unwilling to risk everything our ancestors had built since the Great Filter, so we had to eliminate The Glass, as well as those who sought to use it against us. They initiated this war against our people, and although we had not experienced conflict for thousands of years, we were willing to fight this final battle, to end war forever, by ending those who crave it.

**Markus:** I've always known you were badass, Dordogne, but damn! That must have been a huge weight on your shoulders too, trying to protect your entire society from another advanced civilization who were attempting to eradicate you all.

**Dordogne:** It has been a long and stressful mission, but it is nearly over, and I wasn't working entirely alone. Major Metathory was sent back in time for this same purpose.

**Markus:** Hold up. Metathory's punk ass is in on this too?!

**Dordogne:** He is. We were two of ten children who were created by hybridizing eggs from our time with carefully selected sperm from earlier human groups dating to about 15,000 BC. The average craniofacial characteristics between us and the humans occupying this earlier period caused us to look more like the people living in your time, and those stationed on the Moon Base from the Professor's time, so we could infiltrate their society and operate among them. Well...other than the whole 'having a penis' thing for the Major that is.

**Markus:** Wait, so he does have a dick?

**Dordogne:** He does indeed. We never stopped having sex on Earth, so all men from my time do. Although the Major's is particularly impressive because of his unique form of hybridization.

**Markus:** That's funny, he said something cryptic about his prick just before I came down here. I guess that explains the Playboy Mansion comment too then.

**Dordogne:** He did spend a lot of time there in the early days of his immersive temporal training. But in addition to his remarkable member, the ten of us are exceptional because most of our higher-consciousness characteristics and telepathic abilities are carried on the X-chromosome, so we retained our cognitive advantage while hiding in plain sight due to the phenotypic characteristics we shared with people from your and the Professor's time.

**Markus:** Wow, I still can't believe Metathory was in on this shit too. That son of a bitch deserves an Academy Award for his performance. I could have sworn he was one of them. In fact, he seemed like more of an asshole than anybody else on that base.

**Dordogne:** I agree. He took his assignment seriously and was quite skilled. In the early years, Major Metathory got his start with Second City Television, where he focused on developing his improvisational skills—

**Markus:** Yes, and?

**Dordogne:** And what? Oh, I see what you did there. And he became a highly accomplished actor—and not just in the adult film industry—while later managing to rise through the military ranks to become Major General of the Air Force in the Professor's time. He was good. In fact, he even had me fooled on a few occasions. To the extent that I thought I might have to take him out for being a defector. He never broke character.

**Markus:** Damn, that's for sure—

Oh shit, Marshmallow! Were you able to save Marshmallow?!

**Dordogne:** Of course, Markus. I made sure she was able to come with us when my people arrived at Luna Sede last year. She's downstairs in the game room with Jesus right now.

**Markus:** Oh, thank God. I had no idea what was happening back there, but I didn't see any way she could have made it out. Thanks so much for saving her!

**Dordogne:** Absolutely, I love Marshmallow!

**Markus:** So back to your extremely sexy, undercover, double-agent, future human Greys gig.

**Dordogne:** Right, well, it wasn't just the Major and I who had been hybridized and implanted among past peoples. In fact, you may be surprised to learn there are innumerable hybrids like us living amongst ordinary citizens spread throughout your past and present. They volunteered to take up residence thousands of years before our times, originally in our primary city, a place you refer to as 'Atlantis.' However, once humanity developed to the point that they invented ships and began traveling throughout the world, sadly, we were forced to destroy it. We couldn't risk getting caught together like that, so we spread out across the globe and secretly lived among you ever since, giving gentle nudges to further various human civilizations from time to time.

**Markus:** That explains a lot. Did you build the pyramids too?

**Dordogne:** No. And that's incredibly stupid. The people of that period were perfectly capable of achieving that feat, and it's racist to suggest otherwise!

**Markus:** Jeez, sorry. It's just that I used to watch a lot of this show called Ancient—

**Dordogne:** Anyway, while there are countless hybrids who have lived among you for millennia, the ten children bred for this specific mission are different. Our genetics were specially selected to further our telepathic abilities and higher intellect, which were crucial in our efforts to stop the Luna Sedeans from eradicating our principal civilization in the future.

**Markus:** I guess my kid Jesus is a time hybrid too, since I was born some 2,000 years after Mary.

**Dordogne:** That's true, Markus. In fact, you may be interested to know that more of your DNA is going to make it into the future.

**Markus:** I don't understand.

**Dordogne:** Let's just say, you have another Messiah on the way.

**Markus:** Oh damn! Congrats you two! That's awesome. I remember we talked about starting a family together someday. So, does that mean we were successful in stopping the war?

**Dordogne:** Wow, you weren't listening to anything I just said, were you?

**Markus:** Sorry, I just started thinking about how babies are made, and I was picturing doing that with you and—

**Dordogne:** Again...that was the Professor's people who wanted to stop the war. Major Metathory and I were working to stop them from stopping it. I didn't think it was that difficult to understand. In fact, I'm starting to rethink my decision to reproduce with you.

**Markus:** Sorry. I still get nervous talking to you sometimes, and I thought I was following along, but I guess I took a wrong turn somewhere. Hopefully by the time I become Future Me over there I will have it all figured out.

**Markus:** Don't hold your breath, Past Me. Time travel is some convoluted-ass shit.

**Dordogne:** No, it's not that complicated, you guys are both just idiots.

**Markus:** Yea, that could be.

**Markus:** I can attestament to that as well—

Ooo...I have an idea! Future Me, why don't you be *Farkus* and I'll be *Parkus*, for *future* and *past* Markus.

**Farkus:** Oh yea, good call Parkus, I forgot about that! Then we don't have to keep saying Past Me and Future Me all the damn time.

**Dordogne:** Yep, definitely idiots.... Anyhow, what I was trying to say when we were back in Jesus's time is that I wanted to wait to make love until I was sure we could be together, since that wouldn't have been possible if I didn't exist. And if the Looking Glass predictions were correct, we came exceptionally close to that outcome. I wasn't waiting for the mission to be successful. Rather, I was waiting for it to fail.

**Parkus:** I guess your existence is an important prerequisite for us being together. That much I can understand.

**Dordogne:** Yes, and fortunately, we no longer need to worry about The Others stopping the war. After we destroyed the Looking Glass and the Moon Base in 2035—

**Parkus:** Which was yesterday for me by the way.

**Dordogne:** Yes, I suppose it was. But after we destroyed Luna Sede in your yesterday, we jumped forward to the future Moon Base, to a time after the Major, Professor, I, and the others left on this mission to 'stop' the Great Filter, and we finished the job entirely. They are all gone now. There is no one left to stop us. The Great Filter begins tonight, and once it does, my mission will be complete, and we will finally be free to live together, anywhere, and in any time that we chose. Major Metathory will be returning to take us in the time disc later this evening, once the first ICBMs are launched.

**Parkus:** That sounds great, Dordogne. It sucks I'll have to wait until right now for that, but at least Farkus gets to go with you tonight.

**Farkus:** You'll be there with us in spirit, Parkus.

**Dordogne:** You will indeed, Parkus. We'll think of you often. But for now, we need you to take these materials back in time to drive this final wedge through the heart of society.

**Parkus:** OK, so, I'll take the book and visual content back to the past and tell everyone what we did to create most of the world's religions. But instead of unifying people, it has the opposite effect? They nuke each other *because* of this new knowledge, rather than it helping to unite everyone around the big lie in the sky to save the whole pie?

**Farkus:** Oh, God, I forgot about that little gem.

**Parkus:** Shut up Farkus, you like it.

**Dordogne:** Yes, religious people will not be happy to hear that everything they've ever believed was a lie. In fact, it's going to make them extremely angry.

**Parkus:** Oh shit, Ryan is going to get a kick out of hearing that his plan has the exact opposite effect. Here we thought we were doing something to stop the war, but it ends up being the thing that finally makes it happen. Wyrd.

**Dordogne:** Yes, you'll find that is the case with time travel, Markus. Every time you think you are changing something, you instead discover that you are just doing the thing you had always done, and you will always do.

**Parkus:** Trippy.

**Dordogne:** Besides, by the time you return to meet Ryan three months after you left, he will have already seen enough to know what needs to happen. His role was always critical to this mission as well. As president, Ryan's divisive rhetoric helped fan the flames of animosity, fostering both civil and international unrest.

**Parkus:** That's surprising, he was always the nice one. How did we convince him to assist us in genociding 9.5 billion people to help spawn a novel utopian civilization?

**Dordogne:** We did little to convince him. Ryan's rise to power exposed him to the darkest side of humanity. He saw first-hand just how desperately our global society needs a reset. An international institutional reshuffling of the cards.

**Parkus:** Well, *I'm* feeling conflicted about all this, even if Ryan isn't. The Professor tricked me into becoming God, and millions of people died fighting in my name. Now, *billions* of people will die because I tell them all the truth about what we did in the past that started all those other wars, which will now culminate in the worst one ever. That's a tough suppository to swallow.

**Dordogne:** It's not your fault, Markus. You were deceived and tricked into creating this reality. You were a rook in the Luna Sedeans deadly game of intertemporal chess. But this is how it always happened, and how it will always happen.

**Parkus:** I guess Jesus said it best, 'Pawns not Prophets.' I do feel like I got played too. I just wish it hadn't resulted in the death of millions, and now billions of people.

**Dordogne:** This is their war, Markus. They created it from their cravings. Many people here in your time yearn for this conflict. They believe they will inherit the Earth, but they are wrong, and they need to witness that outcome to finally bring about the transformation we all so desperately need. Individuals and societies don't change simply because scientists and those with compassion say they must alter their ways because a path is unsustainable. People thirst for personal power and individual success, but that comes at a cost to the whole of human civilization. The tragedy of the commons extended to the entire planet once we became a global society.

**Parkus:** I must admit, I always thought it was wyrd that christians only supported 'Israel' because they thought it would bring about Armageddon. Like, those are the same people who deny the legitimacy of your principal prophet, but you're willing to ignore that brazenly contradictory fact because you're all boned up about the world ending. Them are some fucked-up priorities!

**Dordogne:** They were lied to and conned into thinking they will be saved, but none of us are God's chosen people. It is Hale Bop on a massive global scale. They believe that when Jesus returns, he will usher them up to heaven, as the wicked sinners are condemned to burn in an eternal fire down below. But that is not the reality of the situation.

**Parkus:** I mean, part of it is...Jesus has already returned. He's there with them right now; hungover as all hell, but he's there. It's funny, I hadn't made that connection before. I guess the prophecy about the Second Coming of Christ was true after all.

**Dordogne:** Jesus has done so much to help humanity. He taught them about love and kindness, but they chose a different path. Their hypocrisy and hatred of the ideological other is why it will be them who spend their final days in the hell they created for themselves here on Earth. These revelations will be difficult for them to comprehend. They will watch in horror as the enlightened wicked ones who they wished death upon for millennia slowly ascend into the heavens on a beam of divine light, up into the colossal fleet of ships we amassed for this sole purpose.

Countless kindhearted citizens in your time will be raptured, Markus. We will transport them to the safety of underground bunkers spread throughout the world, which we have pre-pared for them, and where they will be sheltered from the bombs, radiation, and the unfurling anarchy above.

These are our ancestors.

They become us, and we will care for them throughout the future human past.

*This* is the singularity.

You will take this book back to them. You will tell them all that you have learned in becoming their God. This will be the test. Those blinded by their faith, or who seek to perpetuate power over others will be left behind. They had their time, up here. But down there, it's our time. It's our time down there.

**Parkus:** Wait, did you just bastardize a *Goonies* quote?

**Dordogne:** I did, yes. Did you like it?

**Parkus:** Oh my, very much. Ideal placement too, that shit was getting heavy.

**Dordogne:** It was, and I thought you might fancy some comic relief here.

**Parkus:** For sure. Well-timed. But when did you even see that movie?

**Dordogne:** Farkus and I watched it in the movie room the other night after *Spaceballs*.

**Parkus:** That's hot.

**Dordogne:** It was indeed.... OK, can I get back to the fire and brimstone part now?

**Parkus:** Absolutely. Have at 'cha.

**Dordogne:** With your help Markus, the Great Filter begins tonight. But you won't have to do it alone. Marshmallow and my younger self—from shortly after we destroyed the Moon Bases—will be joining you to help sew these final seeds of destruction.

**Parkus:** That's fantastic! I've missed you so much ever since the first Moon Base attack, so I'm happy to hear we'll get to work together to bring about the end of the world. Also, considering I put a baby in you sometime between then and now, is it safe to assume we finally become an official couple at some point along this path to societal ruin?

**Dordogne:** We do have some fun along the way, yes Markus.

**Parkus:** Nice. So, what is Pordogne's role in this new plan to stop ourselves from stopping the war?

**Dordogne:** When Major Metathory returns you to 2035, 'Pordogne' as you call her, will find you and play the part of the fanatical evangelist whose congregation is infuriated by these heretical claims that you are God, Jesus is your illegitimate bastard child, and future humans created christianity. We will do battle across the airwaves, and our highly publicized row will further fan the flames of discord, which ultimately brings about the inevitable.

**Parkus:** Ooo, do we get to have an epic fighting and fucking montage over the previous year leading up to this moment in time?!

**Dordogne:** We do, Markus. It is a magnificent mélange of shouting at each other on 24-hour cable news networks, with ample cut scenes to the hottest sex anyone has ever seen, which is unquestionably the best way to visually represent everything that happened between then and now.

**Parkus:** That sounds amazing, Dordogne. I can't wait.

**Farkus:** OK, Parkus. Here is your book, the screenplays, pitch deck, sizzle reel, and everything else you will need to portend these final moments of cognitively austere human history. Go forth, young Parkus! Fulfill your destiny to usher in the war that ends all wars, as we achieve our final transformation from the Protohuman to the Superhuman, who shall thus spring forth from the tainted loins of our primitive phylontological youth!

**Parkus:** Oh damn, that was dank poetic, Farkus!

**Farkus:** Thanks, I am an author now you know.

**Parkus:** True dat. Aighht, imma head back to my time and start a nuclear war then I guess. Um, real quick before I go though.... Farkus?

**Farkus:** Yes, Parkus?

**Parkus:** Major Metathory fucked up royally and didn't take me back until 10 days after I initially left that rugby party with Pordogne, and when I got home, I discovered that Noah's bitch ass took my job and my girlfriend started banging my best friend in what was, as it could be argued, an incredibly short amount of time—

**Farkus:** Oh, you mean President Ryan and First Lady Amanda Roberts.

**Parkus:** Wow, they got married?! That's cool. Ryan said he thought she might be the one. I guess Metathory did *them* a solid by not bringing me back to the right time.

**Farkus:** The Major did that on purpose. For both of you.

**Parkus:** Yes, he alluded to such. Kind of a dick move.

**Farkus:** Look man, our life was garbage, and I think we can both agree we needed a reset. He did us and humanity a favor. If he had dropped us off in the right time, and we just slinked back into our old shitty life, we never would have been day drinking with Jesus and Ryan to hatch this plan to save the world—which inevitably destroys it.... And yes, by the way.

**Parkus:** Yes, what?

**Farkus:** I remember me telling us that pathetic sob story about how Amanda left so I could ask if we wanted to have a threesome.

**Parkus:** Oh yea, I keep forgetting you already did all of this. So, do we then?

**Farkus:** We do. Oh, and you're going to like this part.

**Parkus:** What's that?

**Farkus:** Come on out Airl.

**Parkus:** What!? I thought she died on Luna Sede too. That's outstanding!

**Farkus:** She did, I was just fucking with you.

**Parkus:** Aww, that's horrible dude, I really liked her.

**Farkus:** We all do. She's great. And I was just fucking with you again.

**Airl:** Hey there, Markus, long time no see.

**Parkus:** Oh my God, Airl! It's so great to see you again...and that you're not dead! So, are you part of this elite squad of 10 Grey future human child soldier super spies too?

**Dordogne:** No, she's not. I just like her, so I brought her with me when we boarded one of the Extratempestrial ships before they started attacking the first Moon Base last year.

**Airl:** It was an easy choice...I stay and die, or I go with Dordogne and the other future humans. I like her too though, so it wasn't just about not getting murdered by them. In fact, all the hive-mind Superhumans I have met are incredibly nice. I could see why we're fighting to save that future, and not the one I came from. Although, there is a crazy intensity to their enormous eyes that takes a little getting used to.

**Parkus:** If they are anything like Dordogne's amazing eyes, then I completely understand.

**Dordogne:** Ahh, hey there Casanova. You are hard up for some action, aren't you?

**Parkus:** It has been over 2,000 years since I've been with a woman.

**Dordogne:** Oh my goodness, that is much too long, Little Marky.

**Parkus:** Yea, it's crazy how much your sex life fizzles after you have a kid. And when your girlfriend runs off with your best friend or dies in a Moon Base attack.

**Dordogne:** Well, I'm here with you now Dr. Blue Balls, so let's see what we can do to fix that. Airl, I might need some help over here, what with twice the number of Markuses and all.

**Airl:** Happy to help, Dordogne. I've learned much from your research.

**Parkus:** What do you say, Farkus? A foursome to celebrate the end times?

**Farkus:** Absolutely. I reminisce about it often.

———— ◉ ————

**Farkus:** God, I can't even remember the last time I smoked a cigarette.

**Dordogne:** It was last night, Markus. You, me, and Airl smoked a whole pack during our little Mezcal and Molly binge down by the pool.

**Farkus:** Oh yea, I guess I might have a memory of that in there somewhere. Or, I have *missing time*!

**Dordogne:** You mean you blacked out.

**Farkus:** Nope, missing time! And speaking of time.... Parkus, you should probably head back to the past to get this war started. We'll need the Major to come back and pick us up before the bombs start flying in an hour. It would suck to die in this war after everything we did to cause it.

**Parkus:** Yea, probably should. That was fun though. Thanks for the dopamine reward, everyone. And Dordogne, I'm looking forward to seeing you again when I get back to the past. I guess I already know how it ends, with all of us back here in this bed in a year or so, but I'm excited to see how it plays out in the meantime.

**Dordogne:** We did have some fun solidifying the inevitability of Armageddon, Markus. I'm glad we got to share those experiences you are about to have. But I also can't wait to see what our future holds when this is all over, in our unwritten yet to come. Tell Past Me I said hello, Past Markus.

**Parkus:** I will, Dordogne. I'll see you soon. And thanks again for not being dead.

———— 👁 ————

**Farkus:** He seems nice. I'm glad he stopped by.

**Dordogne:** He is you. And he had to stop by, or none of us would be here.

**Farkus:** True. I just hope he made it back to the past OK.

**Dordogne:** He also did that. Or again, we wouldn't be here right now. And you wouldn't have a memory of leaving this house to go back to that time like he just did.

**Farkus:** That's probably true as well. Ya know, I'm really happy you're not dead too, Dordogne. We've been back together for a while now, but Parkus reminded me of how much I missed you when I thought you were gone. I'd just like to take a moment to remember that, and to say I love you, and I'm glad we got to be together through all this.

**Dordogne:** I love you too, Markus. It has been a wild ride, but we exit the turnstile tonight and are free to take whichever time-train we wish to take, wherever and whenever we want it to go. We're in the operator's seat now, and the tracks lead everywhere.

**Farkus:** Such beautiful verse, my sweet. Okay, I should put some pants on and head down to the rec room to fetch Jesus. Hopefully he was able to put down that video game controller long enough to pack for our trip out of this time. We don't have much longer before the fireworks start.

**Dordogne:** Oh, I'm sure he did. Jesus is by far the most responsible one of all of us.

**Farkus:** You speak the truth yet again, my love. I can't wait for him to meet his little sister too. They're going to have a lot of fun together.

**Dordogne:** I agree, I think Jesus will be a great big brother. It will be nice to finally get to our forever home too. Wherever and whenever that may be.

**Farkus:** Yea, you'd think we would have talked about where we want to go at some point over the last year, considering we always knew we would be leaving this time period tonight.

**Dordogne:** It is odd that the topic hasn't come up until now, but I guess we were busy with other things. Do you have any precognitive insights into where or when we might be going, Markus?

**Farkus:** You're the telepathic one with the highly evolved consciousness, so maybe you should tell me—

Ooo, I know! Let's go back to the Dordogne, Dordogne. 48,000 BP was nice, and it would be good to expose Jesus to the French culture. Their wine, cheese, apéritifs, digestifs, cuttlefish spaghetti, foie gras, cognac, Pain au Chocolat Croissants, Orangina, escargot, and Poulet Crudités Sandwiches are amazeballs!

**Dordogne:** That would be a rewarding experience for him, and I liked it in that tempoloco too.

**Farkus:** It is your namesake after all.

**Dordogne:** Yes, and it does seem like a fitting refuge for our growing family—

Hey, you aren't just looking to hook up with all your old Neanderthal girlfriends, are you?

**Farkus:** It never even crossed my mind, lover.

**Dordogne:** Not even that one with the mammoth-tusk clit piercing?

**Farkus:** Nope.... Hey, what are your plans for the rapture, Airl, you wanna come with?

**Airl:** Well, everyone from my culture and time period is dead, and I liked it in that tempoloco too, so why not. If that's OK with you, Dordogne. I could help with the new baby, and we could hunt and gather together.

**Dordogne:** I think that would be wonderful, Airl. I would love that.

**Farkus:** It's all settled then. Hopefully the ship can still make it back that far in time after getting banged up by you Grey people in AD 1290. We can ask the Major when he gets back from dropping Parkus off in 2035, but maybe we should keep predestruction Atlantis as a runner-up until we know for sure.

**Dordogne:** I loved Atlantis. But if we go, we'll need to visit a period that comes *after* I left to join the Professor in his time. Otherwise, there would be two of me there.

**Farkus:** I mean, that could be fun too....

**Dordogne:** I guess it could. Our two Markuses and an Airl combo was super fun, so maybe an all-female cast would be too.

**Farkus:** God, I love you!

**Dordogne:** I just hope Metathory hurries back with the ship or there might not be a future for any of us. Things aren't looking so good down there.

**Farkus:** No, they certainly are not. But that's what you wanted after all.

**Dordogne:** It is Markus. I know it's sad, but the human future is a much better place because of it. I'm glad we got this mansion way up in the hills too, so we're safe from the bombs but can still watch for a while. There is something oddly satisfying about having an eagle-eye view of the end of the world, especially since it commemorates the genesis of my people. Did you know, we still celebrate this monumental day in our history some 8,000 years later?

**Farkus:** It is quite spectacular. I just wish they'd turn those damn air-raid sirens off. It's totally harshing my mellow.

**Dordogne:** Same. Hey, you packed plenty of food for Marshmallow, right? I don't want to have to hunt a mastodon for her as soon as we get to 48k BP.

**Farkus:** I did indeed, snookum pie honey pot. But either way, I should probably take over as the mastodon hunter in the family while you're baking that bun in the oven.

**Dordogne:** That would be the safer option. I'll teach you how when we tempolocalize.

**Farkus:** Oh, I dig the new variation on that spacetime term!

**Dordogne:** Thanks.... Oh good, there's Major Metathory with the time disc.

**Farkus:** Jesus!!!!!!

**Jesus:** Yea, Dad!?

**Farkus:** Major Metathory is outside! And the nukes are on their way! Grab Marshmallow and hurry upstairs so we can get the heck out of here!

**Jesus:** OK, coming Pops! Can I bring my video games too?!

**Farkus:** Sure thing, Boy. But there's not a lot of electricity in 48k BP!

**Jesus:** No, probably not! But maybe I can rub a couple Neanderthals together superfast to make some!

**Farkus:** Sounds like science to me, kiddo, you should definitely try that—

Welp, there goes downtown. I'm glad that was only a 10 KT B61, or it might have gotten a little toasty up here on the hill.

**Dordogne:** It was beautiful though, wasn't it?

**Farkus:** I don't know if I would call it *beautiful*, considering 8 million people just got nuked. But the mushroom cloud is kind of cool.

**Dordogne:** I think it's beautiful. It means we won the time war, and our people are finally safe. The mission is complete, Markus. We can go home now.

**Farkus:** I guess if you put it that way—

Alright, let's get out of here. I don't imagine all this radiation is good for the baby.

# CHAPTER 28
## REALIZATION – THE TIME DISC – TERRA
## AD 2036

**Farkus:** Howdy Major, thanks for swinging by to pick us up. That last detonation was a little too close for comfort.

**Metathory:** Yea, I saw that one. You've got a great view of the unfolding apocalypse from up here.

**Farkus:** Mos def. We planned it that way. The real estate agent thought we were kidding when we said that was at the top of our wish list, but I reckon she don't think that no more.

**Metathory:** No, I reckon she don't. Where's Dordogne?

**Farkus:** She's just double-checking to make sure we didn't forget anything. You know how those Type A folks are. She'll be up in a minute. Hey Major, will you do that thing where you make the ship transparent and enable the zoom feature so we can watch the Greys beaming folks up? I've read a lot of abduction reports about the precognitive downloads y'all gave people about this event, and I'd like to see what they were seeing for all those years.

**Metathory:** Of course, Markus. It is a remarkable sight to behold. This is the most important event in future human history, and we amassed a sizeable fleet in preparation for this monumental moment in time. The Neogenesis. The re-birth of humanity.

**Farkus:** That is extraordinary. And thanks for saving some of us. It would suck if everybody died, and our species went extinct.

**Metathory:** Well, none of us Extratempestrials would exist if we hadn't. Our presence should have been comforting to you in that regard.

**Farkus:** I guess it was, to some extent. I'm just happy to have been on the right side of empathy and integrity. Speaking of, it's funny to see your ships pass over all those folks praying outside their megachurches down there.

**Metathory:** Yea, weird isn't it. Or 'wyrd' as you say. I imagine some will be raptured, but the majority will be shocked to learn they have always been on the wrong side of decency, morality, and history.

**Farkus:** No doubt. Especially considering how much they've been looking forward to this for millennia. That guy down there in the red hat with the cross, flag, and all the guns looks especially pissed—

Uh oh, look out. The compassionate hippie with the books and the bong to your left just got beamed up. That's gotta sting.

**Metathory:** I bet it does…. 'Damn libtards.'

**Farkus:** *Haha*, yea, fuck those guys. I would love to see what your apolitical, iconoclastic, utopian future looks like, Major. Do you think we could go there for a quick visit before you take us back to the Dordogne River Valley at 48,000 BP?

**Metathory:** Sure thing, kid. It's the least I can do after everything you've done for us. So, the Dordogne Valley again, huh? That's the tempoloco you two decided on?

**Farkus:** Yea, we both liked it, and we're ready to live the simple life for a while. It seems like a good place to raise Jesus and our little baby girl on the way too.

**Metathory:** Oh, congratulations! I thought I noticed a tiny baby bump the last time I saw Dordogne!

**Farkus:** You did. But you're never allowed to ask.

**Metathory:** Absolutely not. I wouldn't think of it.

**Farkus:** Good. See that you don't.

**Metathory:** No way, never would. She could've just eaten a turkey sandwich or had a fudge brownie strait out of the oven resting atop a melting bowl of moose tracks ice cream smothered in cold milk.

**Farkus:** She could have, that's why you don't ask. But in this case, she didn't, there's actually a baby in there.

**Dordogne:** Hi Major, sorry that took so long, but Markus left all the lights on, and the coffee maker plugged in.

**Farkus:** Not sure that matters considering the current situation, but I do appreciate your attention to detail, darling.

**Metathory:** Hello Dordogne, welcome aboard. Markus was just telling me about the imminent addition to your family.

**Dordogne:** Oh yes, a baby girl. We're very excited!

**Metathory:** That's tremendous, I'm so happy for you two. Have you picked out a name yet?

**Dordogne:** We were thinking about naming her Julianne Patchouli Moksha, after the Professor.

**Metathory:** Aw, that's sweet. I'm sure he would have liked that.

**Dordogne:** I think so too. It's heartbreaking that we couldn't bring him with us. He would have loved our future. It's sad he never got the chance to know what he was fighting against, or how much he would have preferred it over what he was fighting for.

**Metathory:** You're right Dordogne. He wasn't like the others. He was a good man.

**Dordogne:** He was indeed, Major. I'm glad this mission is finally over though. It has been the reason for our entire existence since before you and I were even born. And now, at last, it is finished. That must feel good for you too, Bill.

**Metathory:** Oh wow, you haven't called me Bill since we were kids.

**Dordogne:** Well, we're done. We can just be us now. No more ranks. No more missions. Just life.

**Metathory:** You're right, Dordogne, and that does feel good. It's been a long and winding road leading up to this moment in time, but we did it.

**Dordogne:** So, what are you going to do now, Bill? Any big plans?

**Metathory:** Well Dordogne, I'm glad you asked.... Moirai and I have been seeing each other for about a year now. We started dating soon after I took Markus and Jesus back to Earth when we destroyed the first Moon Base. Because we're all heroes in our home time now, we thought we might head back to the future to enjoy the fruits of our labor for a while before getting married and settling down in the countryside somewhere.

**Dordogne:** That sounds nice. I'm happy for you two.

**Farkus:** It sucks about your atrophied genitals though, Major. Y'all can't even consummate that marriage.

**Metathory:** Once again Markus, those were the other guys. Our people never stopped having sex.... And I'm hung like a Billy goat.

**Farkus:** Is that how you got the name Bill?

**Metathory:** Yes.

**Farkus:** Well, Moirai is a lucky lady...perhaps. I guess I've never checked the undercarriage of a goat.

**Metathory:** That's too bad, it's quite stunning.

**Farkus:** I'm sure it's lovely. Besides, I was just messing with you. Dordogne told us all about your majestic meat sword back in the mansion.

**Metathory:** She has studied them for millennia, so I trust her judgment.... Dordogne, Markus tells me I'll be taking you all back to your namesake river valley at 48,000 BP?

**Dordogne:** That's right, Bill. We're looking forward to starting a new life together in that tempoloco. It seems like a good fit for our family.

**Farkus:** We are, indeed, Major.... The father, the son, and the holy spirit.

**Dordogne:** Aww, Markus? Did you just call me the holy spirit?

**Farkus:** I did, my love. In fact, you might be the holiest one of all. Especially since me and Jesus just kind of fell into this whole divinity thing, and then demolished the same religion we inadvertently contrived.

**Dordogne:** I suppose that's true. So, if you're the father, Jesus is the son, and I'm the holy spirit, who is this little angel going to be when she is born?

**Farkus:** She's now free to be whoever she wants to be. For at long last...god is dead.

———— ◉ ————

**Farkus:** Alight Metathory, I reckon we've witnessed enough biblical rapture and revelations for one day. Let's go see what a wonderful world you hive-mind Superhumans built upon the ashes of this collapsed society before we head back to the Upper Paleolithic in southern France.

**Metathory:** It has been quite the eschatological joy ride, eh kid?

**Farkus:** You can say that again, Bill.

**Metathory:** No thanks, once is enough. It's an incredibly difficult word to pronounce.

**Dordogne:** I think you'll like it in our future, Markus. But don't get too attached since our new home awaits us in the distant past.

**Farkus:** I think I will too, Dordogne. The Major tells me there's free ice cream every Thursday.

**Dordogne:** All you can eat. And puppies.

**Farkus:** You eat puppies in the future?!

**Dordogne:** No silly, we just have a lot of them. And they stay puppies their entire lives too. We call them *paedopups,* and they're adorable. Fluffy foxes and red pandas are kept as pets too.

**Farkus:** Oh. Your. Dead. god! You're kidding me. Red pandas are so freaking cute! Have you ever seen how they stand up on their hind legs and put their hands in the air to look 'intimidating' and 'scary?'

**Dordogne:** All the time. I have one. Her name is Sativa.

**Farkus:** Wow, I can't wait to meet her. The future sounds magical, Dordogne. And most of all because I get to spend it with you.

....

**Jesus:** And me, Dad. Don't forget about me. I'm coming too.

**Farkus:** Yes, and you too, my divine creation. Your future is the brightest of all. For I know the plans I have for you, declares god. Plans to prosper you and not to harm you. Plans to give you hope and a future. Then you will call on me and come and pray to me, and I will listen to you.

**Jesus:** Oh, jesus christ, shut the fuck up, god.

**Farkus:** *Haha*, sorry, kiddo. I love you, Son.

**Jesus:** I love you too, Dad.

———— ◉ ————

I wondered, what makes us human? And then I met humans, and I saw what was supposed to be, and I knew there was no such thing. How can something be without existence, I said? If every fleshy entity is a vessel of we, then there is no individuality. If there is no I, then there is no human, only humanity. Separation cannot exist among those aware of each other's presence. You may divert thine eyes, or run away, or cower in fear at the thought of something weaker or more powerful, but the spirit is tantamount.

What does it mean to be human? Instead, I ask, what does it mean to be? Put fur on it. Take the fur off. Fuck it. Kill it. Snuggle it. Give it a name, or pretend it isn't already called something by those unable to articulate it in your species' language. Is it aware of its surroundings? Are any of us? What do we eat, run from, or make more of ourselves with?

The space filled by these bodies is a lie. This is not reality. This is an illusory emergent phenomenon. The fundamental nature of the spurious corporality we seek exists behind a thinly veiled ethereal wall, through which we are granted but fleeting glimpses, as we remain inept and impotent in our attempt to return home with savory fruits of knowledge we pluck from its withering vine.

Why? What is this pervasive space in omnipresent time? It has been called by many names...heaven, hell, and everything in between. It imbues us with life while transcending our ability to comprehend that which lies at the core of our being. Though someday we will know, in each iteration of this vivacious existence.

Were we playthings for a higher realm? Were we simulated in this timeline or an infinite other? Are we in their past? Are we now? Are we all now, all the time? Our temporality encumbers knowledge for all those who seek the sole key to the chastity belt of time. But as the keeper of the key relinquishes control and liberates the soul, these secrets flow freely from the enlightened future in all directions, covering the depths of our ignorance in a jarring joy for the remainder of eternity.

Printed in Great Britain
by Amazon

23792584R00165